WHITE DRAGON

Sarah Jestin

WHITE DRAGON

A DOUBLE DRAGON PAPERBACK

ISBN 978-1-78695-476-3

Double Dragon
is an imprint of
Fiction4All

Published 2020
Fiction4All
www.fiction4all.com

Cover art by Deron Douglas
www.derondouglas.ca

Chapter 1

The door slammed in Leena's face. The tall girl shook her head with a sigh.

"So? Do we have a place to sleep?" asked Meeryle.

Leena shrugged. "We can use the barn. Well, I think that's what she said. She was so busy deciding whether to faint or simply shake with fear that she chewed her words."

"The barn it is, then," said Meeryle. "It's better than sleeping in the open. Besides, it looks like it's going to rain. I'd rather be dry in the hay than wet in the forest."

"Not rain, Meeryle, more like snow," replied Leena with a shudder. "Don't forget, we've been heading north and I think we're far enough for winters to be white rather than muddy like the ones we're used to."

The chubby girl frowned, looking at the clouds. "Are you sure? This looks like rain to me. What do you think, Tikid?"

Tikid inhaled and shook her huge head. As usual, the dragon responded directly in the girls' heads, using mindspeech. "*Snow is cold. Let us see if the barn still has live earth. I am tired and I need to replenish.*" She headed for the barn, wings drooping.

"She didn't answer my question. Leena, we have to teach her to answer questions properly."

The tall girl smiled. "I thought you'd be used to these answers by now, Meeryle. Come on, Tikid's right. If it does snow, it'll be cold. We need to start a fire."

Meeryle's face paled and she bit her lips. "You start it; I'll get the dry fruits and the bread ready."

Leena's heart sank at the fear on her friend's face. No matter how hard she tried, she couldn't get Meeryle near a fire. It hurt to see her best friend afraid of the very thing she used to treasure. Meeryle was a Mage who had lost control of her power, and in doing so, burned down their village's barn and all of its contents, almost killing herself in the process. Since then, Meeryle had refused to use her gift for fear that she might once again lose control of it and harm, if not kill, someone.

Meeryle didn't just avoid fire, she no longer wanted anything to do with things linked to the element. As a result, the most celebrated cook in their village didn't prepare hot meals any longer. She could still make dried fruit and bread taste good, but she didn't use her talent to its fullest. Mealtime was reduced to the barest minimum; Leena had to prepare soup or hot items. Meeryle would only eat those away from the fire. The only positive outcome was Meeryle's decreasing girth. Between the much leaner meals and the constant walking, the Mage had gone from big to chubby. Another few months and Meeryle would probably be a normal size for her soon-to-be eighteen years and her short height.

Leena entered the barn, waiting for her eyes to adjust to the darkness. Evening was already upon them, and the clouds, heavy with snow, didn't help matters. The tall girl took out her small lantern, lit it with the flint and frowned at what she saw. The barn was old and empty, the owner using it to store forgotten objects and garbage that might be useful one day, not grain or hay. The gray sky could be seen through the ceiling in some places.

"Well, let's find the driest spot in here, shall we? I'm surprised this place is still standing."

"*The earth here is useless to me. I will need to go back into the forest for a little while before I sleep*," said the disappointed dragon.

"From what I understand, the closer we'll get to the city, the worse things will get." This farm was a bit of a surprise, really. Since they had decided to take the short route over the mountains to Sharitown, they had met very few dwellings once they had been clear of the forest. The land was rather dry, giving little hope of wielding any crops. The rocky mountains ahead were not a welcoming sight, but they might offer better sustenance for the dragon than the desiccated fields surrounding them.

"Go before it gets completely dark. I'll get a fire going and we'll eat before you get back."

"*Thank you. I do not like the smell of live dead things cooking*," replied the dragon with a disgusted sniff.

Leena smiled. The only smell Tikid liked was that of Meeryle's sweetcakes. Anything else offended her senses. Dragons didn't eat; they imbued themselves with the essence of their environment. Tikid was a Green; she needed the essence of the trees in particular and of plants in general. As earth was crucial to plants, she could also use its essence, but it had to be 'alive', full of minerals and other nutrients. It seemed humans had a tendency to drain the earth of its essence, forcing Tikid to fly into the forest and rest there for a few candlemarks, replenishing her energy. She always came back to sleep with her human friends, and had become a heat source for Meeryle. Since the young Mage refused to warm herself beside the fire, she cuddled Tikid and slept against the big creature, holding the fourth member of the traveling group, Suqi.

Leena still didn't know what to make of the fox-like creature. Suqi was a goupil, the traditional Mage's familiar. Leena could no longer think of the creature as an animal. The goupil could mindspeak, just like Tikid, so she had to be considered a person. Suqi would only speak with Meeryle and sometimes Tikid, but never with Leena, which irked her to no end. She had much to discuss with the goupil, in particular her ability to lick a wound and Heal it. However, Meeryle had relayed the firm message that Suqi's Healing gift was none of Leena's business. Insulted, the girl had decided to ignore the creature, at least for the moment.

Leena prepared the fire and heated the remnants of the soup. She considered their dwindling supplies and sighed. Life was not easy. While they had managed to gather a few coins, money was of no use in the villages scattered in the forest. Trade was the currency both within and between the small communities, so buying food had at times been difficult, especially of late. As they slowly made their way out of the forest and into the mountains, villages were far and between, isolated enough to rarely have visitors, let alone accept coins for goods. Since neither of the girls could offer freshly killed game – they weren't hunters – or fabric, they had to find another solution.

Meeryle did have an idea and for some reason, Leena wasn't comfortable with it. Meeryle had proposed that Leena offer her services as a Healer, but not for people. The village Healer, Corvin, had given Leena her gold-and-green scarf marking her a Healer in her own right, but to make it completely official – and in some areas, legal – Leena had to register with the Healer's Guild. In the meantime, Corvin had told her to limit her Healings to very desperate cases only. Some new Healers who hadn't been sanctioned by the Guild had met with mistrust when offering services. Leena didn't want to take the chance. She was much too young to be a Healer and she knew it.

No, Meeryle had suggested that Leena offer her Healing services for animals in order to pay their way to Sharitown.

Tikid had jumped with joy at the idea. Since dragons spoke with animals, she could ask the cattle or the horses where they hurt or if they felt sick, then relay the message to Leena. The solution was simple and elegant, but it didn't have the success Meeryle had hoped. In order for Tikid to speak with the livestock, she had to show herself. Since the group's goal was to introduce dragons to the human population, they had hoped they could combine the offer for services with the presentation of the eager young dragon, but so far, they had been met with mistrust and fear – and very few farms. Who in their right mind would let a creature as big as the dragon near their animals?

Looking at the near-empty bag of food, Leena was now wishing people weren't so mistrustful. The thought was unfair, as she was herself still intimidated by the large dragons. But now that they probably wouldn't see another settlement before they reached Sharitown itself, Leena wasn't so inclined to be charitable. They already had to ration their food, trying to use whatever could be gathered – which was thankfully a skill they had both developed while they were very young.

The first villages who had welcomed them had been close enough to theirs to have heard about the dragons, so had they been in need, they would have certainly allowed Tikid to speak with their animals and Leena to Heal them. However, the livestock had been quite healthy, so Leena's skill hadn't been required, much to her relief. However, the further away they traveled, the less they were made welcome. Offering Healing services for the cattle had been out of the question, so Leena hadn't have to use her gift at all, on people or animals, for which she was thankful.

Why was she so hesitant to Heal animals? Her pride, that's what it was. Her worst and best quality, Jetyaa always said. Leena missed her stepmother. The quiet woman always knew how to guide Leena in the right direction. Where Parin, Leena's father, would yell or order, Jetyaa would suggest or guide. She had given the girls and the dragon the best advice she could to prepare them for their journey and Leena wished she had come along with them.

But Jetyaa couldn't leave, so Leena hadn't asked. Her stepmother was one of the best hunters and the small, isolated village depended on the hunters to survive the winter. The farmers could only do so much and in the humid winter, grain could rot. No, Leena was walking her own path now.

When she was seven, Parin had told Leena that Jetyaa would now be her mother. He had never spoken of Leena's real mother again. She didn't know if her mother had died or if she had decided to walk her own path, without Parin. Leena almost wanted the former to be true, as she didn't want to think her mother would have left without her. The thought was old and Leena shook her head to stop brooding on it. Eleven years later, she still wasn't sure how she felt about her mother.

All she could remember were the woman's large and green eyes, and her name. Otherwise, her mother was but a ghost. Leena had asked herself if she missed her. Her relationship with Jetyaa was healthy; the woman had never tried to replace Leena's mother. In a way, they had become friends. Watching Meeryle and her mother, who could smother her children with too much attention, Leena had decided that she didn't miss the woman who had given birth to her. Jetyaa had been everything she needed, for both Leena and Parin.

What Leena missed were siblings. She always envied her peers, even the pointless bickering. Where they saw an annoying boy or girl following them around, Leena saw a companion, who could become in turn a partner-in-crime or a shoulder on which to cry. Even the families where sibling rivalry became out of hand seemed richer to Leena. The traveling hadn't helped either. Only once Parin and Jetyaa had settled had Leena been able to form a lasting friendship akin to that of a sibling's. She had never told her, but Leena considered Meeryle a sister.

She smiled briefly and thought that Tikid might be put in that same category. The young dragon, although of similar age in years, was certainly not as mature as Leena and Meeryle. The tall girl had taken to thinking of Tikid as a younger companion, maybe even a younger sister. The dragon was enthusiastic about anything human, yet naïve in so many ways. Leena had started to wonder if Tikid wasn't too young to travel with them.

But the Great One of the Greens had been adamant. He had told Tikid to show her new-found skill. Leena frowned at the thought. Tikid had been extremely vague about the conversation with the great dragon. After all these weeks, she was still hesitant in sharing her experience with her human friends. Yet, as time went by, Leena deemed it more and more important that they learn the young dragon's exact mission. For mission it was; she couldn't think of another word. She decided to ask Tikid about it when she came back. The closer they got to Sharitown, the harder things would become. They needed to know beforehand where Tikid's mission was to take them. Meeryle was to get training for her gift and Leena was to register with the Healer's guild. If Tikid needed to go elsewhere, they all had to know and plan accordingly.

Meeryle came in the barn, arms overflowing with food.

"Where did all this come from?" asked Leena with a huge smile.

"Suqi found a tree and a bush still bearing fruit. They're a bit wrinkled, but she said they'd still taste fine."

"She did, did she?" Leena made a face. It was silly, but anything Suqi did right annoyed her. "Well, I guess we can really use something fresh. The soup's ready. Tikid's gone to 'feed', so we better hurry and finish before she's back."

Meeryle busied herself cleaning and cutting the fruits. She handed Leena her share and took her own bowl of soup. The young Mage sat and slurped her soup, eyes closed with bliss. "This is so good, Leena. I hadn't realized how hungry and cold I was."

Leena smiled. Meeryle was indeed cold: she sat much closer to the fire than she usually did. The tall girl didn't say anything. She wanted her friend to get over her fear of fire. Winter would undoubtedly help.

The soup having taken the edge of her hunger off, Meeryle looked expectantly at Leena. "So, what do you think of the fruits? With a bit of time, I bet I can get them in an amazing salad. I'm sure I can find mint here."

The young Healer shook her head in amazement. No matter what the situation, Meeryle always found a way to think about food. Leena had always envied Meeryle's capability to make out the best in any given situation. Leena wasn't so easy going. She had been fretting over their traveling, whereas Meeryle had just taken in stride, as if she was expecting problems to simply solve themselves. In a way, they sometimes did. For all her physically poor shape, Meeryle had never complained since they left. She just mentioned when she needed to rest, and when she was ready to set out again. She never made it an order or an expectation, but simply a statement. Leena had never felt annoyed by her friend's lack of endurance, all thanks to her positive attitude.

"You know, Meeryle, I wish I could be like you."

Meeryle stared at her in amazement. "What, you want to be short, fat and bald?"

"No, you silly," said Leena with a laugh. "First off, you're not that short. I'm just very tall. And you're not as big as you were, either. Plus your hair is growing back nicely, you know." Meeryle rubbed her short hair. While Leena and Tikid had been able to Heal the terrible burns on Meeryle's body, they had not been able to restore her magnificent long and curly hair, so it was growing back at a regular pace. Meeryle's head was now covered with a two-inch fluffy helmet that stuck out in all directions. "Just give it a few more months and you'll be able to tie it back. No, what I meant is that you're just… positive. You always find the good in everything and I wish I could stop thinking about everything that could go wrong for a change."

"Well, I hope you don't, because, otherwise, when something goes wrong, then we won't be ready for it."

"See? You just found something positive about my negative attitude!"

The two girls burst out laughing. Leena's mood was lifted and they finished their meal exchanging jokes and pleasantries.

Tikid returned at full dark. When she entered the barn, the dragon was still glowing in a faint emerald color. Tikid was usually different shades of green, from dark forest green to a pale, almost yellow green. But when she infused herself with the essence of her environment, the young dragon would glow emerald and gold. She was truly beautiful.

"*Well, I think we will have to stop earlier if I am to fly back to the trees. Dragons do not fly well at night. I nearly bumped into the barn when landing.*"

"You're truly beautiful when you glow like this, Tikid."

The young dragon looked at Meeryle, blinking in bewilderment at the comment. "*But I am only one tone of green when I am imbued. How can you find only one shade of green beautiful?*"

"Well, you don't understand the human standards of beauty, so it's safe to say we don't get the dragon ones."

Leena smiled at the memory of Tikid's description of Rokin. The dragon had found the handsome boy ugly due to his bulging muscles. It seemed Tikid liked her humans straight and soft. Meeryle and Tikid bantered on the ins and outs of human beauty versus dragon standards.

Leena tuned them out quickly. She had never enjoyed these endless fashion talks. Meeryle's mother was a seamstress, so the plump girl had grown up appreciating a well-made garment, as well as its originality. Leena, however, didn't see the point in even thinking how to enhance or even change one's looks. She wasn't very keen on her appearance, but she was who she was. She kept her straight brown hair long to keep her neck warm, as she felt cold intensely, even in the warm season. Her long and thin arms and legs were fit, without bulging in what Tikid called an unbalanced way, thanks to all the physical work she had done as a child and as an apprentice-Healer. Her body remained fairly shapeless, though. Her chest was almost flat and her hips were barely bigger than that of a boy's. Her almond shaped eyes were a bit too big for her face, but according to Meeryle – and everyone else – they were her best feature. They were a deep green and once in a while, when she looked very closely in the mirror, Leena could see gold specks glittering in their very depths.

Leena was actually glad for her physical shape. Her narrow hips allowed her to wear breeches easily, and she didn't attract attention. Clothes were a practical thing, and face paints, ribbons and jewelry, a nuisance. She found them frivolous and just plain boring. As a result, she set herself apart from the other girls in the village, who found her as boring as she found them. Meeryle was the only exception. Whatever it was, she saw something she liked in Leena's seriousness. Leena still didn't know exactly what it was, and she wasn't sure she wanted to know. She accepted Meeryle's friendship unconditionally.

On the other hand, Leena found Meeryle's positive attitude soothing and amusing. Her best friend could be very funny without ever being mean. That was her most endearing quality: Meeryle was nice to everyone, even to people who weren't so kind to her.

Leena clenched her teeth at the memory of Teerane, the village bully, berating Meeryle. The plump girl would only shrug and turn away, whereas Leena would have torn the girl to pieces. Eventually, Leena's cold stare had dampened Teerane's enthusiasm and she had left Meeryle alone. Leena now finally understood why Meeryle was always so nice and turned away from confrontations.

Some had said she lacked backbone; Leena knew for a fact that Meeryle had a very strong personality and quite a temper. She had learned very quickly to hide it, though, since every time Meeryle lost control of her temper, blinding headaches and nausea would incapacitate her. Anger fueled the fire of the Mage gift and made her sick.

Fire was the first manifestation of the Mage gift and the first element Mages learned to control, in particular to purge water of its deadly component. However, since no one had understood that Meeryle was a Mage, she hadn't trained her gift. Instead, she instinctively used her affinity with fire to cook, as well as to burn small things to let her anger out. Unfortunately, at one point, Meeryle lost control of her anger and the gift took her over, nearly killing her. Nowadays, Meeryle kept her temper in extreme check. She didn't seem spineless anymore, but calm and controlled.

Over the past few months, Leena had overcome her jealousy. She had wanted to be a Mage and been sorely disappointed when she had learned she had the Healing gift. She now cherished her gift, as it had allowed her to Heal Tikid's wing. Granted, she had had help from Meeryle, but a Mage could never have Healed the shredded tissue.

Tikid's rumbling laughter made Leena's bones vibrate and brought her back to reality. Meeryle was wiping her eyes, catching her breath, and the dragon was hiccuping.

"Do I even want to know what was so funny?"

"It's just something Suqi did," answered Meeryle was a huge grin. "You had to see it."

"Yes, well, I guess I missed it." Leena looked down at the goupil. The fox-like creature was looking back at her, eyes full of mischief. She seemed to like annoying Leena. The young Healer cocked an eyebrow at Suqi, who barked joyfully and ran bouncily outside.

"*I wonder what the other dragons will make of her.*"

"Why's that?" asked Meeryle as she settled against the warm scales of her friend.

"*We know what goupils are, but only the Greens ever really see them. As we are heading north, I think we should meet Whites, and they certainly have not ever met a goupil. It is too cold where they live.*"

Leena took in a deep breath. "Tikid, you've been avoiding this, but now that you mention other dragons, will you finally tell us about your mission?"

The dragon harrumphed and turned her head, trying to evade the question. Meeryle came to the rescue and poked Tikid in the belly. "C'mon, out with it! What's the big mystery? We'll be with you, so we're going to find out anyway. You might as well give us the details beforehand so we don't end up making you look like an idiot."

Tikid grunted and shifted, finally setting her head on her front paws and looked pointedly at the wall. "*Well, I am not sure if I should. The Great One made it clear he did not trust humans.*"

Leena threw up her hands. "Oh, please! If he doesn't trust humans, then why let you come with us in the first place?"

Meeryle quelled Leena with a warning look. "Tikid, you know you can trust Leena and me. Whatever you tell us here, today, we promise not to talk about it to anyone else without your permission."

The dragon made faces Leena would have found funny under other circumstances. Her reluctance was starting to grate on the girl's nerves. They were a team; secrets should not be allowed.

Tikid made up her mind and resolutely sat on her haunches. "*While you were recovering, Meeryle, I went back to my home. My sire had a message from the Great One; I was to fly and meet him.*" She closed her eyes and projected feelings of happiness. "*I do not know if you can understand how great an honor this was for me and my kindred.*"

"Well, my guess is, this would be like meeting the King in the capital."

"What King?"

"Oh, Meeryle, didn't you listen in class?"

The big girl shook her head with a smile. "I usually phased out during history and geography. Too boring for me."

"Never mind. Go on, Tikid. I think I understand."

"*I had to fly for two days before I reached his mound. The Great One lives amongst the oldest and biggest trees of the world. It felt so... good to be there. I was really alive. For the first time in my life, I was almost too full of essence.*" She stopped, lost in the memory. Leena's loud sniff brought her back to reality. "*Sorry. I think about that moment a lot. He was waiting for me in the middle of a clearing. I had never appreciated how big a Great One can be. I had only seen him through Rutad, so I was surprised by his height. He was taller than most trees here. And if you find me beautiful when I am imbued with the trees' essence, Meeryle, then you would have found him amazing.*" The dragon stopped, her eyes glazing dreamily. The girls smiled at each other, hearts warmed by their friend's wonder.

Leena spoke softly; she didn't want to spoil the dragon's rare mood. "Can you describe him to us?"

"*I will try to show you. Look into my eyes, Leena.*"

The tall girl obeyed. Meeryle had described to her once how she could lose herself into the dragon's red eyes. Leena finally understood her friend. She was pulled in and fell into the red pools. Soon, pulsing green energy surrounded her and Tikid's voice called. "*Watch, Leena, look at the essence of the Greens…*" Leena looked. As the green energy engulfed her, it changed, becoming lighter, until it was almost white. In the middle, Leena could make out a shape. It slowly became bigger, until it was clearly a dragon. Although she had no reference point, Leena knew that this dragon was huge; its head was as big as Tikid and its tail a long sinuous track that lost itself behind the great half-opened wings. The creature was pulsing with emerald and gold light. Its scales were never colored with the same range of greens like Tikid and her fellow dragons; this one remained a lighted emerald beacon in the middle of the forest.

The big head turned and great red eyes bore into Leena's. They were filled with kindness, just like Rutad's when he had been filled with the Great One's essence. Leena knew that she was looking in the same eyes that had looked at them that day. She smiled. Seeing her pleasure, the big dragon nodded and said: "*My name is Murod.*"

Leena gasped. She blinked and broke the contact. She was now looking at Tikid, who was beaming with pride and happiness.

"*Did you see him? He taught me how to do that, you know. I did not know I could project my memories like that until I met him.*"

"What? Can I see?" asked Meeryle impatiently. Tikid turned her head and Meeryle locked her eyes into the dragon's. A few second later, she gasped and backed up. "Wow. This is… amazing. He's beautiful, Tikid! He spoke to me."

"*No, he was speaking to me. The image I showed you is the memory of when I met him the first time.*"

Something nagged at Leena. "He said his name was Murod, not Murad. How come?"

"*The Great Ones are ods.*"

Meeryle rolled her eyes. "That explains everything."

"Meeryle, give it up. Tikid, you said males were ads and females were ids. So what's an od?"

"*The Great Ones*," answered Tikid, puzzled.

The girls exchanged a look. The young dragon was an expert at giving cryptic answers. Over time, they had found out that Tikid was not good at giving explanations, particularly about things that were obvious to her.

Leena sighed and braced herself. "Tikid, bear in mind that humans don't have any 'great ones', at least not like dragons. It doesn't mean anything to us."

The dragon snorted in frustration. "*I do not know how to explain. Once a dragon has been chosen to become the Great One, he or she becomes an od.*"

"And who picks a dragon for that?"

"*The Great One.*"

Meeryle threw her hands up. "I give up!"

"I'm not. Tikid, what exactly does the Great One do?"

"*Each kind of dragon has one Great One, one od. That dragon is the receptacle of the essence of the Color he or she represents. If a Great One dies, another dragon must immediately take his or her place, otherwise, the*

Color no longer has its essence and all the dragons will die too."

"And what is the actual process for this?" Leena was getting excited. She found anything about the dragons' physiology fascinating.

"*I...*" Tikid blinked in surprise. "*I do not know. I think I am not old enough to have acquired this knowledge yet.*"

"When were you going to find out?"

"*I am not sure. I am sure that eventually, one of the wise ones would have spoken about it. Such things are not often discussed.*"

"Well, if you ask me, we're getting away from the original question here," interrupted Meeryle. "I don't care how the Great One became an od, I want to know what he told you."

Leena was briefly annoyed. To her, the subject was very interesting. She sighed, acknowledging that Meeryle was right. She would have plenty of time to question Tikid on the ins and outs of dragon biology while they were traveling. She nodded encouragingly to the dragon, who seemed hurt by Meeryle's outburst.

Tikid blew air out of her nose and turned a haughty head to Leena. "*Well, Leena, since you wanted to know...*" She was interrupted by Meeryle, who hugged her.

"I'm sorry I snapped at you." The girl looked up and smiled. "You still have to work on that expression, though."

"*I did not fool you?*" The dragon seemed disappointed. "*I think you know me too well. Another human would have felt differently, I am sure.*"

Leena took a sudden interest in the hem of her thick tunic. She wanted to hide her smile from Tikid. The dragon was trying very hard to mimic human expressions; all she managed were the stereotypes. The girls found her efforts hilarious, but since she was so eager to learn human ways, they never told her she would never fool anyone. Leena guessed her dragon friend would soon learn that the dragons' range of expressions was very efficient and that she had no need to human substitute.

"All right, then, continue, will you?"

"*Well, it turns out that the way I fed you the essence of the Greens is a very special skill, Leena. And same thing for you, Meeryle. The fact that we can both give Leena power to Heal is a skill that has not been manifest for a long, long time. What the Great One wants me to do is simply to seek the Great Ones of the other Colors and show them how to do it.*"

"Do what? Feed power to me?" Leena wasn't sure if she liked the idea. She was a Healer, not an experiment. "I'm not sure it would work with anyone else but you and Meeryle. You're my friends. I don't know if I would accept to link myself so closely with anyone other than the both of you."

"*That is what I said to the Great One. Meeryle fed you the power of the earth and I the essence of the trees. Both have something to do with growing. I do not know if another element or the essence of another Color would be compatible. He thought it was well worth the try. I also got the impression he thought it was time humans knew about dragons. I am not sure why, though, seeing as we have been forbidden to speak with humans for so long.*"

Leena and Meeryle were the first humans Tikid has encountered. At the time, she hadn't been sure what they were. To Green dragons, humans were mythical creatures to be avoided. To humans, dragons were stuff of legend. Leena approved of the idea to introduce dragons to humans – after all, the Green dragons had only been beneficial to the villagers – but she found it disturbing that the leader of the Greens would have a hidden plan on that subject.

Meeryle cut her brooding short. “Well, I don’t think it matters. The important thing is that we’re together and that we’re all doing what seems right to us. Obviously, Tikid needs to meet with any dragon we come across. Since we want to meet new dragons, this is perfect. From what Tikid says, we probably will get to see White dragons. And then, we can go to Sharitown, introduce Tikid and show what she can do for crops. After that, we just need to find a Mage to take me in and the Healer’s Guild for you, Leena. See, it’s perfect!”

Maybe it was her constant negative attitude, but Leena couldn’t help finding Meeryle statement naïve. She shrugged and pushed the thought away. It was useless to worry about it right away. They were still far from Sharitown – or any other real town, for that matter. Tomorrow would be soon enough to start worrying.

Chapter 2

The next morning, the sky was still gray and laden with clouds. The snow had yet to fall though, and the ground was still dry and firm. The four companions set out as usual, Leena and Meeryle on foot, Suqi frisking at her side and Tikid flying ahead and coming back to tell them in which direction the road turned and what to expect in general. Leena had forbidden the dragon to fly ahead too far for fear that someone might see her and shoot an arrow. Tikid had shuddered at the mention of the weapon. An arrow had torn her wing and only Meeryle's idea of feeding Leena the power of earth had allowed the then apprentice-Healer to restore the wing to its fullest. For a brief time, Tikid had thought she wouldn't fly again. She therefore took Leena's recommendation very seriously and never flew out of the girls' sight.

They had found out that Tikid didn't have to be close in order to hear her in their head; the dragon could speak to them from aloft. Much to their amusement, both girls had a running commentary from their friend about the terrain.

"*Well, today, I cannot see very far ahead. The clouds are very low. The road turns abruptly in order to avoid a large boulder, then it twists again because someone decided to build something. I do not know what it is, though. A strange and long wooden barrier...*"

At first, Leena had found the comments annoying. Tikid was like a child; everything was new to her. Eventually, as the dragon got used to human point of view, her running news became useful. The girls knew ahead of time if the road turned to mud, if a tree had fallen... they would also know when to expect company and get ready to explain Tikid's presence. Ever since they had left the forest, that particular event hadn't occurred. The road leading them through the mountains didn't seem to be frequented by many travelers; in fact, they had yet to meet anyone on the road. At this point, Leena didn't think it could be called a road anymore, as it had become narrow enough to be considered a trail.

It meandered in the fields, which had already been harvested, making it impossible to know what they yielded. Leena didn't think they were very productive, because some of them were overrun with weeds. Her experience with the village fields told her this place was poorly chosen to grow anything but the tough pastures favored by goats.

They proceeded as usual, walking at a brisk pace, entertained by Tikid's descriptions of every single thing ahead of them. Suqi would run ahead and turn back, hunting mice and making comments about her meal that disgusted Meeryle. Leena was glad she couldn't hear the goupil. Both girls would take the time to stop and gather plants and edibles for their meals. When the occasion rose, Leena would pick medicinal plants. She had learned to use them thoroughly and planned to continue. Healing with magic was not always the answer. Meeryle or Tikid may not always be around to give her power, so Leena couldn't rely only on her gift.

As the morning wore on, the sky became darker, until the first snowflakes made a lazy appearance. Leena's heart sank. They weren't prepared for the cold and had to find shelter. However, Meeryle and Tikid's delight soon cheered her up.

"Look, look! It's snowing, Leena! I can't remember the last time I saw snow."

"Well, it hasn't snowed since I moved to the village with my parents. So it's been more than ten years for sure. It is beautiful, isn't it?"

"*It is strange. Soft, but wet too, like weird rain. See how it moves with the air!*" The dragon proceeded to dance in the sky, twirling in a mist of snowflakes. The snow, flowing with the movement of her wings, made elegant lines around Tikid, the contrast of white against green stunning.

They continued on in the light snow, with Tikid beating her wings in their direction, forcing the snow to move towards them in small squalls. They ran to escape them, laughing and cursing.

"You just wait, Tikid! Eventually, there will be enough snow to pick up. Then you're in trouble!" threatened Meeryle. The only answer was the deep resonating laughter coming from the sky – and another snow squall.

They walked on for another candlemark, until Tikid landed in a flurry of snow. "*I can no longer see ahead.*"

Leena frowned. "Is it just me, or did it suddenly get colder?"

"You're right." Meeryle wrapped her cloak tighter. "And the snow's a lot whiter, too."

"*Not whiter, denser. Otherwise, I would still be able to fly. It is now too dangerous for me. What do we do, Leena?*"

The young Healer was at a loss. Since she had been too young when she was last in a snowstorm, she wasn't sure what to do. Meeryle and Tikid had never seen snow before, so they looked to her. She knew they needed shelter, but in the open fields, nothing could protect them.

"Tikid, did you see anything that could give us some shelter? We have to stop and protect ourselves somehow."

The dragon blinked, thinking fast. "*The mountains are very near to the west. I saw the beginnings of a tree line.*"

"Well, we don't have a choice. How far is not very far?"

Tikid shrugged the dragon way, her wings moving up and down briefly. "*For me, it would be a few wing strokes. For you, I am not sure how many footsteps.*"

"Well," said Meeryle, "I don't care. Let's get moving. I'm really getting cold. Suqi says she can smell the woods, so we should be all right."

Leena had her doubts. They were in the middle of the poorly tended fields. Would it be possible for them to stop so abruptly? She shook her head at her silliness. Panic was slowing her mind; of course such a thing was possible. Their village was a plain surrounded by trees, after all. Reassured by the thought – though she found it silly – Leena motioned the group on.

"Tikid, you will have to lead us. You know the directions, we don't."

"*I am not sure I will be able to guide you in this snow.*"

Meeryle rolled her eyes. "She doesn't want you to guide us from above, silly. You'll walk with us." The goupil barked. "And Suqi can help her too."

Leena sighed and shook her head. Apart from the previous night's find, she had yet to see any use to the creature. However, if the goupil was to be Meeryle's familiar, Leena guessed she had to accept her. She refrained from making any comments, as she didn't want to see the disappointed look that filled Meeryle's eyes whenever Leena made a disparaging comment concerning Suqi.

They made their way through the empty fields, following Tikid who walked slowly, her head down. The wind became stronger and snow whipped their faces. The flakes doubled quickly in number and soon, Leena could barely make out the dragon in front of her. As the wind got stronger and stronger, they could hardly hear one another. Only Tikid's voice in their heads was loud enough.

Leena feared they would lose track of one another. She grabbed Meeryle's hand, who in turn took hold of the dragon's tail. Tikid spread her wings a little in order to take off the edge of the wind, but the cold was seeping in quickly. Meeryle stopped and yelled in Leena's ear. "We have to get warmer. Do you think our blankets will help?" Leena nodded vigorously and gestured for Meeryle to turn around. She removed her friend's blanket from her pack and Meeryle did the same for Leena. A few minutes later, both girls were as muffled as they could manage.

Giggling at their appearance, Leena grabbed part of Meeryle's blanket. "Well, we're a nice bundle, aren't we? Let's go!" Once again, Meeryle took hold of the dragon's tail and they plodded on.

How long had they walked? How far? Leena couldn't tell. Everything was white. Each step was becoming harder in the accumulating snow. Her feet were slowly getting colder, as were her hands. The extra blanket soon became useless; the cold had penetrated through it.

Tikid stopped suddenly, surprising a yelp out of Meeryle. "*I cannot go on. I am too cold. Suqi is also not faring well. I cannot carry her, as I need all my paws to walk.*"

"I'll take her, of course," replied Meeryle in an offended tone. She gave Leena a guilty look as she scooped up a shuddering Suqi. The tall girl smiled weakly. Neither of them had noticed that the goupil was lagging behind.

Leena put her hand on the dragon's shoulder. "What about you? We don't have anything to wrap you in, Tikid. Tell us how to help you stay warm." Leena didn't know what to suggest. Normally, people huddled together and shared body heat. But how did two human girls hug a creature three times their size?

"*I will imbue myself with the essence of the trees. It should help*."

Leena looked around. "What trees? Tikid, this is a field! You've complained that you have to fly back to the forest to replenish yourself."

"*I think I can find enough essence around here to protect me for a while. I guess I should say I will use the essence of the plants*."

Meeryle sighed. "Just do it. Leena, stop asking for details will you? We need to get moving."

Leena bit back a harsh comment. Meeryle was right. She would have time later to ask questions. She had to learn to curb her curiosity. Her endless questioning had almost cost Meeryle her life once, when the burning barn had collapsed on her, and now, she might be making the dragon freeze to death.

Tikid had quickly concentrated and was now a glowing emerald light. The snowflakes surrounding her were glowing, making the dragon seem unreal. Meeryle laughed with delight. "Well, now you'll be lighting our way too! Come on, let's get moving."

Once again, Leena grabbed Meeryle's blanket. Tikid wrapped her tail around the plump girl's arm. Suqi had wrapped herself around Meeryle's neck, warming her. Leena instantly regretted her negative thought on the goupil. Suqi took care of Meeryle and protected her when she could. Leena almost wished she had a familiar of her own to provide a bit of much needed body heat.

Her envy was soon curbed when she estimated the goupil's weight. A mere seven pounds can become very heavy with time, especially in such harsh conditions. Leena knew the goupil would quickly become dead weight, so she suggested Meeryle take a break. Meeryle refused to put Suqi down. "She didn't stop licking me until I was completely Healed. She had used up so much of her strength, I thought she would die. This is nothing to me."

Brave words, thought Leena. Meeryle's head and shoulders were drooping with the effort. The young Mage's body wasn't used to such toil. At this point, Leena knew that sore muscles were well worth the heat, though. She simply nodded, and they moved on.

An eternity later, the first trees loomed over them. The storm hadn't let up at all. Leena even had the impression that the wind had become louder and the snow even thicker. She knew something was wrong. They were not north enough for such an early winter. When they had left the village, the harvest had been done, but the cold rains hadn't started yet. However, a quick calculation showed that indeed, back at the village, winter would have set in. They had been on the road for three months now, enough for the weather to worsen. She could only conclude that they had been lucky so far weather-wise; the sun had shone more often than not, and the clouds had barely let any water down. Their luck was down and the weather had decided to catch up. All she could do about it was to wish they had prepared better and brought mitts and warmer clothes.

As the trees got thicker, Leena looked for shelter. They were at the edge of the forest, where the ground was covered with the fallen leaves, which made footing treacherous. The snow made them very slippery, and both girls nearly fell more than once. The trunks were too wide apart to offer a hold or protection from the wind. The few copses they saw were too small for their purpose. They had no choice but to continue.

The ground was slowly going up. Each step was made more difficult as the slope made the footing even more slippery. Leena had yet to spot anything that could provide them with even the smallest shelter. Tikid's size was truly playing against them. Leena was starting to despair they would ever find a place to stop and wait out the storm. The day was going by, and she fancied it was getting darker. They couldn't stay in this weather throughout the night, otherwise, they would die. Yet she had to accept it was becoming a strong possibility. The storm hadn't abated; it was become a bit worse with each candlemark. Should she tell Meeryle? Would Tikid fare better than they in such weather? Probably not. The fact that she had to imbue herself with the essence of plants didn't bode well at all. The dragon might last even less time than the humans.

Tikid interrupted her dark thoughts with a joyful grunt. "*Look! An elf! We will be fine.*"

Meeryle yelped as Suqi struggled and landed on the ground. Leena was blinking furiously, trying to see the elf creature. Only the cold – her chin was frozen – kept her mouth from dropping open. A huge cat was looking at them with green eyes. When he blinked, Leena lost sight of him. He was white and blended in with the whipping snow. Those eyes were as intelligent as Suqi's; she wasn't looking at an animal. A thought struck her. How did she know the elf was male? She certainly couldn't by sight. She shook the thought away. Once again, she was letting her curiosity get the better of her.

Luckily, Meeryle had her feet on the ground. "So how are we going to be fine, then?" Suqi said something and Meeryle nodded. "She says all we need to do is follow him."

"*Yes*," added Tikid, "*he will guide us. He is a scout and knows the closest shelter. He says it is not very far*."

Leena bit the inside of her cheek. Why didn't she hear the elf? Was this going to be another creature like Suqi who only communicated with specific people? She was too cold to ask the question aloud. She nodded and motioned warily for them to move on.

The next candlemarks were extremely difficult. Leena couldn't feel her feet or her hands. The wind whistled in her ears, whipping snow in her eyes, blinding her to sight and sound. Her grip on Meeryle's blanket was slowly slipping. Fear chilled her further. She had to hold on, she had to trust Tikid. She could barely make out the bulky shape of the dragon. Tikid was almost back to her normal color, no longer an emerald shining beacon. Only her voice in Leena's head made her real.

"*Meeryle, you must hold on tighter to my tail. I can feel your hand slipping*."

Leena jerked at that comment and yelled over the wind. "We have to stop for a few moments, Tikid!" She pulled on Meeryle's blanket to stop her. The plump girl turned to Leena, her lips blue with cold.

"*Now is not a good time, Leena. We must go on.*" Tikid hovered over the two human girls.

"I'm so tired, Tikid. I just want to lie down for a few minutes and rest," complained Meeryle, her eyes closed.

Panic rang in Leena's mind. "No, no, you can't. I'm sorry, I shouldn't have said anything. Make sure you hold Tikid properly. Remember, I'm holding on to you, so I'm counting on you. Now go."

Meeryle shook her head warily. "It's just so cold, Leena. I can't feel my feet anymore and my fingers are so stiff, I think they'll break off. I need to rest!"

"You can't. If you sit down, you'll fall asleep and die, Meeryle. Go!" Leena gave her friend a gentle push.

"*We will be warm soon.*"

Leena hoped Tikid was right. They had put their lives in her claws and in the paws of that strange white cat, the elf. The cold must be muddling her mind. How could she have possibly agreed to such a ludicrous idea? How could Tikid be sure that the stupid creature would lead them to safety? She wanted to go home, where things were safe and warm.

Lost in her thoughts, Leena didn't notice when Meeryle stopped and she bumped into her friend, sending them both sprawling in the snow. For a second, Leena relished the fact that she wasn't on her feet anymore. She hadn't realized how tired she was, how much her muscles hurt.

When she had been out in the forest collecting plants for the Healer during the rainy winter, she had thought she was cold. Rain had a way of finding its way into clothing, no matter how waterproof the cloak. With the usual wind, she had been chilled to the bones. It was nothing compared to this. Every part of her body had stiffened and was becoming hard as ice. If lying down was a relief for her legs, she soon found that other parts of her felt just as abused. Her back was locked in place, her neck couldn't turn anymore… her arms from her elbows down were non-existent. Better to close her eyes and rest, to allow her body to relax for a few minutes. She just couldn't go on any longer.

"*Leena! Do not fall asleep!*"

Leena jerked awake. She couldn't see anything but snow. Something was shaking her shoulder. She turned, finding her head heavy, and saw Tikid's large paw. The dragon had lost all her shininess, which meant she was now as much at the mercy of the cold as Leena and Meeryle. The young Healer shook herself fully awake and sat up with the help of her friend.

"*Come. Get up. Meeryle is already in the… house, with Suqi.*"

As weary as she was, Leena didn't miss the hesitation. "Are you sure it's safe?"

"*Oh, absolutely. I am just not sure what to call this shelter.*"

With the help of the dragon, the girl got to her feet. Her muscles screamed in protest. Leena ground her teeth and willed herself to move. Tikid supported her and wrapped a wing around her, partly relieving the human from the fury of the wind. Soon, Leena was able to walk, albeit very slowly. She refused to think about how close she had been to dying.

"Over here! Hurry!" Leena could barely make out Meeryle's voice. The wind seemed to make a special effort to befuddle her. As she moved on, she was finally able to make out a faint yellow light. She frowned at her advanced state of tiredness; she was having hallucinations. The light was coming from a round opening in the middle of a snow heap. Yet instead of disappearing, the mound became sharper as she got closer.

Leena blinked furiously. She was not hallucinating; she was really seeing Meeryle's head coming out of a heap of snow. "Well, come on! You'll see, it's nice and warm in here."

Tikid gave her a gentle shove. "*I need to get warm, Leena. I am not feeling well.*"

The dragon's quiet voice in her head shook her out of her trance. The tall girl walked stiffly up to the entrance and stepped in, almost losing her balance in the process. The warmth hit her and she sat down carefully, giving Tikid as much space as she could to allow the dragon to make her own way in, and sighed with relief. Suqi poked her seemingly boiling nose on her hand and gave her a smiling look. For once, Leena was happy to see the goupil.

As she slowly regained the feeling in her extremities, Leena took in her strange surroundings. She was sitting in a hut made out of snow. The walls seemed blurry, as if the snowflakes were moving. Her finger found a solid surface, though. She frowned, focusing intently on the flakes.

"A shield holds the snow, which provides the necessary protection."

Leena yelped. She looked up and faced a man. He was a complete stranger, yet Leena had the impression she had seen him before. His appearance was strange: his pale skin was almost white and his hair so blond, they looked like silver. His eyes… his eyes were green and almond-shaped. She realized she had already gazed into these eyes. At the time, they had been the eyes of the big white cat who saved their lives.

"What… What are you?"

"I am an elf. My name is Jatoron. I very rarely see humans this far up the mountain." His voice was soft, yet deep, and his words had a strange lilt.

A strange feeling overcame Leena and dizziness threatened for a few seconds. She quickly closed her eyes and felt herself again. When she opened them, Meeryle was looking at her with concern. "Are you all right? You look pale. Come closer to the fire."

She tried to get up, but her legs were weak. The man gently took her elbow and helped her up.

His touch sent energy through her.

Leena stared at him in amazement. Never had she felt such a jolt of pure Healing energy coming not only from anyone, but from a casual touch. "Are you a Healer?"

Jatoron's face crinkled with amusement. "No, I'm not. What gave you the idea?"

"Did you not feel it when you touched me?"

"Feel what?" Meeryle looked intently from Leena to Jatoron.

"A… I can't describe it. Almost like he Healed me, but not quite." The jolt had enabled Leena to regain some strength and she moved close to the fire, analyzing what she had felt.

Meeryle had yielded the spot immediately, putting as much space between her and the fire as she could. She was preparing soup with water and dried strips of meat. When came the time to heat the soup, the big girl hesitated. Leena didn't say anything; she had tried over and over to help her friend to regain her confidence with fire. It was up to Meeryle to take the first step.

Apparently, the young Mage had decided she was too cold to be squeamish. Leena clearly heard a strange beat interfere with Meeryle's song of life, and the soup was steaming. Tikid was radiating pleasure. She had echoed Leena's encouragements. Girl and dragon smiled at each other. It might take a while, but Meeryle was definitely on the way to recovery.

Jatoron's gasp brought them back to reality. "You are a Mage?"

"Well… yes, I guess." Meeryle was staring at the soup, stirring it with stubborn determination.

Leena sighed. The pangs of envy were getting fewer with time, but she still wished Meeryle would accept her gift. Leena's dream had been to become a Mage. The Healing gift had seemed a pale thing in comparison. When she had learned that Meeryle had the coveted gift, Leena had flared with jealousy. Only time and Tikid had helped her accept that the Healing gift was just as precious – if not more in some situations – than the Mage gift. Leena had demonstrated exceptional Healing talent when she Healed Tikid's wing. Even the village Healer, Corvin, had grudgingly admitted to her that he had never met or heard of anyone with her ability. All these comments and assurances had been of tremendous help, but sometimes Meeryle's attitude would bring the envy back. Leena knew that Meeryle's feelings towards her gift had been implanted by fear when she was a young child, but some days it just didn't help. Meeryle tried very hard to train, to use her gift, to overcome the fear; since she lost control of her gift and almost died in the process, she knew she had to train and become a Mage openly.

However, while she could now talk about her gift without getting cold sweats, Meeryle was still recovering from the loss of control over fire.

Pushing aside any comment towards Meeryle's attitude, Leena turned to Jatoron and explained who they were and why they were traveling. The tall man sat beside them and listened intently. He stared pensively at Leena when she finished speaking. When his gaze transferred to Tikid, Leena noticed his ears were pointed.

"This is a very strange encounter indeed. I have scouted this mountain for many years, yet I have never met a Mage." He nodded at Meeryle. "The duke of Sharitown keeps his Mages well hidden within the city." He looked at Tikid and smiled. "I have met many a dragon, yet, although I knew of Green ones, they were but a mystical creature to me. Imagine my surprise when I saw you!"

Tikid's laughter rumbled throughout Leena's body. "*I almost did not recognize you for what you were, Jatoron. Elves do not come into the heart of our forest.*"

"Now wait," said Leena. "When we first saw you, you were a cat, were you not? Your eyes are the same. How is that?"

Jatoron gave her a dazzling smile. "This ability is a close-guarded secret, particularly from humans. Only the dragons know of it. Every elf can shift from humanoid form to cat form at will."

"Really? What does it feel like? And why would you change shapes?" asked Meeryle. Now that the discussion was steered away from her, she had suddenly lost interest in her soup.

"I trust you will not divulge this information." Both young women nodded. "For a scout like myself, the ability to shift makes life much easier. I can hunt more easily than as a humanoid. My sense of hearing and smell are much better, and the fur is a more than adequate protection against the cold. Not to mention the speed if I need to run."

Something bothered Leena. "Why do you need to scout?"

"The humans from Sharitown are not very fond of elves. We try to avoid contact as much as possible, because it unfortunately ends in bloodshed."

Leena was horrified. Even if her parents had many heated arguments, she had never seen violence. It had been a near thing between the villagers and the dragons in the spring, but they had managed to come to an agreement. She had to admit that the sheer size of the dragons might have had an influence. But the elf looked just like a human, aside from the paleness and the ears. "Why are you at odds with humans?"

Jatoron didn't answer immediately. He gave Leena another of his pensive gazes. When he looked at Meeryle's face, who was just as curious as Leena, he seemed to reach a decision. "Have you never met elves before?"

Leena shook her head. "Until today, I had never heard the word."

"Well, Tikid mentioned it to me once, not long after we had met the first time," answered Meeryle. "I just remember wondering what kind of animal an elf was. We had none in our village, and I don't think they were covered during school."

"I knew of elves, of course. All dragons do. But I know you like the quiet of the mountains, which are a

harsh environment for the Greens. I am very glad to meet an elf in person."

"Well, I find it very strange. I am not one to travel much beyond my mountain, but other elves do, and they all report that humans know what they are. Some are nice, but some are not."

"That can be said of anyone, Jatoron. I'm sure some elves aren't as nice as others."

He smiled. "You're right, Leena. I can think of a few troublemakers among my peers. Here's what I propose. If you're going to be traveling to Sharitown, it is past time you learned about my people. We should wait out the storm, which will probably last the night, then go to what you would call my village, where I'm pretty sure you will be more than welcome. The sight of a Green dragon will be quite the sensation, but a Mage and a… Healer? My people will all benefit from your presence." He looked at them expectantly.

Leena and Meeryle exchanged a look. The short girl shrugged. Leena wasn't so sure. Why had he hesitated about her being a Healer? Maybe he didn't trust her. "We need to go to Sharitown. I have to register as soon as possible if I want to get set up as an official Healer. Meeryle can't delay her training, either."

"*You forget, Leena, that I need to meet with the Whites. Jatoron said a group of Whites live a few days away from his settlement. This is a great opportunity. They can get my message to their Great One.*"

She wasn't pleased with Tikid's interruption. Jatoron was hiding something, she was sure of it.

The elf shifted his attention to Meeryle. "We have Mages of our own. They might be able to train you. They all speak your language, though some not as well as others."

Meeryle's face was blank. Leena wished very hard that her friend's reluctance to training would prevail once again. But the chubby girl's curiosity won. Leena's heart sank as Meeryle nodded slowly. "If this makes your life easier, Tikid, then I'm willing. But do they all speak the same way you do?"

Jatoron smiled. "If you're referring to my accent, I'm told I have little of it. Some have a stronger one, but nothing to impede communication."

"I'll try my best," replied Meeryle with a shrug.

"Good. It's settled. If you want, I can hunt for a more filling supper. Your soup smells fine, Meeryle, but it will not be enough. You need to recover your strength."

Tikid groaned. "*I hate the smell of cooking meat. Can they not restore themselves otherwise?*"

Jatoron laughed. "I had forgotten. My bread supply should help." He got up and rummaged in his packs.

Leena was not pleased with Meeryle. Yet she couldn't pinpoint the reason for her suspicions, so she didn't voice her disappointment. If the elf proved to be treacherous, she would act then. Corvin had taught her that a Healer had the ability not only to restore life, but also to take it if need be. She wasn't keen on the thought, but she would overcome her squeamishness to save her friends' lives. She deliberately pushed any such thought away as Jatoron handed her a flat and dark bread. Instead, she pointed at their shelter and asked how it was built.

"Our Mages set the spell for such things in small objects, such as stones. When the storm started, I triggered it and the dome appeared. It traps snow between two layers of air. I can make it bigger by pushing it. I have to admit it's the first time I have needed to make it so big. I've never sheltered anything as big as Tikid before."

Despite herself, Leena was intrigued. "With air? You can make a solid wall out of air?" She got up and touched the wall. It was still hard. But when she pushed, the wall moved with her hand. She gasped and moved back. "Are you sure your spell is safe? There's no risk that it will collapse? I mean, it moved. What if we lean on it during the night?"

Jatoron was looking at her, slowly nodding, as if she had just confirmed something. "The shelter can only collapse if I say a specific word. We are safe for the night."

At Leena's gasp, Meeryle had also pushed against the wall, but it hadn't budged. "Why did it move for Leena but not for me? Tikid, what about you?"

The elf interrupted them. "I don't think this is the right time to experiment." Strong wind gusts emphasized his words. "We should finish our meal and settle for the night. You all look exhausted. Your goupil was particularly out of shape when she came in and we should follow her example."

Suqi had rolled up against Tikid and was sound asleep. Leena suddenly realized how tired and sore she was. The food had made them all drowsy. She wasn't even sure if Suqi had eaten. She shrugged and figured the little creature know would how to take care of herself.

Both girls finished their bread and Jatoron banked the fire. They rolled themselves in their blankets and cuddled Tikid. Meeryle was leaning against her shoulder and Leena, back against Meeryle's, used the dragon's lean belly as a pillow.

The wind's low whistling, the heat of the fire and the pressed bodies lulled Leena. Her heavy lids were slowly closing. Yet she saw Jatoron staring at her. She didn't have time to even phrase the question in her mind before sleep claimed her.

Chapter 3

The next morning, Leena awoke to the happy chirping of small birds. She took the time to laze, eyes closed, and listen to their bickering. A loud gurgle spoiled the moment.

"Mfff… I'm hungry."

Leena sighed and sat up. "You're always hungry, Meeryle. Come, let's feed you and find out where Jatoron wants to take us." The night's rest had cooled her anger down at the man's presumption. She had to admit being curious about the elf.

As if summoned, Jatoron poked his head in the shelter's entrance. "Good morning! Have you all thawed out?"

"*Yes, thank you*," answered Tikid with a yawn. "*I need to get out and stretch. Then I will replenish among the trees*." The dragon made her way out awkwardly, almost toppling over the pot holding the remainder of their soup.

Suddenly feeling the shelter closing in on her, Leena followed her friend outside. She never really liked closed spaces. Last night, she hadn't cared, but now, Leena needed the open sky.

She gasped at the beauty of the forest. The trees were indeed spaced out, offering little shelter. What the snow had hidden was their age and their grandeur. These trees were old and wide. They were very tall, their trunks almost black, and each had grown taking its personal space quite seriously. Leena recognized them as the strange pines that shed part of their needles during the winter. Her father had told her about them, but she had never seen them before except in illustrations; they didn't grow in the forest around the village.

These huge trees were planted in the pristine snow, giant black sticks on a gleaming white blanket. The sun lit hundreds of sparkles on the snow, little lights winking playfully at the birds landing on the snow-laden branches. How could something so deadly the day before be so beautiful?

"Wow. I had no idea snow looked so nice," whispered Meeryle. The two girls stood side by side, taking in the quiet landscape. The snow muffled all the sounds of the winter forest, making it an incredibly peaceful place.

The crackling of fire and a most appetizing smell interrupted their musing. With a smile, Jatoron gestured for them to join him. Two rabbits were roasting above a small fire. After weeks of eating dried meat, Leena's mouth watered instantly.

The elf had cleared up the area around the fire and sat cross-legged on a blanket laid out on the ground. Meeryle sat beside him and stared intently at the cooking meat. "That one's done. The other one needs to be turned."

"Is that so?" replied Jatoron with a smile. "I did not know Mages were cooks."

Meeryle threw him a dirty look. "I'm a cook who happens to be a Mage, not the other way around. So, are we going to eat or not? Because that other one is now ready, by the way. More, and it'll be burned."

The elf grinned, obviously amused by Meeryle's reaction, but didn't answer. He simply tore the first rabbit apart and handed each girl a share. Meeryle devoured hers in an instant and quickly busied herself in heating the leftover soup. Leena and Jatoron ate their share at a more leisurely pace, in silence.

Leena enjoyed the quiet immensely. She had never realized until now how noisy her friends – and everyone she knew – were. Meeryle usually had a running comment on the finding and preparation of food, and Tikid's shuffling on the ground had become a constant background noise. Only Suqi had been quiet. Now that the young Mage was in the snow shelter seeking herbs from her bag for the soup and Tikid was aloft, Leena was able to truly relax in the silence. For the first time in a long while, she could hear branches lazily clanking against one another in the slow wind. She could even make out the slight sound of the snow falling off branches. Closing her eyes, she smiled and reveled in the new sensation.

Jatoron's sharp breath interrupted the moment. When she opened her eyes, the elf was looking up at Tikid, who had replenished herself. She landed in a flurry of sparkling snowflakes, a blazing emerald sun.

"You look truly amazing, Tikid."

"*I thought you had seen dragons before, Jatoron.*"

"Ah, yes, but not Greens. Only Whites. And they do not look like you at all, especially not when you are as now."

The young dragon cocked her head. "*Do they not imbue themselves as I do?*"

"Indeed, but they do not shine emerald, but silver," answered the elf with awe.

Meeryle joined them, holding the soup. "Really? I can't wait to see them!"

"*Are you not done eating?*" asked Tikid with a definite whine.

Meeryle laughed. "Yes, we're done. I'm just adding the rest of the rabbit for later."

Relieved, Tikid turned her attention to the landscape. "*It is much warmer today. I will not need to remain so imbued with my essence.*" She immediately changed from emerald to forest green. Leena marveled at the beauty of her friend. The dragon's scales ranged from a deep green to a lighter green that looked almost yellow in the sun. The light gave hints of gold. Jatoron was staring with wonder at Tikid, who preened and extended her wings in the sunlight, casting green shadows.

Meeryle burst out laughing. "You're a vain thing, you know that?"

Tikid sniffed loudly. "*I told you I look much better when I am different colors. You seem to think the shining emerald suits me better, but it is obvious from Jatoron's reaction that you are wrong.*"

The elf was trying very hard not to laugh. "To each his own, Tikid. But since this is the first time I have seen a Green dragon, you cannot judge on my reaction alone. Now come, and take everything out of the shelter before I collapse it. Then we will leave."

"*Can I fly ahead? In which direction?*"

Grinning, Jatoron pointed to the north, at the mountain. "That way. We will be there in the evening. However, I'm sure you will be welcome if you arrive before we do."

"*I will go, then. That way, you can finish your food, Meeryle, so you won't have to carry it.*"

The dragon was soon a green dot in the sky. Jatoron shook his head and smiled. "Your friend seems very young. I've only met bigger dragons, so I'm guessing her size is an indication of her age."

Leena nodded. "I think she's my age, almost eighteen. But she's not as… mature as we are. I don't know if it's the same for all dragons, or if it's Tikid's nature."

"I met fledglings. They were very small and sounded just like every little boy and girl I've known. They were so cute!" explained Meeryle. She had taken Tikid's suggestion seriously and was scraping the bottom of the soup pot.

"Well, Meeryle, thank you for offering!" Leena shook her head. When would her friend learn to take it easy with food?

"Did you really want some?"

"Forget it! There's probably not enough left for me, anyway."

"Don't worry," said Jatoron. "Tonight, you will have plenty of food."

Leena helped the quiet man to pack the rest of their things and watched as he touched the outside of the shelter. He mumbled a word and the heap dissolved. Of their spacious shelter, only a small pile of snow remained. Jatoron fumbled in the snow and retrieved a flat rock. He pocketed it and smiled. "For the next storm. Now, let us leave, if we want to arrive before nightfall."

Leena loaded her packs onto her back, and helped Meeryle with her own. The plump girl was carrying the now empty soup pot. Leena refrained from making any comments. Jatoron was waiting for them, his pack much smaller and more efficient than theirs.

"If you want, tonight I can show you how to pack."

"It would be much appreciated. We're not very good travelers, I'm afraid. My stepmother helped us, but it's something else entirely when you're on your own."

The elf nodded and started to walk. Leena fell behind him, then Meeryle behind her. Suqi followed them by leaps and bounds in the snow. She was having a grand time either hunting unseen mice or simply enjoying the feeling of the snow on her belly.

They walked in silence. The snow was light and fluffy, allowing them to move at a good pace. Leena was truly enjoying herself. The sun kept her face warm and they were moving fast enough that her feet didn't get cold. It took her a while to realize they were moving too fast for Meeryle. Leena stopped and waited for her friend. "Are you having a hard time in the snow?"

"No, not at all. You're just moving faster than you usually do. What's the rush?"

Leena didn't answer. Jatoron had turned back, a questioning look on his face. Was she really going faster than usual? She didn't feel tired at all. "I guess I was going at Jatoron's pace without noticing it."

"Well, remember, my legs are shorter than either one of you." Meeryle didn't seem annoyed, but she was such a good-natured girl that she wouldn't complain. Yet Leena had never had the impression that Meeryle had been holding her up during their travels.

Jatoron interrupted. "I apologize. Elves tend to be much faster than humans. I will slow down." He turned and moved on. The girls followed suit, Meeryle first. Leena wanted to make sure they didn't outdistance her once again.

Meeryle turned her head back, a puzzled look on her face. "That was kind of strange, don't you think? I mean, you're human too."

Jatoron heard her and stopped. Leena could tell he was burning to say something, but he simply shook his head and moved on. The tall girl was once again getting annoyed with the elf. He was hiding something, and it had to do with her. However, since she was in the rear, she couldn't ask questions without having to shout. Jatoron had slowed his stride down, but he remained far enough ahead. Leena walked on, refraining from grumbling.

The silence wore on Meeryle's nerves, tough. The big girl asked Jatoron to slow down, and once they caught up, she questioned him on his status. "So, what does a scout do, exactly?"

The elf laughed. "I walk around the mountain and check for strangers, enemies, people in need… When I can, I help, otherwise, I seek others. If I see enemies, I report them, if I meet strays, I guide them back to the right track."

"So you're a type of guard, then. Surely, you're not the only one to scout?"

"This mountain has many scouts, but this part is all but deserted, though, so one person is enough."

Meeryle smiled. "Yes, we noticed. We only met a woman on a pretty beat up farm. Otherwise, we had the road to ourselves once we came out of the forest. Do elves farm too? What about craftsmanship?"

Jatoron seemed taken aback by the questions. "You really don't know anything about elves. I find it very hard to believe. Where do I start? Your village seems to be a remote one, so I'm not sure if your community functioned like a typical human one."

"Why would that matter?"

"Then I can give you points of reference."

"Oh." Meeryle had clearly never thought this over. Leena was amused. Aside from food and dragons, Meeryle cared about very little else. Geography and politics were unknown to her. Leena was not particularly interested in them either; Healing was much more important. However, she had an idea of the complexity in the governing hierarchy. Was the elven society as intricate?

Her curiosity was not to be satisfied, though. Meeryle quickly changed the subject. "Why are you fighting with humans?"

Jatoron hesitated. "I'm not sure I should be the one to tell you this, for the simple reason that my explanations may not be adequate. The center of it all are precious stones. The humans want them for profit, but elves use them for energy. We therefore don't want them to go to waste, so we refused to trade. The duke tried and tried, until he resorted to force. But there again things didn't go his way. We're very good fighters. So for the past, oh, two decades or so, the duke has been trying to take over our mountain."

Leena was worried. What if they were to walk into a battle? "When was the last time you fought?"

"Don't worry. Things have been very quiet for the past year. The rule is to ignore each other."

"This is not reassuring, you know." Why had she agreed to come? Jatoron obviously thought his words were nothing special. Leena closed her eyes and plodded on. Why had she left the village? This white world, so beautiful a few candlemarks ago, was now completely alien, a dead and bleak monochrome place. Homesickness washed over her and she swallowed back tears. Leena hated to cry, and longing for home was not worthy of tears.

She stayed silent for the rest of the trip. Since the trail was becoming steeper, Meeryle was too busy trying to move on without slipping, so she didn't speak either. The elf seemed naturally taciturn, allowing Leena to remain in her gloomy thoughts.

By the time they had reached their destination, the sun was getting low in the sky.

Meeryle suddenly yelled. "There's Tikid!"

Leena smiled at the sight of the incongruous green spot amidst the whiteness of the snow. "Well, she seems warm enough. She's not glowing."

"I just hope the trees around here will be enough for her. I mean, look at them! They're all scraggly."

"We are getting high in the mountain, Meeryle. On this side in particular, only these small ones can survive with the weak earth. Maybe Tikid's visit will bear fruit in the spring," explained Jatoron.

Meeryle turned to Leena and shrugged. "Right." Leena laughed. Trust Meeryle to say such a thing. Anyone else would have asked for more details. The plump girl avoided any such tedious conversation. True to herself, she quickly changed the subject. "Look, there's a welcoming party!"

Unruffled by the sudden change in the conversation, Jatoron nodded. "Of course. The arrival of a Green dragon must have been quite the event. I'm sure Tikid warned them of our arrival."

Leena had to blink when she looked at the crowd awaiting them. The last rays of the sun shone on the elves, highlighting the silver in their hair. Their green eyes were bright lights against the white skin of their faces. They were beautiful. Leena forgot her bleak mood, her homesickness and her resentment in that moment. She smiled and moved on, eager to meet these people.

The huge terrace before the entrance of a cavern was crowded by hundreds of elves. At first, they looked similar, but Leena was soon able to see the differences. They were generally tall and slim, but some were shorter and stockier. The hair was usually worn long, either loose or tied back. She spotted some females with more intricate hairdos, but generally, the various heads were adorned simply. Some had cut their hair, one had almost shaved it.

The dress was just was simple, yet each one seemed to make it unique. Most wore a long tunic overflowing breeches in soft colors, and boots made of a soft-looking material. All in all, the elves made a very pleasing tableau to the eye.

Jatoron made the introductions. "This is Meeryle. She is a Mage, and Suqi here is her goupil. This is…"

He was interrupted by a much older man. His blue tunic was embroidered with a subtle gold pattern. "I don't believe this," he said with the same lilt as Jatoron. He approached Leena and gazed into her eyes. He smiled slowly and Leena was shocked to see tears in his eyes. His hand brushed her cheek lightly and she jumped. The same feeling she had experienced when Jatoron had briefly touched her sparked. "Yes, you felt it, didn't you? You look just like Lyandrin."

Leena was hot and cold at the same time. How? How could this stranger know that name? She had never told anyone, not even Meeryle. Yet this old man acted like he knew her, just like Jatoron. The ground no longer felt stable. Was she going to faint? A woman's scream helped her gain control of herself.

"Leena!"

Jatoron hadn't had time to say her name. Yet this woman knew it. The tall girl looked beyond the old man to the woman who was running towards her in the parting crowd. The elf stopped just before her. Leena thought that the old man was right; she did look like Lyandrin. Soon, she couldn't see much through the tears. All she could make out was the shape of the woman standing in front of her.

"Leena," Lyandrin repeated softly. She opened her arms and Leena threw herself in her mother's embrace.

Chapter 4

The crowd had given them relative privacy by moving inside the cavern, leaving mother and daughter alone on the terrace. People still hovered at the entrance, wanting to see what would happen, Meeryle and Tikid among them.

Lyandrin's eyes were now dry and she smiled. "Everyone is curious, but your friends more than most. If you wish, they can join us."

"Not yet. What I want to know and ask you is private. I will share with them later, if I feel up to it."

Lyandrin nodded her understanding and sat on one of the many benches adorning the terrace. Leena sat beside her, barely acknowledging the beauty of the bench; it could wait. Her mother was much more important.

"What I want to know is why. Why did you leave us?" She didn't voice the long-standing doubts: did Lyandrin hate her? Did she find her so unworthy, she had discarded her? Fears she had thought mastered resurfaced with an intensity that brought tears to her eyes.

The tall woman sighed. "They're both valid questions, Leena. Did your father never explain?"

"No. Until yesterday, I didn't know elves existed, let alone the fact that I was one of them."

Lyandrin's eyes went wide. "I did not know he hated me so much," she whispered. She was silent for a while, and when she spoke again, her voice was normal, if a bit shaky. "The first thing to know about elves is that they live in pairs, much like humans. However, an elf doesn't choose with whom he or she will spend his or her life; we are two halves of one soul; only once we find our soulmate are we complete. My soulmate was Danpiron.

We lived on another mountain, a few weeks travel in cat form from here. Did Jatoron explain that we are not on good terms with the humans from the city close by?" Leena nodded. "Good. The conflict between this particular elven enclave and the duke of Sharitown is an old one, almost twenty years. At the very beginning, the best elven negotiators were called in to find a mutual agreement. Danpiron was one of these negotiators. Naturally, I went with him." She stopped and closed her eyes. When she opened them again, they were so full of sorrow, Leena's eyes filled with tears. "I still do not know if it was by design or accident, but Danpiron was killed during the duke's welcoming feast. I do not believe a butcher's knife can accidentally find its way in a person's heart, but to this day, the duke maintains it's the truth. Assassinating Danpiron couldn't have served any purpose for the duke, so he might be saying the truth. Any chance at peaceful trading disappeared with Danpiron. Open warfare wasn't declared, but the skirmishes begun that same week. My enclave left and returned to their mountain, but I couldn't bear to return to my home without my soulmate. I stayed behind, fully intending to join him."

Leena took Lyandrin's hand. She couldn't believe she was looking at her mother, touching her. All the questions and doubts that had plagued her over the years were gone. Many times she had tried to remember her mother, to imagine what she would be like. The woman whose hand she was holding was everything she had hoped and completely different at the same time. Her sadness and her sorrow were palpable and erased any doubt. This woman had loved her soulmate so dearly, how could she have not loved her child?

While she waited for Lyandrin to compose herself and continue, Leena truly looked at her. She indeed looked like her mother, but where Leena was tall and gangly, Lyandrin was grace itself. Her eyes were exactly how she remembered them: almond-shaped and a deep green. Her face was like Leena's, only smoother, sweeter-looking. Even the hand she was holding looked like her own, just better honed. The hair was pale, the almost-white blond typical to the elves, whereas Leena's was brown. Her human heritage, she gathered. Just like her eyes: Lyandrin's held no golden specks.

Leena gazed into her mother's eyes and smiled. "What changed your mind?"

Lyandrin smiled back. "I didn't, at least not at first. I sought to fly off the mountain, but a man saw me and found me before I died."

"Parin."

"Yes. He was the complete opposite of anything elven. But like the elves, he liked the peace the forest can offer. He was hunting here, on the other side of the mountain, where no one really goes because the forest is too sparse. He had been following a huge deer. He lost the animal and found me instead. I found a sort of refuge in his presence at first, then is his arms later. And you were born two years after that." Her smile grew sad. "With a child came the necessity to settle among other people. I couldn't possibly bring him to the enclave, so we sought a village of humans. Things did not go so well after that. I was unhappy with humans. The noise, their screeching voices… Parin and I argued more and more, to the point where I could no longer endure it. So I left." She was quiet again, and looked at the darkening sky. "I thought of Danpiron. It was past time I joined him, I thought. But when came the time, I couldn't." Her gaze bore into Leena's eyes. "I kept on seeing your lovely face and I knew I couldn't leave you. However, when I came back, Parin had already left with you and, I learned, another woman."

"Her name is Jetyaa. She... I want you to know that she never tried to replace you."

Her smile was weak and her eyes, full of tears. "That's good to know. I was afraid she would make you hate me."

"She never mentioned you, at least, not with me within hearing distance. Neither did Father."

"I am not surprised. I hurt him deeply. I just didn't realize how deeply. To hide the very existence of elves... Had your schooling not covered it?"

"No. And now that I know, I think Parin might have arranged it that way. Our village is very small. We didn't really need to know about elves. They don't come that far south, I think."

"Then, you truly do not hate me?"

Tears blurred Leena's vision and a huge lump blocked her words. How could she hate this beautiful woman? She wasn't sure she understood the relationship of a soulmate, but from the sorrow in Lyandrin's eyes, she could well imagine the longing to join him beyond. Only love could have held her back. No, she couldn't possibly hate Lyandrin. Since her mouth wouldn't work, Leena embraced her mother in a tight hug, letting the tears flow freely. When Lyandrin's arms returned the embrace, Leena's bottled up feeling broke loose and sobs wracked her body.

She didn't know how long they stayed interlaced, two women crying. Feeling the cold, she shuddered and reluctantly disengaged herself from her mother's arms and looked around her. The sky was dark and the elves were still standing in the cavern's entrance, respecting their privacy. Not so for Tikid and Meeryle.

The two friends took Leena's gaze as a signal and ran to her. Meeryle stopped just before the mother and the daughter, torn between her awe of Lyandrin and her desire to hug her friend. The elven woman smiled and beckoned Meeryle. The big girl threw her arms around Leena. "I'm so happy for you!"

"*As am I. Jatoron had asked me not to give out your names, saying that he would rather do it. Now I see that he knew who you were, Leena. Everyone here knows your name.*"

Lyandrin nodded. "Yes. I had made sure of that, just in case someone met you. Then they could let me know you were fine." New tears fell down her cheeks. "I just never dreamed I would get to see you again."

Before any of them could speak again, the old elf with the blue tunic came out and gestured for them to come it. "It's almost full dark and the cold will no doubt affect our Green friend."

Lyandrin simply nodded and wiped her eyes. Leena and her friends followed both elves into the great cavern. Leena had to blink from the light, which told her darkness had indeed crept up on them.

After a few moments, her eyes adjusted to the light and she stared around in wonder. She'd never been in a cave before, so she didn't know what to expect, but what she saw was nothing she'd ever imagined. A cave was made out of rocks, yet here, she couldn't see anything that reminded her of it. Every surface was smooth or carved, painted or bleached in some way.

The lights coming from regularly spaced-out niches high up on the walls shone very brightly, making it hard for Leena to really see any details. She was sure they weren't candles, though.

"Hey, Leena, come on!" Meeryle pointed to an area surrounded by gauze-like hangings, in the center of which a long table had been erected. The old elf beckoned them with his hands.

"Come, it is time for the feast. My name is Risalon, and in the name of the enclave, I bid you welcome, Leena, long-lost daughter, Meeryle, first human Mage to enter our presence, and Tikid, daughter of the trees." Each time he said the name, Risalon bowed to the person in question. His was a quiet voice, but it carried very well despite the crowd. Maybe the cave was made to carry sounds in a special way. Leena soon realized that the acoustics had nothing to do with it; the old man's voice was heard simply because the crowd was quiet.

She looked at them all and was shocked by their number. More than three times the number of people in her village stood silently, welcoming smiles on their faces. Only some shuffling broke the silence when Risalon finished talking, and most of that noise was made by Tikid.

Leena closed her eyes and smiled, wallowing in the quiet. When she opened them, she stared into many expectant green eyes. She wasn't too sure what to say; she'd never been one for speeches.

Surprisingly, Meeryle came to the rescue. "Thank you, Risalon. We're really glad to be here and really happy that Leena found her mother. Honestly, we don't know much about elves, so I'm not too sure on how to proceed." Leena bit back a giggle. The statement didn't sound like Meeryle at all. She usually found a quiet place and observed from the side, letting Leena handle situations. Yet becoming officially a Mage and a dragon ambassador had made her friend gain assurance and allowed her to become quite the diplomat.

If Risalon took exception to Meeryle's attempts at diplomacy, he didn't show it. He simply smiled and presented the table with his hand. "After the welcome, we feast. I realize this isn't much for such a short notice, but I think it will do."

The table was covered with pastel-colored bowls filled with unknown types of food. Both Leena and Meeryle approached eagerly, as their stomach rumbled. It was the signal for everyone to start helping themselves.

Leena took a plate and discreetly examined it. She was disappointed; it was just like the plates she'd always used, except for the swirling patterns in the center. Apparently, elves didn't have special dinnerware, but it made them a bit less strange in her eyes.

The food was another story. The bread Jatoron had served them had tasted fine, if a bit strange, but it was close to the bread Leena was used to eating. Apparently, it was scout-fare only. Here, the bread had a tangy, almost bitter taste to it. The fruits and vegetables were very acidic, to the point where Leena had to force herself to swallow them. She hoped that the meat would be better, but the spices were burning her throat.

Leena glanced at Meeryle. The Mage's eyes were watering from the mix of spices and vegetables' acid. The girls exchanged a look, not daring to say anything out loud, fearing their words would be heard in the silence.

This once, Leena fervently wished for noise and to be elsewhere. The elves weren't exactly looking at them, but they would surely notice if their guests didn't eat. Leena suddenly envied Tikid. The dragon had been shown to an area deeper into the cavern in order to remain warm and to be away from the smell of food in general and cooked meat in particular. Suqi had followed her; Leena now wondered if the goupil had known about the food.

"You must be tired from your journey here," said Risalon. "Did you wish to finish your meal in your alcove?"

Not caring if the man truly did think they looked tired or if he was aware of their problem, Leena got up and nodded. "I hadn't realized how tired I was until I sat down to eat. Resting would really be nice right now, thank you."

"Come with me," said Lyandrin with a smile. "I will show you where you'll sleep." Meeryle got up and kept her plate with her. She even refilled with a few pieces of bread before following Lyandrin. Leena did the same, but for show only. She knew she just could not swallow another bite.

Lyandrin led them behind the gauze walls of eating area, which hid numerous tunnels.

Meeryle stopped. "Wait! Will Tikid be able to fit through here?" The tunnel did indeed seem narrow for the dragon's bulk.

Lyandrin frowned. "You mean you share sleeping space with a dragon?"

"What's wrong with that?" Meeryle's voice had taken an edge Leena didn't like. The last time she had heard it, the Mage had lost control of the gift. The barn had been isolated enough that no house had been touched, but if the same were to happen here in the cavern, everything could burn.

Her mother had read the danger or she simply had not meant to sound insulting; Lyandrin shook her head and laughed. "Not at all. It's just… no one here has ever done it. We'll make arrangements later. Right now, I think you both want to be in an alcove, far away from any elf, and eat human food."

Leena arched an eyebrow. "Were we that obvious?"

"Only to me, I think, and that's because I've lived with humans. Remember, this enclave has not had any contact with the humans for over twenty years! I'm sure no one remembered how our spices affect humans."

Meeryle sighed with relief. "I only took the bread to be nice. I can't get that burning sensation out! Do you think we could get some of the bread Jatoron had?"

Lyandrin smiled at the Mage's plaintive voice. "Don't worry, I'll get fresh meat and scout bread. You can cook the meat any way you like. That's why I thought the arrangements with Tikid could wait."

"Yes, she would complain on and on about the smell," replied Meeryle with a roll of eyes.

The elf laughed and left to get their food, taking with her the foodstuff both girls had brought with them.

"Whew, even the smell was getting to me."

"Come on, you're pushing it, Meeryle."

"Maybe. I have to say it's the first time I didn't find anything good to eat."

"Like you've had a lot of experience in exotic foods."

Meeryle blushed. "You're making me feel like a country bumpkin."

"Sorry, but we are. This place is overwhelming."

The young Mage sat down with a sigh in one of the low chairs, while Leena took in their surroundings. The alcove was a recess in the rock wall furnished with three low and cushy chairs, a small table and hand-woven rugs. The beds were thick mattresses laid out in a rectangular hole carved into the wall, flanking a hearth in which a fire roared. Everything was simple, really, yet managed to look both beautiful and strange. The material used for the blankets was very soft, almost like silk. She'd never held silk before, but she was pretty sure this was something else.

"Meeryle, what do you think this is made of?" After all, the Mage's mother was a seamstress; she should recognize it.

"Hm." Meeryle peered closely at the cover and rubbed her hand over it. "All I can tell you is that it looks really comfortable!" She let herself fall on the mattress with a sigh. "Leena, you have to try this. I've never had such a comfortable bed!"

"Well, compared to our sleeping rolls for the past three months, anything would be blissfully comfortable, no?" Yet when she sat on the bed, Leena's shoulders slouched in contentment.

"Well, well, you are enjoying elven hospitality, I see," said Lyandrin as she walked in with a plate of uncooked meat and a basket filled with bread. "That is something that gave me such a hard time with your father, Leena. I am not a Mage, so can't grow the plant used for making all our material and filling. Human-made beds never quite measured up, except for wool-skins. Elves don't use them that way; I've started quite the trend here."

Leena reeled with the information Lyandrin imparted. So many things to explain, so many things to understand. She didn't know where to start. Luckily, Meeryle's stomach took the situation in hand. Before Leena could even start to organize her thoughts and question her mother, the young Mage took the meat platter and stood in front of the fire, looking for something to use for cooking the meat. Only because Leena was watching for it did she see Meeryle hesitate when Lyandrin handed her long skewers. Not wanting her friend to show her discomfort, Leena took the skewers as Meeryle put meat on them and put them in the fire into grooves made for that very purpose.

"You tell me when they're done." Meeryle nodded without a word. She was gaining confidence, but Leena wasn't sure it would be a good idea to push her at this point. They were both tired and feeling at odds with themselves.

Lyandrin had simply taken a chair and was watching them in silence. The only noise came from the crackle of the fire and the sizzles of the cooking meat. Once again, Leena marveled at the peaceful quiet, and once again, it bothered Meeryle.

"Tell me, Lyandrin, are elves always so quiet?"

The woman smiled. "Yes, we are. We find humans very loud. We enjoy the quiet sounds of nature. I've had time to think on this quite often, and I think it has to do with the fact that we need to spend time in cat form. When we are, every sound is magnified, so we avoid noise then, and it continues when we're in humanoid form."

"Mother…" Leena savored the word and Lyandrin grinned.

"It is so good to hear this word."

"And it feels so good to say it!"

Mother and daughter hugged tightly. This time, no tears made their way out, but Leena's throat was nonetheless tight.

"The meat is ready." Meeryle spoke quietly. Did she miss her mother at this point? She had told Leena she was glad to leave her parents' home when they left the village, but surely seeing the two women embrace must twinge. When Leena looked at Meeryle, the chubby girl just smiled.

Leena took the meat out of the fire and put the skewers on the plate Meeryle held for her. They both helped themselves and sat to eat the juicy meat. As always, the Mage had known exactly when the meat was cooked to perfection and Leena closed her eyes in pleasure as she bit into the flavor-filled food. With the bread, it was perfect.

"Do you mind if I have some? It's been so long since I had human food, I think that now that I smell it, I've missed it."

Meeryle's mouth was full, so she nodded, while Leena smiled. "Of course! Anything prepared by Meeryle is usually quite the feast." Her friend blushed. Leena left out the part about her new fear of fire.

"Oh, I have to keep a piece for Suqi," said Meeryle as soon as she swallowed her food. "She went with Tikid to get some sleep, and I'm sure she'll be starving when she wakes up."

Leena nodded and kept eating. She felt guilty for assuming the goupil had run away from the food. She always thought the worst of the little creature simply because she wouldn't talk to her. It was petty, but the young Healer really resented the fact that someone – or something – would refuse to speak to her about Healing.

She rolled her eyes at herself and shook the thought away. She was with her mother; it wasn't the time to examine her faults.

"Mother, can you tell us about elves? We know nothing of them."

Lyandrin sighed. "Your father was very angry with me, then. I wonder who in the village knew about you."

Meeryle shrugged. "I imagine that our bullies would have picked on Leena if they had known, so I think no one from our age group knew. Maybe some of the adults. My parents certainly never mentioned anything."

"Like I said, mother, our village is very isolated, and from what Jatoron said, elves don't venture in that area."

"It's too warm for us in the South. We crave the cold and the snow; I think it has to do with our cat form. I am not a researcher, so I can't tell you exactly why that is."

"Elves have professions?"

Lyandrin laughed. "Of course, Meeryle. Otherwise, what would we do? I am a painter."

Leena didn't say anything, but she was a surprised as Meeryle. She shouldn't be, though. People have to occupy themselves somehow, and for the most part, in every situation, they have to see to their survival. Even dragons had a profession, though Tikid had been very unclear as to the details so far.

"Will you show us your painting?" What did an elf paint? People? Animals? Landscapes? The village had no resident artist of the kind. Decorations were done in patchworks, not paintings. Leena knew next to nothing about this form of art. Country bumpkin indeed, she thought bitterly.

"Tomorrow. You are all exhausted. We will see to sleeping arrangements with Tikid, and in the morning, you can ask all your questions. Be warned that many here will have questions of their own. You are the first human

Mage they've ever met, Meeryle, so our Mages are very curious."

Meeryle gulped. "I'm not a real Mage," she said in a weak voice.

"Meeryle. Enough with that! Mother, Meeryle is an untrained Mage, so she may not be able to answer many questions."

"Well, then, you may be able to give them information when you start your training with them. But before that happens, they'll have to determine if your gift is compatible with theirs."

Meeryle gave her a blank look. Leena was suddenly afraid her friend would refuse the offer Jatoron had made. The young Healer was no longer in a rush to get to Sharitown and register with the Healers Guild. She had found her mother!

Much to her relief, Meeryle shook her head and smiled. "You see, you just lost me with what you said, Lyandrin. Compatible? I'll have to understand that in the first place. But don't worry, Leena will help me. So, where's Tikid?"

Lyandrin gave Meeryle a strange look. As usual, the chubby girl had managed to change the subject as soon as it came to her gift. The life-long habit was very difficult to shake, and while Leena understood it, others didn't. Leena bit down a smile. If her friend was true to herself, the elven Mages would find life interesting indeed.

Lyandrin didn't comment on Meeryle's abrupt change of subject. She finished the meat on her skewer, nodded her compliments to the cook and gathered the remains of their impromptu meal. "Come, let's find your friend and make arrangements."

The girls followed the elf back to the huge entrance cave. The bright lights were dimmed and the place was deserted. The gauze walls were still there, as well as the table. Before Leena could ask, Lyandrin explained.

"This is the gathering place. A meal is prepared here at midday, and all who want, attend it. However, in the evenings, most eat in their alcove. Your arrival was a special occasion. I think everyone left shortly after you did. All the alcoves lead here." The back of the cavern was riddled with tunnels similar to the one from which they had emerged.

"Is there no other way out?" ask Leena.

"Yes. The mountain a bit of a maze, but you can find your way out in different ways. This cavern is what you would call the official entrance. The other ways would be the equivalent of your back door."

"Um… our house has no back door, Lyandrin. Why would anyone need a back door?"

Leena laughed. "Sorry Meeryle, I shouldn't make fun of you, but it is funny. The houses at the village were too small to need back doors, but the inn has one."

"Well, I've never been to the inn, so I certainly didn't go in any front or back door."

Lyandrin watched the two friends with a frown on her face. "You sound like you've had a very sheltered life indeed. I'm not sure I like this. You say you've been on the road for three months? It's a wonder you haven't run into problems."

Leena bristled. "Mother, we were prepared. Jetyaa had warned us and I'm not easily fooled. I know someone who means trouble when I see one. We also had Tikid and Suqi with us, which helped." Recognizing the goupil rankled, but she had to give credit where it was due.

Lyandrin smiled. “I see you have your father’s pride. It would seem, however, that your step-mother didn’t warn you about the suddenness of snowstorms in this area.”

Leena clenched her teeth. Her mother’s comments stung. Proud, her? And she hated to hear anyone belittling Jetyaa in any way. Before she could say anything, however, Meeryle diffused the situation by yawning.

“I’m sorry, but I’m really tired. Can we go to Tikid?” Leena smiled. She *was* tired, but also didn’t want to get into a fight with her mother. Lyandrin must have thought the same thing because she beckoned them to follow without another word.

The dragon had been housed at the end of the largest tunnel. Leena was sure that if Tikid had been an adult, she wouldn’t have fit. Dragons really didn’t visit elves all that often, it seemed. The tunnel was rather short, with only two alcoves on each side. They were filled with fragrant drying herbs. Leena wanted to ask about them, but Meeryle gave her a warning look. “You can ask later,” she whispered.

The elves had given Tikid privacy by hanging a thick gauze-like curtain across the width of the tunnel. When Leena pulled it to the side, the dragon opened her red eyes with a lazy blink.

“*Oh, you are finally here. Suqi is sleeping; the cold was hard on her. I asked where you would sleep and they gave me a strange look. But they brought in sleeping things for you when I insisted. Come, it is nice and warm here.*”

A fire was burning in a quickly built hearth. Meeryle pulled one of the two mattresses piled on the side close to Tikid and promptly lay on it with a sigh of satisfaction.

Suqi was nestled against Tikid's neck and remained there. The little goupil was either exhausted or ignoring them. Leena was leaning towards the latter.

Lyandrin smiled at the sight of the young Mage curled against the dragon's stomach. She bade Leena goodnight with a smile and left in silence. Since Tikid had gone back to sleep and Meeryle was already halfway there, Leena pulled her own mattress closer to the fire and lay down without removing her clothes. She promised herself she would ask about bathing in the morning.

Lulled by the dragon's regular breathing, the popping fire and the comfort of the mattress, which seemed extraordinary after all the nights spent outside on the hard sleeping roll, Leena closed her eyes and quickly fell asleep.

Chapter 5

Leena was awakened by a rumble. Any other time, she would have known what the sound was; however, this morning, the comfort of the bed made her forget where she was and she panicked, thinking an earthquake was rocking the ground. She was on her feet in an instant, looking for shelter from whatever would fall on her, when Meeryle and Tikid's astonished faces stopped her in her tracks.

"Oh. Yes. Good morning," was all she could say.

Meeryle arched her eyebrows. "What's the matter? You had a bad dream?"

Leena jumped on the line her friend had unknowingly thrown her. "Yes. About an earthquake. I'm fine now." She also figured out that the earthquake was really Tikid laughing.

"Well, are you ready to meet your relatives?"

"They're not relatives, Meeryle. They're…" What were they?

"*They are part of you, Leena. You will learn about elves, right? What about the cat form? Will you try to change?*"

Tikid's suggestion stunned her out of straightening her clothes. It hadn't occurred to her that since she was part elf, she might be able to change forms. "Well, first I have to find out if I can change at all. I mean, I'm half human too, and humans don't change shapes."

"Still, wouldn't it be fun? I could pet you!" Leena threw her friend a dirty look. "Oh, come on, Leena, for once I can tease you about something other than Rokin."

"Be serious, Meeryle."

The chubby young woman sighed. "That's your problem, Leena, you're always so serious. I'm not even sure you'd have laughed at Suqi's joke!"

Leena didn't want to know, so she just shrugged; at least she now knew what had made Tikid laugh in such a way that her sleeping mind thought an earthquake was going to kill her.

"*I need to stretch my wings.*" The dragon shuffled to get up, unwittingly pushing her friends to the side.

"Tikid, wait! We'll get out first." Meeryle pulled her mattress to the side for fear that the dragon would drag it out of the tunnel, and Leena did the same. She pulled the curtain to the side at the last minute to make sure the thing survived the dragon's passage. Leena suddenly longed for the house they had built specifically for Tikid in the village: no walls, no floors, no furniture to move around.

Meeryle echoed her thoughts. "You know, Tikid, it's a good thing we never tried to put you up in a house. I think you would have destroyed the place!"

"*This place is too small for a dragon*," replied Tikid with as much dignity as she could muster. She would have left, but her friends were blocking the way. Trying very hard not to laugh, Leena walked very quickly out of the tunnel, followed closely by Meeryle. By the time the dragon made it out to the entrance cave, Leena was able to keep a straight face. The dragon was very proud when it came to certain things. Meeryle had explained that Tikid was clumsy and resented it. Recalling their first encounter with the dragon, Leena had to admit her dragon friend had indeed something about which to worry: she had stepped on her tail and fallen in the bushes.

As soon as Tikid stepped out of the tunnel, she extended her wings as much as she could. "*I had not realized I moved them so much during my sleep. It feels so good to move!*" The dragon was about to shift her wings up when Meeryle stopped her.

"Wait, you might bump off some of the lights."

"*Oh.*" The young dragon was crestfallen. "*I am really not meant to be in here, am I?*"

Leena smiled. "Don't worry about it. We're here to help you. Now, let's see if the weather is warm enough for you this morning."

Their voices had carried in the quiet cavern and soon, they were surrounded by elves, bidding them good morning. The closer they came to the entrance, the cooler the air. Leena shivered.

"Ah, I see our guests are up." Risalon made his way to their side. "Come, Lyandrin has helped us prepare a human breakfast."

"*I will fly out and replenish.*"

"Yes, we know dragons' aversion to food, friend Tikid. You will be happy to learn the day is most sunny. I hope it helps to keep you warm."

"*Do not worry about me. I have enough energy left to infuse myself if necessary.*" With these words, the dragon flared from green to bright emerald and left the cavern.

Risalon smiled and herded them towards the food table. Much to Leena's relief, it was covered with familiar things like apples, bread rolls and even sweetcakes. "Lyandrin went to trade with farmers on the other side of the mountain very early this morning," explained the old elf.

Leena's eyes widened. "I thought humans didn't welcome elves around here."

"They don't," answered Lyandrin. "However, I know how to pass for human when needed. A well-placed headdress and lowered eyes work fine, especially when the sun isn't completely up."

"Thank you very much!" Meeryle looked and sounded eager, and Leena hoped it would be attributed to hunger rather than to relief.

They filled their plates and a repeat of the previous evening took place. People were standing, eating their food in silence. The difference lay in the number of people attending; apparently, either the novelty of their presence had decreased, or work was taking precedence. The elves present amounted to about a quarter of the previous night's crowd.

Leena also noticed that Meeryle was slowly being herded towards a group of four elves, whereas Leena was being left to her own devices. Lyandrin followed her eyes and smiled. "These are our Mages. They've been very eager to speak with Meeryle and Suqi."

"Ha! I doubt she'll talk with them. She's been ignoring all my attempts at communication with her."

"Oh, she'll probably only tell them to take it easy. Meeryle doesn't look comfortable talking about magic, does she?"

"She hates anything that has to do with it and she has good reason. She was… threatened by another Mage when she was a child, so she suppressed her gift, in a way. She's now learning to cope with it. It's driving me insane, though. I mean, the Mage gift was my dream. I was sure I had it. Instead, it's the Healing gift I have."

Lyandrin gave her a penetrating look. "You're a Healer?" The last words were said rather loudly and echoed in the cavern. Heads turned their way, eyes full of questions.

"What's wrong with being a Healer? And why didn't Jatoron mention it? He knew about it." She remembered how the scout had hesitated when talking about her status as a Healer. She thought it had to do with the fact that she was half-elf and that he knew her. Now, she wasn't so sure.

"No, Jatoron didn't mention you were a Healer. I guess he forgot; your being Leena was probably more important to him. However, Healers are very rare amongst elves, much more rare than Mages."

At that point, everyone present had gathered around her. Meeryle seemed relieved to have escaped the Mages, but she nevertheless sent a questioning look to her friend. Leena shook her head discreetly, hoping she'd understand everything was fine. She wasn't even sure herself if it was.

"If you don't have Healers, how do you Heal injuries and sickness?"

"We share it amongst ourselves by touching. An injured elf will feel better and eventually heal when he or she touches another elf. The more people we can touch, the faster we heal."

"Remember when Jatoron touched you? You said you felt something like Healing." Meeryle had managed the elbow her way to the side of her friend. "You weren't looking good at all when we made it to his shelter. As soon as you touched him, you looked better."

"Yes, and he nodded." At the time, Leena had been too weary to really think about it, but now, she recalled the scout's reaction. Touching Leena and seeing her feel better had probably confirmed that she indeed was Lyandrin's daughter. "But now that I touch you, mother, I don't feel that jolt."

"Jolt! What a wonderful way to describe it," said Risalon. "I never really thought about it; it's part of our lives, just like breathing. You didn't feel that 'jolt', as you say, because you are fed and rested; you're not injured or sick."

Leena finished the thought. "So I don't need any healing…"

The old elf nodded. "That's why Healers are not as common amongst elves. The rare ones we have are precious indeed; not every enclave houses one. We seek them when a person cannot find relief in others' touch, or if the same people have touched the injured too often. Then each one risks falling ill. We share the wound or illness, you see. You can only share so much."

Leena's mind reeled. The very concept was so strange, she couldn't even begin to make sense of it. She needed to sit and think it out, even talk it out with one of these rare elven Healers.

The old elf laughed. "You look as if I had clouted you on the head!"

"Almost. This is so new to me, I don't know where to begin."

"You are in luck, Leena. You see, we are amongst the lucky enclaves. Not only do we house a Healer, but he is one of our own. It gives our enclave much prestige and pride." Risalon gestured and a younger elf approached. "This is Kilaron. I hope he can answer your questions."

Leena's eyes widened. The elf wasn't any more beautiful or different than the others, but for some reason, the very sight of him sent shivers throughout her body. She felt both hot and cold. Something in her body tightened, but she couldn't say what or even pinpoint where. When heat crept to her face, she looked down. She was blushing! Embarrassment cooled her down every effectively. She took in a deep breath and quickly regained her composure. When she felt her face should be back to its normal color, Leena looked up wearing an expression that she hoped was neutral. She was shocked to see that Kilaron's pale face had turned completely white.

His eyes were wide open. Leena couldn't decide if he was angry or surprised. "Impossible!" he whispered before turning around and leaving the cavern.

Risalon stammered an apology for the young man's behavior and hastened to follow him. Several elves went along, including the Mages, until only Lyandrin and four other women were left with Leena, Meeryle and Suqi.

The goupil barked, startling the elves. "I don't know," said Meeryle. Suqi had spoken, apparently. Leena could easily guess the question, though.

"What just happened, mother?"

Lyandrin tapped her nose thoughtfully. "I was looking straight at our withdrawn Healer when he arrived. As soon as he laid eyes on you, for the first time, I didn't only see one emotion cross his face, but all of them. The one that stood out the most was horror. Why, I don't know."

"Face it, Lyandrin, that little twerp was probably appalled to see he wasn't the only Healer here," said one of the women who had remained. She was older than Lyandrin, and stood with authority, yet her accent was so pronounced, Leena had to think a few moments before she understood her words.

"I know, Caliana, I know. It just seems strange, that's all. If he were so horrified, why come at all?"

The older woman harrumphed. "Because Risalon asked him to come. No one refuses him when he makes a request for the enclave. Even Kilaron wouldn't dream of disobeying his enclave leader."

Suqi barked again, but this time, Leena was sure the goupil was laughing. She turned to Meeryle, hoping her friend would tell her what the creature thought so funny.

Meeryle, however, wasn't laughing. She stared from Suqi to Leena, mouth open. "She said 'Soulmate'."

"What?"

"Suqi says Kilaron is your soulmate," explained Meeryle, a stunned look on her face.

"Impossible!" said Caliana. "You're half-human, Leena. Humans do not have soulmates, do they?"

Leena didn't answer. Her thoughts were a jumble. Her mother hadn't seen her when she first saw Kilaron. She'd never felt like that before, not even with Rokin – much to the boy's dismay.

"Leena?" asked Lyandrin. "Did you feel something?"

"Yes. I just can't explain it."

Caliana laughed in delight. "Could it be? Finally!" The woman left, followed by the other three. They were all very excited, but unlike humans, they didn't chatter on their way out of the cavern, which made the entire situation very strange.

"Come with me, all of you. Let's go back to your alcove and talk about this." Lyandrin almost dragged them to the end of the short tunnel and quickly drew the curtain. The girls sat on the mattresses while Lyandrin put some life back into the fire.

"What is going on, mother? I get the feeling Kilaron is not someone people like. Why did Caliana seem so pleased with this soulmate thing?"

The tall woman sat beside her daughter. "Well, the first thing you need to know is that Kilaron was really influenced by his mother all his life. The fact that he's a Healer made his parents treat him like royalty, you would say among humans. Don't get me wrong, he's a good boy, and a very good Healer, but his attitude…"

"Like Teerane. He sounds like he thinks everyone owes him everything."

"Not really, Meeryle. It's almost as if he's afraid of everything and everyone. He seems haughty to some, but I've seen the look in his eyes – he stays apart because he fears something. Now the second important thing is that children born of elf and human are very, very rare, Leena. I think you may be the only one. And here, where humans and elves hate each other… I'm afraid that after you all went to sleep, the word 'halfbreed' was in many mouths."

"So that's why Caliana was so happy. The seemingly mighty Healer has a halfbreed for a soulmate," said Leena bitterly.

"Something like that."

"Wait, wait. Lyandrin, you had a soulmate, no? Was it not great? Shouldn't we be happy for Leena?"

Lyandrin smiled. "In any other circumstances, this would be yet another event to celebrate. However, I'm afraid politics and prejudice will get in the way."

Meeryle shook her head. "I don't get it. What politics?"

"Think, Meeryle! Who would want a precious Healer to be the soulmate of a halfbreed?" Leena's tone was sharper than she had intended, but it was one of those times when her friend's lack of interest in things other than food and dragons got on her nerves.

"Don't yell at me! It's not my fault your soulmate is a cretin. You should've stayed with Rokin! At least he worshiped you."

Her lack of interest in the young hunter now made sense. She had always known he was wrong for her; now Leena knew why.

"Sorry, Meeryle. You're right, it's not your fault. I think I need to take it up with the one concerned."

***

Leena wanted to do this by herself, so she had stared at her mother until she relented and gave her directions to Kilaron's alcove. Now she regretted her decision; she was lost, and for some reason she was alone in the tunnels. Where were all the elves? She couldn't call Tikid for help, as the dragon was too far to hear her.

A bark brought her back to reality. "*Come, this way.*"

Leena yelped at the voice in her head. She had heard it only once before, but she knew immediately who had spoken. "So now you deign raise your voice!"

The goupil snorted. "*You're lost and I'm probably the only one whose help you'll accept*."

"Well. I'll have you know that I would have asked for directions if anyone was around."

"*You could just call out for help.*"

Leena had nothing to answer. Yes, she could have, but her pride prevented her from admitting to strangers she didn't know where she was. "Just lead on, will you?" The fox-like creature snorted again and guided Leena to a backward alcove without another word.

The curtain was closed. Leena was sure it was the right place because Suqi sat in front of the closed entrance. As soon as she nodded her thanks, the goupil ran back from where they had come.

She was now on her own. On the way to Kilaron's alcove, Leena had deduced that people were around; they were just busy in their working alcoves. She had heard noises proving the presence of busy elves. Suqi was right; she could have called out at any time. She sighed. Maybe Lyandrin was right and she had inherited Parin's pride.

Leena told herself sternly to get on with it. She had no idea on the protocol for entering someone's alcove. She couldn't knock, so she cleared her throat.

An irritated "What?" answered her. That was enough to anger Leena. Who did he think he was to treat someone thus? In her experience, anyone showing up at her door could be a patient.

She grabbed the curtain and pushed it aside, almost tearing it off in her anger. Any scathing words died as soon as she saw him, though. Kilaron was sitting on the floor, legs crossed, and had been holding his head in his hands. His head came up at Leena's sudden entrance, but the hands remained opened, elbows on his knees.

"You!"

"Yes, me. We need to talk." Leena made her voice as icy as possible, hoping all the while that it hid the flutter of her heart. Now that she could see past the signs of her physical desire, she realized how right he seemed. The young man had reached the same conclusion because his face briefly softened, making Leena ache even more to touch him.

He quickly got up, breaking the eye contact, and when he looked at her, his face was blank. "Close the curtain, I want privacy."

"It's only a curtain. Anyone will be able to hear."

"Only if we yell. The Mages spelled it to block out normal conversation."

"Oh."

"Yes, oh." He frowned and looked at her. "You don't know the first thing about elves, do you?"

Leena ground her teeth, ready to bristle, when she realized he seemed puzzled. He stared at her, biting his thumbnail. She couldn't be sure, but for a fleeting moment, fear lit in his eyes.

"It doesn't change anything," he muttered to himself.

"What do you mean?" asked Leena, confused.

Kilaron jumped, startled by her words, almost as if he had forgotten about her. He was starting to annoy her.

"I can't have a soulmate."

Leena blinked. "You're not making any sense. Don't all elves want to find their soulmate?"

He gave her an affronted look. "Of course they do! It's the only way one can reach one's full potential." As he said the words, hope lit his face, but he shook his head and it disappeared. "But what if it takes too much concentration, too much time? Focus is so important…" Pacing, Kilaron continued to mutter to himself. Leena only caught a few incomprehensible words, and surmised they were in the elven language.

The pacing and mumbling soon got on her nerves.

"I hope you're not this indecisive when it comes to Healing," she said.

"What?" He started, confirming that he had forgotten about Leena. What was wrong with this man? Was he as self-absorbed as Caliana had said?

"I hope you're not this hesitant with your patients. Healers need to be a lot more focused than you are, you know."

He blinked a few times, as if puzzled by her statement. "How can you know anything about Healing?"

Annoyance suddenly gave way to fury. How dare he?

She looked around and spotted a writing stick on the table. In one smooth move, she grabbed it and slashed Kilaron's cheek with it. He gasped in shock. The very act sickened her; she dropped the stick with a shudder. How could she have let anger get the best of her?

"You..."

"Shut up! You're hurt, now I'll Heal you." As she moved to put her hand on his cheek, Kilaron backed up and tripped on one of his chairs. He sat down abruptly in it with a resounding "oomph". His eyes filled with fear as Leena bent towards him. All anger left her. "I'm sorry," she whispered. "Don't move, I'll make it better." She now truly felt bad and disgusted with herself; she had never hurt anyone in her life and in a moment of anger, she had wounded her soulmate.

Her guilt must have shown as Kilaron relaxed. Leena let her hand hover over the wound, listening to the elf's life song. The screech of the wound wasn't all that important; she had only scratched him. Under normal circumstances, she would have simply cleaned it; Healing wasn't warranted in such a situation. But in this case, she had to prove to him she was truly a Healer. She therefore reached inside her, in the spot where her life energy rested, and pushed some of that energy out. Once it reached her hand, she put it on Kilaron's cheek, willing it to go inside his skin and grow it back together.

Normally when Leena Healed, she felt a jolt once the person was whole. This time, not only did she feel that jolt, but it was so much more intense, she gasped. Kilaron did the same and they stared at each other, with Leena's hand still on his now flawless cheek. For a moment, life sang through Leena's body. She closed her eyes and wallowed in the feeling. She felt right, complete. This young man really was her soulmate.

She opened her eyes, hoping to find the same feeling of rightness reflected in his eyes. His lips trembled on his blank face. They remained thus, without moving, for a long moment, until Kilaron pushed her hand away. He slowly got up, shaking his head, muttering in his language. At that moment, Leena didn't know what to feel: remorse for having been violent, sad because he obviously didn't feel as she did, or simply anger for the principle of it.

They stood beside each other, Kilaron biting his lips and staring at the floor, Leena slowly starting to seethe, when the elf looked up and gave her a penetrating look. He blinked a few times, a slow smile forming, when he shook his head.

"I don't know what my mother will say," he whispered.

Leena was taken aback. "What do you mean?"

"You're a halfbreed!" he yelled before leaving Leena on her own.

Chapter 6

Leena started down the corridors to return to her alcove, confused by Kilaron's parting words. Since he had obviously felt good when she touched him, he must be glad to have found her. But the hesitant look he had given her and his parting words implying prejudice left a cold feeling in her belly. Having physically hurt him also twisted something inside her. She was not a violent person; the only time she ever hit someone before was to slap a woman who had fainted.

Yet something in her, something she didn't know existed, had uncoiled itself and made her strike. What did it mean? That she wasn't fit to be a Healer? Healers never harmed anyone, unless they needed to defend their lives. In the village, Leena had never been in such a situation. If Corvin were here, would he once more declare her unworthy to wear the Healer scarf?

Refusing to let herself sink into the despairing memories, Leena listened to the song of life around her. That exercise always helped her clear her mind. She let the sound of healthy elves engulf her as she walked. Many were indeed present behind the closed curtains, their song much different from the human one. Whereas the dragon life song was overpowering, the elf life song was a quiet one, reflecting the race's apparent liking to silence. It was very strong, though. She didn't detect the typical wavering she heard amongst humans. Maybe it had to do with the touching they did…

As Leena entered the big cavern, Tikid's voice resonated in her head. "*Quick, Leena, Meeryle is not well at all and Suqi does not know how to look after her.*"

The young Healer broke into a run and passed the dragon. She didn't stop; Tikid would follow at a much slower pace and it might mean Leena would be too late.

Meeryle was lying on her mattress, face white, eyes closed, shivering under a pile of blankets. The fire was roaring, heating up the small space, and Leena almost immediately broke into a sweat. Lyandrin was sitting by her side, a worried frown marring her smooth face.

"Ah, there you are. Suqi looked like she was about to go looking for you. Meeryle doubled over in pain suddenly a few moments after you left. She said her stomach hurt, then soon after, the fever broke out. She was speaking up until a few moments ago. This is so sudden, Leena. In a case like this, I would send for Kilaron…"

"But he probably doesn't know the first thing about humans, does he?" She allowed bitterness to show in her voice. Her mother arched an eyebrow, but Leena shook her head. "Later. Let me attend to Meeryle." As she knelt beside the young Mage and put her hand on her stomach, Leena listened to her life song. The discordance was general, though not screeching as it would for a wound. However, around the stomach area, the discordance was more marked.

It was also familiar.

Leena dug into her memory, thinking back to each particular sound diseases and wounds made, and to each face associated with it. A little girl's face sprung up: she had drunk out of the small pond which formed after a heavy rain. She was too young to understand that unboiled water was very dangerous. Corvin had Healed her very quickly while Leena listened. Meeryle's life song sported the exact same discordance.

"Did she drink unpurified water?"

Lyandrin gave her a blank look. "What do you mean?"

"Mother, you mean to tell me you don't purify your water?" Leena was shocked. Everyone knew that to drink water straight out of a pond or a river was deadly. The water boiling was a tedious, but also a very necessary task.

The elven woman's eyes widened. "I remember now! No, elves have no need of preparing drinking water. It always amazed me to see Parin boil water. You both had tea this morning and water last night."

Meeryle had drunk the deadly liquid twice. Panic briefly overtook Leena, but she fought it hard. She needed to focus on Healing her best friend.

The tall young woman closed her eyes and drew in a calming breath.

"What are you doing, Leena?" asked Lyandrin.

She bit back an exasperated sigh. She was having a hard time staying calm, so interruptions were not welcome at all. "I need to Heal her, mother. Very quickly."

"Can I watch?"

The hope in her voice and the very question surprised Leena. "Of course. Why couldn't you?"

"Kilaron demands to be alone while performing a Healing. He might allow the soulmate to be present, but only if he or she insists."

He did, did he? It went against the principles Leena had learned. The only time Corvin would bar someone from witnessing a Healing would be if the person would cause distress to the patient. A friend or a family member's presence usually reassured the patient; a lot of people, though they knew about Healing, were very anxious when they needed it. That Kilaron would work without onlookers was so wrong in Leena's eyes that fury threatened once again. The hesitant smile he had given her doused her anger; could it be that something – or worse, someone – required him to be alone when Healing?

She tucked away the questions forming in her mind and smiled at her mother. "Well, I would be honored if you'd watch. But please do not speak, as I'm having a hard time. This is the second time I've seen Meeryle close to death."

Lyandrin smiled her encouragement, but stayed quiet. Leena figured her mother's presence would be very calming, but more for her than Meeryle.

Once again, Leena closed her eyes, telling herself this was just another Healing. Her self-confidence nevertheless waned. She had only ever done two complete Healings in the past; one for Tikid's wing, and Meeryle had been there to help her, and the other on Meeryle, with the dragon's help.

"*I am here, Leena. You must hurry, Meeryle's color is wrong. Do you need me for this?*"

Leena choked down a sob of relief. She was so taken with the situation, not only had she not heard the shuffling of the dragon along the tunnel, but she had also forgotten that the creature who could feed her healing energy was nearby. "Yes, Tikid, yes. I do need you. This is really bad, and I'm afraid I won't have enough life in me to Heal Meeryle."

"*Then I will provide it. We have Healed her before, we can do so again.*"

Lyandrin followed the discussion with widened eyes, yet she stayed quiet. Leena was thankful; she didn't want to give lengthy explanations at this point.

The dragon shone bright emerald and lit the tunnel in the strangest way. She extended a front paw, against which Leena leaned, both for the comfort and to receive the energy her friend would wield. Tikid sent a burst of Green energy, changing the life song around them briefly, and somehow pushed it into Leena. For the second time in her life, the young Healer was engulfed by the power of the Green dragons. Her entire body pulsed with it, boosting all her senses. She could smell the burning wood, the stench of sweat, and taste the sickness coming from her friend. She could hear her mother's breath, the dragon's heartbeat, the young Mage's labored breathing, the life song around her. She could feel Meeryle's trembling body under her hands, the twisting of her laboring stomach, even the flutter of her closed eyelids. Most of all, she could see the harmful things making her friend sick. They were dark brown, almost black, whereas the area around them was lighter brown. Only the very extremities of Meeryle's body shone the green of health the way dragons saw it.

Leena harnessed all that strange energy and willed it to extinguish the dark spots. A Healer didn't kill things that didn't belong in the body, but rather either pushed them out or accelerated their growth until they wilted. The spots became darker, creating a screech in Meeryle's life song, until they faded. The song was still a bit discordant, but it was the sort announcing recovery. Meeryle's breathing came easier and her fever would soon break.

"*She is fine, Leena. You did it.*"

"We did it, you mean. Without you, I wouldn't have been able to get rid of all the poison."

"Will she really be fine now?" asked Lyandrin quietly.

Leena smiled. "Yes. The danger is gone, now we just need to let her body heal the rest on its own. She will be very tired and weak for the next few days, but this is all. Mother, we must make sure our water is boiled."

These elves truly didn't know much about humans and it had almost cost Meeryle her life.

"*Leena, what about you? You drank, did you not? You told me more than once that all living beings need to drink.*"

Lyandrin's eyes widened. "You will be sick as well! We must seek Kilaron before it's too late."

Leena grabbed her mother's arm, preventing her from getting up. "Wait. I feel fine. How long did you say it took for Meeryle to be in pain?"

"Well…"

Suqi interrupted Lyandrin with a bark. "*She was not feeling well when she awoke. That's why she was still lying down when you got up.*"

Leena hadn't noticed it – probably due to her fright about an earthquake – but the goupil was right. Normally, Meeryle got up as soon as she woke; hunger had made the young Mage an early riser over the past few months.

"But I feel fine."

"*You are part elf.*"

"Tikid, that doesn't mean I'm immune to water. Which brings me to this question: why can elves drink unpurified water and humans can't?"

"*I was taught that it is because humans are not part of this world.*"

Leena and Lyandrin exchanged a puzzled look. "What does that mean?" asked Leena, all the while checking for the signs of water poisoning. "Humans are here, right? How can they not be part of the world?"

"*I do not know, I only say what I was taught. Talking about humans was always brief since we did not know them.*"

Leena smiled. The first time they had encountered the dragon, she hadn't know what Leena and Meeryle were. Tikid had never seen humans before.

"Well, let's not worry about this for now, it's not important. What we need to worry about is you, Leena. Are you feeling fine? I'm trying to remember when you were small if I ever gave you unboiled water, but it's been too long."

"Yes, mother, I'm fine. And I couldn't tell you either if ever drank unpurified water before now."

"Don't forget: you have been touched by other elves. It might have made your body immune."

"Or it always was and I never knew."

A groan from Meeryle stopped the conversation from going in circles. "I'm thirsty," she said in a hoarse whisper.

Lyandrin got up. "I will get water and give instructions to have all drinking water boiled while you're here. It won't change anything for us, but at least, you'll be safe to drink the water in any alcove you visit. I also need to report on the Healing that took place here. I wasn't aware that a Healer glowed so during the process!"

"Mother, this was special. Tikid can give me energy; it's something dragons haven't done in a long time and part of the reason why we're here."

"No matter, the entire enclave has to know about it. It might also help the prejudiced ones to overcome their dislike towards you."

***

In the end, Lyandrin's word wasn't enough. The entire enclave was asking for a demonstration of Leena and Tikid's skill in the great cavern. In itself, it wasn't surprising. Leena expected that anywhere they would go, people would need to see for themselves what it was a Healer and a dragon could do. The problem was the attitude a lot of elves had towards her as a Healer.

Apparently, Healing was a very special skill, one that a halfbreed simply could not have. No one explained where the dislike for halfbreeds came; Lyandrin herself didn't really understand it. The fact that she brought one up now made her partially an outcast.

Everyone in the enclave knew about her lost daughter, but she had never told them that the father was human. In her eyes, it was irrelevant, so in a way, she forgot to mention it. Presented with Leena's gold-specked eyes and light brown hair, the evidence was undeniable: Lyandrin had given birth to a halfbreed and hadn't bothered to tell the human-hating enclave that had welcomed her. When she had explained about her relationship with Parin, they had assumed Leena was Danpiron's child, and that Parin had accepted the child as his own.

Listening to all the arguments, Leena could not believe that elves could be as close-minded as humans. When Danpiron and Lyandrin had arrived to negotiate peace between human and elves, they did not have a child with them. Maybe they thought Lyandrin became pregnant just before Danpiron's death, but that would make Leena over twenty years of age, not her mere eighteen. Did she look older? Maybe elven children took longer to mature. Leena had to admit she was totally out of her depth on that one. She needed to speak with someone who knew about elven physiology, in other words, to a Healer.

It always came back to Kilaron. If only Leena could speak with him, she might understand better how things were, and she might be able to reason with this group of elves who were becoming very annoying indeed. But in the eyes of some, her status as welcome guest had changed to unwanted abomination. She couldn't count on her mother's influence – as Danpiron's soulmate, she had had a special status until now. In the day and a half that Leena had been at the enclave, Lyandrin's own status was now precarious.

Leena quickly noticed that this entire situation was stirred up by a small number of elves, who shielded Kilaron with their bodies as soon as Leena looked like she might get closer. That was so insulting, she almost yelled at them. Reason held her back. If she started to scream like a lunatic, she would lose even more of her already poor standing with these people.

She called for support. "Tikid, I know this'll sound strange, but I need you to roar."

"*It is not strange at all. I am reminded when you Healed my wing and the humans thought dragons were animals. It was very insulting; I was surprised my kin were not louder.*"

At any other time, Leena would have laughed at her friend's tone. The dragon tried to sound haughty, but she was still hurt by the very thought. However, this time,

Leena felt exactly the same way. "Your roar will have more impact than mine."

Tikid, who had been lying down, reared up on her haunches and lifted her head, stretching her neck to its fullest. She opened her toothless mouth and let out the most fearsome roar Leena had ever heard. In it, not only did she hear the dragon's frustration and anger at seeing her friends treated so, but Leena could detect the fear of having almost lost Meeryle because of the elves' ignorance about water.

Elves were a quiet lot, but apparently, up until now, they had been noisy in their silence. After Tikid's heartfelt roar, the cavern was so silent, Leena had to check to make sure people were still there.

Now that she had their undivided attention, Leena spoke. "I am not here to debate whether Lyandrin is a criminal for having given birth do me. As a Healer, birth is a daily miracle, no matter who or what the mother is. And I *am* a Healer." She glared around. Normally, she would have been able to look down on the people she was chastising, but for once, she wasn't the tallest person about. She didn't let it deter her. "Tikid and I have a special bond where she can channel the energy of the Green dragons to me, which allows me to Heal without drawing from my own life reserves. It also means I can Heal a great deal."

"Impostor! A halfbreed couldn't possibly be a Healer!" yelled one of the women who shielded Kilaron. From her looks, Leena guessed she was his mother. For a fleeting moment, she recalled Kilaron had said something about her…

Tikid roared once more. "*You doubt my word and through it, the word of Murod, the Great One of the*

Greens? When I seek Kiqod of the Whites, I will tell her that the elves no longer honor dragons. She will not be pleased."

The young dragon's words silenced the woman, but also stirred panic in Risalon. "We do not doubt you, Green dragon. Dragons always speak the truth. But you see, the discussions around a half-elf are… difficult."

"*Well, you need to explain, then.*"

Leena was thankful for Tikid's forwardness. She wanted desperately to understand why her status was so despicable. Lyandrin didn't know herself; the enclave from which she came sported multiple human-elf couples. However, when pressed, she had admitted none had ever had children. Those came from soulmated couples.

Having established that the most damage the dragon would do was make a lot of noise, the crowd had returned to its quiet noisemaking, while Risalon explained the aversion to halfbreeds. "As you probably learned, elves each carry one half of a soul. It is every elf's fervent wish to find his or her soulmate. Some find them in the same enclave, others need to travel. Some even find love with other unsoulmated elves, but when one finds his or her soulmate, they can love no other person. One does not choose his or her soulmate: when the two halves meet, they become one. Once an elf finds his or her soulmate, he or she can reach full potential.

"Humans do not have soulmates. They have lifelong mates, but they do not share a soul. This means that a child born of an elf and a human would have a fragmented soul, with only half of the elven part. That child would never come to full potential, you see. And that in itself goes against the very foundation of the elven ways."

“But… from what I can tell, Kilaron is my soulmate, meaning that I’m complete.”

Risalon turned to the elven Healer. Under his stern gaze, the elves guarding Kilaron parted. “Tell me, boy, is what Leena says true? Did you feel the tug of your other half?”

Leena’s held her breath. She knew they were one, but he seemed so unsure about her, she wasn’t sure he would admit it publicly.

Kilaron moved forward and faced Risalon. “Yes, I did, elder.” His words gave way to gasps, some outraged, and others, like Caliana’s, pleased.

“It is good. This means you will now reach your full potential as a Healer.” Yet he said nothing about Leena’s potential. Congratulatory noises were whispered, but only addressed to Kilaron. Leena’s pride dictated that anger was warranted. Just as she was about to object to this dismissal of her abilities, Kilaron resumed his advance and stopped right in front of Leena. He stood taller than her, just enough that she had to look up to meet his gaze, but he didn’t tower over her. His face was resolute, as if he had made a decision and his eyes were sparkling with interest.

He held out his hands and said: “My name is Kilaron. I greet you as my soulmate.”

A renewal of the gasps told Leena these words held special meaning. She had attended enough hand-fasting ceremonies to know ritual words when she heard them. Usually, they had to be repeated, so she complied. “My name is Leena. I greet you as my soulmate.” She put her hands over his, and everything stopped.

She was engulfed in bright light, surrounded by a resonating life song. Her body felt like it was torn apart, then brought back together, after which it somehow felt like something that had been missing without her knowledge was now present.

Then nothing. Total silence, total darkness.

Chapter 7

Leena opened her eyes slowly, enjoying the comfort of her bed. The rock ceiling was very close, though… recalling all at once what had happened, Leena sat up abruptly, banging her head very hard on the rock. She saw stars for a brief moment, but managed to blink them away quickly. Where was she? Why was the ceiling so low?

A chuckle startled her. "Are human beds so different from elven ones?"

Leena turned her head and stared into Kilaron's amused eyes. For a moment, not a word was uttered. Leena simply basked in the feeling of rightness the sight of the elven Healer brought. The sensation of being complete reaffirmed itself, and Leena smiled. Kilaron returned it, hesitantly at first, then fully, lighting his face. He truly was beautiful.

"So tell me, how do I get out of here without hitting my head?" They were in an unknown alcove, lying in the bed carved into the wall, just like in the alcove Lyandrin had shown the girls when they first arrived. The difference was the size; this bed was made for a couple. Leena blushed and checked herself. She was wearing the same clothes in which she had arrived, meaning she didn't smell so good. However, she was at the end of the bed and couldn't get out while Kilaron was there.

"Here, allow me, my lady," he said shyly as he got up.

Leena was surprised by the longing in his voice. She shuffled out inelegantly under his watchful stare. Very self-conscious of her grubby appearance, the young woman straightened her tunic and breeches, all the while avoiding Kilaron's eyes. Once she regained her composure and once she was sure any hint of blushing was gone, she stood straight and looked into the elf's eyes. "So, will you tell me what's going on?"

He opened his mouth, but no words came out. Mortified, he closed his mouth and for an instant, Leena thought he wouldn't answer. He quickly recovered his composure, and took in a deep breath. "I'm sure you know that we've acknowledged each other as soulmates." Leena nodded. "The bond only comes truly into effect once both halves openly accept it. Ours was apparently very strong because we were very much overwhelmed by it." He looked at her with eager expectation.

How could she know this? She didn't know him well enough to read his expression, and if she trusted her sight, he was looking at her, but his face was rather blank. Yet the feeling of anticipation and hope was there, and it wasn't hers.

Kilaron smiled. "You're curious."

"Well, of course. Aren't you?"

"Yes, but I'm more hoping that you can… help me." With his words, Leena suddenly felt a longing so deep, she almost wanted to weep.

"What is going on? I can feel emotions that aren't my own."

The longing abated as Kilaron nodded. "It's the bond. Soulmates share emotions. I can feel your curiosity, your frustration."

"Frustration? About what?" she bristled.

"You'll have to tell me; we can feel each other's emotion, but we don't share our thoughts."

"Oh." She *was* a bit frustrated with all this. Leena liked to know things, how they worked. The concept of soulmates was completely unknown to her, and so far, information about this bond had been sparse. “You’re right, I am a bit unsatisfied.”

Panic filled Kilaron’s face. “Not with me, I hope.”

The feeling was also threatening to overwhelm Leena. She concentrated to block it out; otherwise, she couldn’t think.

“Calm down. Why would I be unsatisfied with you?” She wanted to add that she was the halfbreed, not him, but caught herself. He definitely wasn’t an arrogant man; something else was going on.

“How did you do that?” he asked, eyes wide. Thankfully, she couldn’t feel his emotions.

“Do what?”

“Block your emotions? My mother said that she can always know what her soulmate is feeling, even when she doesn’t want to.”

“It’s just like when I have to concentrate before I can listen to the life song. I just close everything out.” How could anyone possibly function while feeling someone else’s emotions? It was rather unproductive.

He smiled. “See? How could I be unsatisfied with you? You just taught me something new.” For a moment, his desire to learn, to know, was so intense that it passed through Leena’s block. “The bond is right, no matter what anyone else says,” he muttered.

Curious about what he meant, Leena dropped the barrier blocking her emotions and was taken aback by the jumble of feelings coming from the elf: gratification, elation, guilt and fear. She didn’t know what to say or where to begin in order to address these conflicting emotions.

Instead, she changed the subject. “Are soulmates expected to teach each other new things?”

Kilaron smiled. “I have no idea and honestly, I don’t really care. I’m curious about the strength of the bond… It is a good thing, isn’t it? I’ve heard the descriptions, but I had no idea it would feel so…”

“Invigorating?”

“Yes! The word is perfect.”

Carefully erecting a slight block to let some emotions come through the bond without overwhelming her, Leena was glad to feel his happiness. Was she happy about the situation? She wasn’t sure. As usual, she needed more information before making any decisions.

“So, where are we? Is this to be our alcove? I couldn’t help notice we were in the same bed.” The telltale blush was threatening, but she managed to keep it to a minimum. She knew everything there was to know about intimate relations, but she had never experienced it herself. She suddenly regretted having refused Rokin; if she had accepted, she might not feel so silly.

He laughed. “Come now, it can’t be that bad. My mother told me many a girl would wish to be in your spot right now.”

Why a mother would ever say something like this to her son baffled Leena so much that she didn’t wonder if many girls had indeed found their way into his bed. “Except that I’m not just any girl, am I?”

This time, he was serious. “No, you’re not just any girl. You’re my soulmate. Truthfully, this is a most happy time for me. I’ve searched, I’ve been to other enclaves, so I’ve met many an elf, but none tugged my soul.” His eyes filled with despair. “I thought I would never find my soulmate, and that was an unbearable thought.”

Leena knew she was seeing his true feelings. Her heart swelled with sympathy and her first instinct was to take him into her arms, yet something held her back and told her to tread carefully. “Now you have me,” she said very quietly. The haunted look in his eyes was immediately replaced by a joy so intense, Leena thought she would cry. He truly was happy to have found her.

“Yes, I have you. And now, thanks to you, I will reach my full potential, even if you are not fully elven.”

All the good feelings disappeared. Leena made a face. “Now you managed to make an insult out of a compliment.”

He was serious. “Well, it works both ways, you know. I’m just not sure if I’ll be of any use to you. To answer your question, yes, this is now our alcove. It might be hard for you to bring your human friend here; my mother would be quite cross if you did. She’ll probably be asking that your mother doesn’t come either, seeing as she loves humans. And you really must do something about your clothing and your smell.”

Leena didn’t care about the feelings of guilt she felt from him through the bond; she simply let the fury loose. She spoke very quietly, but put as much venom as she could in her words. “Who do you think you are to dictate what I should do and whom I should invite in *my* home? Since we share it, it is also mine, isn’t it?” Kilaron stared at her in shock. She arched a mocking eyebrow. “Oh, has no one ever spoken to you this way before? I’m surprised. You’re such a spoiled brat, someone must have broken down and told you before now.” She put her hands on her hips and gave him the best haughty look she could manage.

Surprise and insult battled on his face and through the bond, but in the end, laughter won, much to Leena’s surprise. “I should have known that my soulmate wouldn't be one of these soppy girls that my mother pushes in my path whenever I leave my alcove."

"I wasn't aware I even looked like one!" Leena was proud of her no-nonsense approach to clothes and hair. To even suggest she could be like one of these attention-seeking fools boosted her fury to new levels.

"No, you look nothing like these simpering fools, nor do you behave like one. I've been trying to avoid many of them over the past few years, and none of them filled me with the quiet power I feel now. You do, however, look a bit worse for the wear," he added with a smile.

"Well, yes. I've been traveling for the past three months, I almost froze to the death on my way here, and between exhaustion and everyone's disgust with me, fancy that, I didn't get time to wash or change. Oh, and let's not forget almost losing my best friend because elves don't know humans can't drink unpurified water. I touch you, feel both the worst and the best I've ever felt all my life, black out completely and find myself beside a spoiled brat who thinks so highly of himself, he couldn't even fathom why I do not want to be in the same bed as him, and on top of all, refuses to acknowledge that I'm a Healer. So yes, I may lack a bit of polish. Sorry." The harsh words came out all at once before Leena could stop herself. She tempered her tone. "Put yourself in my place, Kilaron. I don't know a lot of people who like to be totally out of their depth. Up until we met Jatoron, I didn't even know elves existed. Now, all of a sudden, I'm one of them because my mother – who I thought was dead – is an elf. Apparently, I'm missing part of my soul, yet as soon as I saw you, I felt complete. How would you feel if our situations were reversed?"

"They would never be! My son would certainly never find himself amongst humans." Two elves had entered the alcove without announcing their presence. Apparently, this entrance curtain wasn't spelled for privacy. The woman who had spoken was the same one who had call her an impostor. She clearly could see her features in Kilaron's face, but the lines around her eyes and mouth betrayed a suffering which didn't seem to be reflected in her son.

"Mother," said Kilaron with a forced smile, "I present Leena, my soulmate."

"She is wrong and you know it!"

"*She* is here. And she hates it when people speak as if she weren't." Leena tapped her foot. "What is your name?" The woman stared without a word. If looks could kill, Leena had no doubt she'd have been reduced to a pile of ashes by now.

The man answered. "This is Safyn, and I am Candron, her soulmate."

Leena frowned at the wording. "You are Kilaron's parents, then."

"No. My father is from another enclave. My mother found her soulmate after I was born."

The young Healer's mind worked furiously. "I thought children only came with soulmated couples."

"Ha! Yet you're here, halfbreed, are you not?" Safyn's words were so full of rage, Leena was afraid the woman would soon be spitting.

"Mother, enough!" yelled Kilaron. His anger was pumping through the bond, its sudden intensity almost choking Leena. Safyn stared as if she couldn't believe her son had raised his voice at her. He didn't give her a chance to retort. "You come in here without announcing yourself, making it clear you've been eavesdropping. You would never do it to anyone else, so why would you be allowed to do it to me? You will acknowledge my soulmate and treat her with respect; otherwise, you are no longer welcome in our alcove."

Leena fought back the childish urge to say, "so there!" Thinking back on some of Kilaron's comments, she was beginning to suspect that her soulmate had been trying to overcome his mother's hold over him, without much success – at least until now. He had mentioned that Safyn had been pressuring him to take a mate, and he hadn't been interested. What does someone who can't deal with some attention do? That person retreats into his or herself, which can seem as being haughty. Leena had seen it with some of the younger children in the village, especially the ones who were at the mercy of the bullies. Kilaron had become more and more distant because he hadn't found a way to tell his mother how he felt. Apparently, when it came to his soulmate, things were quite different.

The elven woman was gaping at her son. Candron, however, didn't seem affected, but rather tired. "Come, Safyn, we will return later." He took his soulmate's arm and dragged her out of the alcove, almost stepping on Suqi's tail in the process. The goupil barked indignantly, which startled an ugly yelp out of Safyn.

Leena could hear the woman's angry muttering as the couple walked away and she bit her lip to keep from laughing. She looked at Kilaron, who was torn between amusement and annoyance. "Your family is even worse than mine," she said.

The elf shook his head. "You have no idea." A deep sadness seeped through the bond.

"Why don't you tell me, then," she said softly. She hoped learning about his family would help both of them understand each other.

But Suqi wasn't interested. She barked once again, calling for attention. She did not deem it necessary to address Leena, so the goupil simply stared at the tall girl.

"Let me guess, Meeryle's awake."

Suqi barked happily and left.

"What was that?" asked Kilaron, eyes wide with curiosity.

"That, as you say, is Suqi, who is a goupil. These fun creatures serve as familiars to Mages. Suqi is Meeryle's familiar, though so far, aside from being annoying and having Healing abilities, I haven't found her to be very useful in general or to a Mage in particular."

Kilaron burst out laughing. "I think you just sounded like my mother for a few moments."

"That's not a good thing, right?"

"No. But I'll forgive you this time."

Anger was about to surface when Leena saw the sparkle in his eyes. "Why, thank you, kind sir. Now, seriously, I need to see Meeryle. The Healing went fine this morning, but she still needs care. Knowing her, she'll be up and about, trying to stuff her face."

"Let me come with you. I do acknowledge you as a Healer, by the way. You did Heal that scratch you gave me…"

"I'm so sorry about that. I've never hurt anyone before. I don't know what go into me."

Kilaron smiled. "Oh, I do! You had the exact same look I've probably had more than once when facing my mother during a harsh conversation. It did prove you can Heal; it just felt different than what I know. Though I admit I've always done the Healing, rather than being on the receiving end."

"Come then. I'll tell you about how I can work with Tikid on the way."

***

While she followed Kilaron in the maze of corridors, Leena explained about Tikid's wing and Meeryle's injuries when the burning barn had collapsed on her. By the time they reached the entrance cavern, Leena had finished retelling the morning's Healing in the small tunnel.

"I can't believe it was only this morning." She looked outside the cavern, where snow was falling idly in the declining evening light. She found snow fascinating, so she moved toward the mouth of the cave to look out. The flakes were carried by wind gusts and moved up and down in an unpredictable dance.

She felt Kilaron's presence behind her, who spoke with a smile in his voice. "You tell extraordinary things, Leena. Notwithstanding the fact that you're half human, I understand why Lyandrin had a hard time convincing everyone."

She turned, surprised. "You hadn't heard about this? I thought I was filling in details."

"Oh, no. My mother dragged me to the main hall saying there was some nonsense that had to be straightened out. Once there, all I heard were arguments of the possibility of a halfbreed being a Healer and whether or not we wanted her here. Nothing about a dragon; I guess that had been mentioned before I got there."

"Well, now you know."

"Yes, I do."

"And?"

Kilaron was interrupted by a group of young elves. Leena remembered seeing them in the cavern the first evening she had arrived with her friends, but she hadn't seen them since. They all sported a mocking smile reminding Leena of Teerane, her village's bully, at her worst.

"Ah, will you look at that. The Healer and the halfbreed. It sounds like a nice title for a representation, doesn't it?" Now that Leena had been amongst elves for a little while, she could see the physical differences. The one who spoke was thicker than Kilaron, more like Jatoron. His face was on the square side, rather than the elegant oval of her soulmate. All in all, she thought that if an elf could be called ugly, this one was it.

Kilaron greeted the speaker coldly. "Saylun." He looked at the others and cocked an eyebrow. "Ulina. Nice to see you."

The elven girl was the only one not sporting a mocking expression. She was furious. "You remember my name. I'm surprised."

Ah, thought Leena, one of the simpering fools. She examined the girl and quickly came to the conclusion that it was a good thing she didn't care about her own appearance. Ulina was probably the most beautiful girl Leena had ever seen. Compared to her, she would feel very inadequate if she cared about such things.

Ulina, however, did. She looked Leena up and down with scorn, which worsened the more she looked. By the time she got to Leena's feet, the elven girl was sneering. "Well, I guess you did good, didn't you, Kilaron? You could have had me, and look what you got. I'm *so* happy for you."

For the second time in her life, Leena felt the urge to strike another person. At this very moment, she was glad she wasn't a Mage, otherwise, she would have burnt the girl to a cinder. Leena suddenly appreciated how much work Meeryle had to do in order keep her temper in check.

Oblivious to Leena's raising anger, Ulina stepped forward and stood directly in front of the young Healer. "You're nothing but a halfbreed, girl. Look at your hair: it's brown! And your eyes… yuck. You manage to ruin the effect of green with those specks of yours. You disgust me." And Ulina spit in Leena's face.

Never had anyone shown her such lack of respect. Leena let her fury rule her and she slapped Ulina as hard as she could. The elven girl reeled and backed up, hand on her cheek.

Saylun moved, fist raised, followed closely by the rest. "You little…"

Leena didn't give him a chance to finish his insult; she also didn't want him to see that her anger was now replaced by fear. "Saylun, you do know that a Healer can stop the heart from beating, right?" She extended her hand and curved her fingers slightly, looking for all intents and purposes like she was about to squeeze his heart for a distance.

The young elf hesitated. Unconsciously, he looked to Kilaron to confirm. Leena had no idea if elves could, but human and half-human Healers certainly could not do what she claimed – one had to touch the subject to Heal or kill with the gift. She hoped that no matter what, Kilaron would go along. This group had murderous intents.

Kilaron simply cocked his head to the side and smiled, sending chills down Leena's back. It was all

Saylun and his friends needed. They ran inside the cavern, dragging Ulina with them.

"Are you mad?" yelled Kilaron as soon as they were out of sight. "You never, ever threaten anyone like that!"

"What else did you want me to do? They were ready to throw me down the mountain, in case you didn't notice."

"Why did you have to slap Ulina?"

Leena was shocked. "You'd let people spit in your face and do nothing?"

He hesitated. "No, no, I wouldn't. It's just…"

"It's just what? Kilaron, these people were very dangerous. It's extremely easy for a crowd like that to do very stupid and permanent things." Leena had witnessed such an event when she was young, before they moved to the village. She didn't know why the crowd had been so angry, and she never asked her father, but she never forgot the sight of the man being literally torn apart. Parin had carried her out of the crowd as quickly as he could, but it hadn't been quickly enough. The memory made her shudder.

"Leena, this is all wrong. I need to think." Using what she had taught him a bare candlemark ago, he blocked his emotions from her and left her on her own.

The snowflakes, so beautiful moments before, were now just cold things getting into her face and hair. Fighting down tears, Leena ran to the safety of Tikid's tunnel.

Chapter 8

Meeryle was sitting, drinking something and talking with Lyandrin and Tikid when Leena entered. The sight of Meeryle awake and alive broke the dam that was holding the tears away. Leena crumbled to the ground, fists and teeth clenched, tears running down her cheeks.

"Leena! What's the matter?"

"Meeryle, you need to stay seated." Lyandrin's tone was stern, but kind. She put her arms around her daughter and hugged her tightly.

"*Leena, I cannot move and hug you too.*"

She laughed and hiccupped. "I'll consider myself hugged, Tikid."

"Well, will you tell us what brought this on? I was told you now have an official soulmate and that you fainted. I wasn't expecting you to cry about it; I thought it was supposed to be a happy thing," said Meeryle with a frown. The chubby young woman was still very pale, but her eyes were alert.

Lyandrin gave her a knowing look. "I gather this has to do with your soulmate."

"Well… not him, exactly. I think that in a way, he and I have the same goals; he just doesn't know how to go about it. No, the problem is elsewhere." Leena told her friends and her mother about Kilaron's mother, Saylun and Ulina.

Meeryle's eyes were wide open in horror. "You really think they would've hurt you?"

Leena nodded. "I pretty sure Kilaron wasn't feeling too brave either. They looked like they hated him as much as they hated me."

"They do, you know. Unfortunately, Kilaron's aloofness has brought him very few friends. His mother didn't help matters."

"*Then why not talk to him about it?*"

Lyandrin smiled. "Things aren't so simple, Tikid. You see, people were so thrilled to have a Healer born in this enclave that they didn't care that their attitude towards him could be detrimental. They only care about the prestige."

"*Oh.*"

Meeryle giggled and Leena bit down a smile. Over the past months, whenever Tikid didn't understand something about humans, all she would say was "Oh". After a few hours mulling over it, she would come back with endless questions about the subject. Leena wasn't sure if she should warn her mother or not.

"*Well, then maybe you should stay with me. You would be safer.*" The dragon had come to terms with the fact that she frightened people, but she didn't like it. However, this time, Leena got the impression Tikid wouldn't mind scaring a few elves.

"What bothers me is the thinking time Kilaron needs. What does he need to think about, anyway?" asked Meeryle with a frown. "And for how long? Is this going to change our plans?"

"*Well, we cannot seek the Whites just yet. Today, you were sick and Leena was soulmated, so it was not a good time to leave. From what I can tell, the snow fall will get worse. I cannot fly in a snowstorm, so maybe you should speak with the elven Mages, Meeryle.*"

The short woman groaned, but Lyandrin held her hand up to stop her from speaking. "I can tell you exactly what Kilaron needs to think about: his situation here.

Being soulmated to a halfbreed has made him quite unwelcome, especially given his aloofness. The people who were so proud to have a Healer in their enclave no longer will. And now, he has you to think about too, Leena; he's not used to that at all."

"He isn't all bad, mother."

"I know, but he has a lifetime of yielding to his mother to overcome. She has been ruling his life and through him, the life of this enclave for a long time. When you're comfortable with something, you don't really want to change it."

"But now he has no choice."

"No, he doesn't. What bothers me is the fact that he didn't consult with you on this. He should have; you're both part of the whole."

Meeryle scratched her head. "All right. Let's do the Mage thing, then. I mean, Tikid can't go anywhere, and apparently, neither can you, Leena. Lyandrin, I'm hungry and dirty. Do you think we could have a bath? I'm sure things will seem a lot better once we're clean."

Lyandrin smiled. "Actually, Tikid, if you can make yourself small, you can join us."

The young dragon could indeed squeeze in small spaces. She followed Lyandrin through endless tunnels, shuffling along, at times scraping her wings, while Leena helped Meeryle in the rear. Suqi sauntered along, peeking in the open alcoves they passed. Tikid grumbled in their heads about the lack of thoughtfulness when digging tunnels. The girls didn't comment, but just smiled. The dragon was patient with most things, but apparently lost her composure when it came to tunnels.

The grumbling stopped as soon as Tikid stepped out of the tunnel. The dragon was speechless. Leena quickly understood why; her eyes widened in amazement at the sight of the huge cavern lit with thousands of sparkling lights. In the middle, a steaming lake of clear water welcomed them. The ambient air was very warm and soothing.

A very old elf greeted them. "At last, our distinguished visitors. I've heard much about you, but I despaired you'd ever need my services!"

"I bid you good evening, Mundriana. This is my daughter, Leena, her friend, Meeryle, and Tikid, a Green dragon."

"Ah! This is one of the times where I wish I could leave my cave." The old woman smiled at Leena's questioning look. "These old bones need the warm air. I've been in charge of the pools all my life, but now, I must make the pools my alcove also. No matter, I hear everything there is to know. Everyone comes here at least once a day. You are long overdue for more than one reason." Mundriana punctuated her words with a wrinkled nose.

"Well, I for one will be glad to wash up all that sweat from the fever."

"Ah, yes, the poisoned human. When news came that you were sick, that was my first question. They just looked at me like I was crazy, but I remember when this enclave walked among humans and them among us!"

"*Can I go into the water? It seems most warm.*"

The dragon's eager question surprised Mundriana. "Why, I don't see why not. Are your bones like mine, then?"

"*Greens are not accustomed to cold. It will feel good to be warm once again.*" Without further comment, Tikid jumped into the lake, creating a huge wave that came crashing against them.

Mundriana shrieked. "You disrespectful creature! This is a tidy place! You have…"

"Peace, Mundriana. Tikid didn't mean anything by it. Since you are wet, will you join us?"

Lyandrin's smile won the old woman. She shrugged off her robe and motioned Meeryle to join her. "This way, girl. The steps will make it easier for you and me. Leena, if you wish to follow your dragon friend, dive over there. Just don't make a wave like hers."

Leena left Meeryle into Mundriana's care and quickly took off her dirty clothes. She jumped in without checking the temperature and was shocked by its heat.

"*This end is very deep, Leena. You are not tall enough to reach the bottom, I think.*" The dragon scooped up water with her wing and sent it Leena's way. The girl retaliated by pushing as much water in Tikid's face, thus starting a monstrous water fight.

***

Much later, clean, rested and wearing elven clothes, Leena enjoyed a cold meal with Meeryle in what they now called Tikid's alcove. The dragon was also lounging with them – hence the cold meal. She claimed cold food didn't smell as strongly.

"It feels so good to be clean!" said Meeryle. "And these clothes are so nice."

Leena had to agree. As much as she avoided any discussion having to do with clothing, she had to admit the long robes given by the elves were not only comfortable, but also very beautiful. For the first time in her life, the young Healer felt elegant.

"*Will you be sleeping here, Leena, or in your new alcove with Kilaron?*"

"If you don't mind, Tikid, I'll stay here."

"*Not at all.*"

"You're angry with him," stated Meeryle.

"Well, yes. He left me standing on my own like an idiot when I was really scared. What kind of man does that, anyway?" As she spoke, her indignation grew, to the point where she wanted to scream.

"Hey, you're right. Just… calm down."

"I am calm!"

Meeryle crossed her arms. "Really."

Leena sighed. "All right, I'm not calm. I'm angry. Here I'm supposed to have this soulmate who makes me complete and all that, and all he cares about is himself."

"Do you have to stay with him?"

Leena grew thoughtful. "Good question, Meeryle. I don't know and I haven't asked my mother. I don't feel like I need to be with him right now, so I know I don't have to be in the same room as him. But don't forget, I'm only half elf, so maybe the normal rules don't apply to me."

Tikid shuffled forward and leaned her head onto her front paws. "*So far, aside from your hair and eyes, everything about you seems elven. I would not think you are different when it comes to soulmates.*"

"Probably not," she responded, tugging at her robe. It was a pale yellow, which, according to Mundriana and her helpers, brought out the gold in her eyes. Who cared? Not her. Maybe if Kilaron had… Leena shook out any thought of her soulmate out of her mind. Before she stooped so low as to pretty herself up for him, he'd have to change his behavior and grow a stronger spine.

"Hey, I just had an idea," said Meeryle. "What about the cat thing?"

"What about it?"

"Can you change into a cat?"

"*You should, Leena. If you have a soulmate, then you have all the elven attributes. Changing into cat form is one of them.*"

The very idea pleased her immensely for some reason. Cats were quicker on their feet than people, weren't they? Their sense of smell was also quite something. She'd never imagined what it would feel like to be an animal, but now that she thought about it, the cat was a very appealing form.

She looked from Tikid to Meeryle. "How do you think one changes into a cat?"

Meeryle's eyes lit up. "You're going to try it? Right now?"

"Why not? Now is as good a time as any, no?"

The young Mage shrugged with a smile. "Go for it, then." She frowned. "Um… Leena? How exactly are you going to go for it?"

"Good question. I don't have a clue."

"*There is something inside you, Leena. Look for it.*"

She wanted to respond that there were many things inside her body and that as a Healer, she was very familiar with them, but she kept quiet. Tikid had seen her potential as a Healer before Leena even knew about it; if the dragon said that something inside her would make her change into a cat, she must be right.

"Let me think on this." She closed her eyes and took in a deep breath.

"What are you doing?"

Leena snapped her eyes open. "Meeryle, be quiet. I'm trying to concentrate." The chubby woman made a face at her. Leena smiled and resumed where she'd started.

She skipped over any physical part of her; she was pretty sure changing into a cat had nothing to do with muscle aches, her stomach or the number of heartbeats. The life song also didn't seem right; it was for Healing and something with which she was very familiar. She dug deeper, seeking something new, but found nothing. Yet she knew it had to be there.

Meeryle yawned, breaking Leena's concentration. She opened her eyes and assessed her friend. She was now fine, but the water poisoning had drained her. She needed the rest and…

Leena was struck by the thought. She had drunk unpurified water and she hadn't been sick. She theorized that whatever made her able to drink the water might have something to do with the ability to transform. What was it that allowed her to drink pure water? People got sick from unboiled water because whatever was in it overwhelmed the body's ability to heal itself, the immune system. She'd never examined hers before, just other people's systems.

With the sense that allowed her to hear the life song, Leena sought her immune system. It sang true, but as she listened more closely, it rang different from what she knew. To confirm her hunch, she quickly listened to Meeryle's. The song was quieter than usual, but that she attributed to fatigue. Otherwise, it was normal, and it didn't have that strange ring Leena had found in herself.

She concentrated on that new sound, digging into it until she did find something completely new, a purring sound. Leena was so surprised, her eyes flew open.

"What is it?" Meeryle and Tikid were watching her with an intensity she found a bit disturbing.

"Have you two been staring at me all this time?"

"Well, we want to make sure we see if you suddenly start growing hair all over your body."

Tikid laughed, sending Meeryle into a fit of giggles.

"Oh, hush, the both of you. You're being silly."

"*But you did find something.*"

How did Tikid know? "Yes. Now if you'll stop laughing, I might be able to find it again."

"Sorry," mumbled Meeryle between giggles.

Leena closed her eyes once more, and sought the purring sound. It was still there, warm and welcoming. It was so strange to have something inside her that felt warm and soft like fur. She liked it; it made her feel safe for some reason. Suddenly, Leena wanted that warm feeling not just inside a small part of her, but throughout her body. She wished for it with an intensity that surprised her, to the point where something in her reached for it. She couldn't tell what it was exactly, but the result was astonishing.

The purring sound spread from the center of her being to every extremity. As it got louder, the sense of warmth and safety spread, filling Leena with a relaxing sense of well-being. She felt every one of her muscles relax and she sighed with relief. It didn't last: her arms twitched. Then her legs. Soon, all her muscles were stretching in strange ways, and her bones were cracking.

Meeryle gasped. "Leena! Something's happening!"

Leena wanted to slap her friend silly for stating the obvious, however, she wasn't sure she could move at all, let alone make any move needing coordination on her part. All that stretching and moving went from being uncomfortable to painful, until she wanted to scream. She didn't; this was her doing, so she stubbornly clamped her teeth and didn't make a sound.

Her back did strange things and her shoulders moved forward, while her arms became shorter. Her lower back and buttocks shifted and her legs cramped in a strange angle.

"Leena!" Meeryle was sobbing. "Leena, this is wrong."

Leena had to admit she wasn't feeling too confident anymore. The pain was too intense and continuous for her to bear. She moaned, but something like a growl came out instead. Only Tikid's apparent lack of concern helped her keep the panic at bay. If this was wrong, she was sure the dragon would do or say something.

The pain stopped completely all at once. Relieved beyond belief, Leena collapsed to the ground.

"Leena?" whispered Meeryle. "Oh, Tikid, what are we going to do?"

The rumble of Tikid's laughter shook the alcove. "*You did it, Leena. You are now a cat!*"

She opened her eyes. Until that moment, she hadn't realized they were still shut. She almost closed them back; the light was very bright. She opened them slowly, allowing them to get used to the brightness. The first thing she saw was Meeryle's stricken face, still wet with tears. Leena opened her mouth to tell her friend that she was fine, but all that came out was "Mreow."

Tikid rumbled once more. "*You do not have a mouth made to speak anymore, Leena. You must use the same speech as mine, in your mind.*"

Easy for you to say, she thought. How did one speak with one's mind, anyway?

"Can you get up?" Meeryle's voice still quavered, but she was no longer crying. "Leena?"

Meeryle was getting on her nerves. She was fine! All she needed was a few moments to get used to her new body.

"Leena? Answer me!"

Leena growled in frustration. The sound started at the bottom of her throat and erupted through her open mouth, resonating against the tunnel's walls.

Meeryle jumped, startled. "Well, no need to be rude. I'm worried about you, all right?" She looked expectantly at the young Healer. "Well? Say something, will you?"

"Meow," answered Leena.

"Oh, that's nice. You can't speak?"

"*No, Meeryle, she cannot. She will have to learn the mind speech.*"

"Ah. Well, I'll try to stick to yes or no questions. Can you stand?"

Leena tested her new limbs and nodded. She put the front paws on the ground and shifted the hind leg in order to sit on her haunches. Getting up felt a bit strange, but she didn't lose her balance. However, the elven robe was very much in the way.

"Oh, good, you can move. You can see, right?" Leena nodded. "Obviously, you can hear." Leena rolled her eyes. "Yes, well, I'm trying to remember everything you ask patients, all right? I have to be the Healer here. Tikid's just smug…"

"*I have a right to be. Leena changed, and she is fine.*"

Leena laughed. It came out as a cross between a rumble and a cough.

"*You see? She is fine, I tell you.*"

Meeryle still looked doubtful. "Is she right?" Leena nodded. "So I can stop the Healer talk?" Another nod. "Oh, well, good then. So, how does it feel?"

How did it feel? Leena took in a deep breath and was assailed by the combined smells of her friends. Meeryle still had a bit of the sweat scent on her, but Tikid was like the pines, the earth, the moss… like the forest. She wanted to smile. Meeryle had tried to describe it to her once, and she had dismissed it. Now she understood. She wondered about the smell of a White dragon.

She stood, but the robe hampered her movement. Her efforts to remove it were in vain and Meeryle took pity.

"Wait, let me help you with this," she said. The two friends managed to remove the garment without tearing it, but it was frustrating. "Next time, get naked before you change shape, all right?"

Leena snorted and immediately reveled in her freedom of movement. She stretched and the sheer bliss of it made her purr. Stretching had always felt good, but this was something else! As she put each limb forward and allowed the muscles to extend, she felt better and better. She finally stood on all fours and took stock of the room.

The strangest thing was getting used to the change in height. Leena had always been amongst the tallest in the village since the age of fifteen, so seeing things from what amounted to half her height was a new experience. She was a bit afraid of moving forward, as she wasn't sure if her brain would know how to move four legs at once, but whatever allowed her to transform also knew what to do in order to move around without making a fool out of herself.

Moving her ears back and forth was amusing. It also allowed her to understand why animals heard things so well. The whiskers were the funniest. As soon as Tikid breathed, the change in the air tickled her whiskers and sent pleasant vibrations in her cheeks. She flexed something, and the whiskers moved.

"Oh, Leena, you should see yourself! You're beautiful. Your hair is almost golden, not white. And the tail is nice and fluffy."

She had a tail! Leena turned – the sheer angle of her head seemed impossible – and indeed, the appendage was there, unmoving. With a thought, Leena flicked it.

"*Ha! Now make sure you do not step on it*," said Tikid with a rumble of laughter.

"Hey, can I pet you now?" Leena hissed at her friend and threatened her with newly discovered claws. The chubby young woman roared with laughter and rolled on her mattress. "Watch out, hissy fit!"

Leena joined her and coughed her laughter with her. Meeryle pulled her ears, then her tail. At first, Leena couldn't evade her, but her brain soon showed her it had all the cat-like abilities. Within moments, Leena had pounced on her friend and was nuzzling her neck, ticking her mercilessly.

"Enough, enough! I surrender! I promise I'll never pull your tail again." The very statement sent Meeryle into another fit of laughter. Once she managed to calm down, she wiped her eyes. "That felt good, Leena. I'm still tired, but nothing sleep won't cure. I'm still hungry though. Do you think there'll be any food left?"

Leena rolled her eyes. Meeryle was indeed feeling better if her stomach was back in full action.

Meeryle had seen Leena's expression. "Hey, I'm allowed to be hungry. You haven't eaten that much either, and I'm sure changing into a cat was hard work. So come on, change back and let's go find food."

Leena nodded. The mere mention of food made her stomach gurgle. She sat and sought the purring feeling inside her, bracing for the upcoming pain of the transformation.

But the feeling wasn't there.

Leena search for it, everywhere within her body, but she just couldn't find it. Without it, she couldn't change back.

She was stuck in cat form.

Chapter 9

Leena fought down panic and tried reason. Surely things like this happened all the time with elves when they transformed for the first time. Dragons didn't learn to fly in one day, so elves must need a few tries before succeeding in switching from one form to the next.

But no matter what logical thought she called forth, no matter what calming technique Corvin had taught her to use when facing gruesome wounds she tried, Leena was slowly losing the battle against fear and panic. Everything was hammering down the fact that she was no longer in human form. Every noise, every scent was magnified, each a hard reminder that she was a cat. She couldn't speak, she couldn't cry, so she didn't even have the natural outlets to allay fears. For a brief instant, she wished she was a dog so she could howl her despair. She held on to the idea simply because it was something tangible. If a dog could howl, why not a cat? Leena tried it, but the only noise she made was a pitiful mew.

"Leena? What's the matter?"

Meeryle's question jolted Leena into realizing her friends didn't know what was going on. She could feel sorry for herself all she wanted, but it wouldn't amount to much if she didn't tell anyone what was happening. The panic was replaced with intense worry, and Leena could now think. She was a Healer! She should know better than just giving in. This problem had a solution; all she needed was to think calmly about it and to get her friends' help.

Communication was, however, a major problem. How did one tell her friends that she was stuck in cat form with only head shakes and nods?

"*Something is wrong. Leena, can you not change back?*"

Leena sighed with relief. She didn't understand how the dragon could know these things, but right now, she was very glad. Nodding vigorously, Leena sat in front of Meeryle and stared at her expectantly. She needed to ask questions for Leena to answer.

"Oh. How come?" squeaked Meeryle.

Leena growled with frustration. Ask yes or no questions, she yelled in her mind.

"*Leena?*" Tikid approached her head until all Leena could see were the red eyes. "*Look into my eyes, Leena.*" She did, and plunged into the red pool of the dragon's gaze. It lasted only an instant. Tikid blinked and Leena was back, unfortunately still in cat form. "*From what I can tell, everything is fine with you, Leena. Your colors are normal, so you should be able to change back.*"

How could she tell? Did dragons have Healer abilities? Dragons saw Mage and Healer potential through the colors each individual emitted. Did the color extend to the life song? The very thought made Leena automatically listen to Meeryle and Tikid's song. Meeryle's was a bit off, this time probably due to the anxiety over Leena's state, and Tikid's was the overwhelming, rich song it always was.

The life song further calmed Leena. Panic was such a useless thing, she thought. She needed her mother. Lyandrin could guide her. Now, all she needed was to find out where her alcove was, which could be problematic. No matter, she'd use her nose. She was bound to pick up her mother's scent somewhere, though she wasn't sure if she'd recognize it. She was still new at being a cat, after all.

She got up and left, when Meeryle's panicked voice stopped her. "Leena! Where are you going?"

Leena cocked her head and stared at Meeryle with what she hoped was a look that conveyed her intentions.

"Um… you're going to ask Kilaron for help?"

Leena rolled her eyes. Given his misgivings about himself, she doubted he'd know how to help – or if he'd be willing. She sighed in frustration and stared once again at her friend.

Meeryle bit her lip. "I don't know what you're trying to say!"

"*She's going to find her mother, dimwit,*" cut in Suqi.

Normally, Leena wasn't into insults, but this time, she agreed with the goupil.

"No need to be rude. Where were you, anyway?"

"*You know, looking.*"

"Snooping, you mean."

"*A goupil goes where she must, Mage mine. Now enough about me. Leena really needs help. She can't change back. Though why she'd want to change without any guidance in the first place is beyond me. Silly girl.*"

Leena stared, astonished, at Suqi. At first, she thought the goupil was talking to her, but the last comment made it clear that Suqi had not directed the words her way. She wasn't meant to have heard them.

Did the cat form allow her to hear all creatures in animal form? She knew Tikid could cut her out. Did it mean she would now hear everything she'd say?

Another thought crossed her mind. If she could hear Suqi, could the goupil hear her if she thought the words hard enough?

Leena gently put her paw on Suqi's back to get her attention. The goupil jumped. "*Careful! That thing's huge. Keep the claws in, will you?*"

The young Healer stared into Suqi's eyes and formed a question: Can you hear my thoughts?

Suqi blinked. "*Why, yes.*"

"*Oh, good.*"

Suqi kept on blinking. "*I shouldn't.*"

"*Why not? I can hear you.*"

"*Only when I wish you to. The only one who can hear me at all times is Meeryle.*"

The young Mage was standing, hands on her hips, foot tapping with impatience. "Well, this discussion sounds really stupid, you know? Who cares if Leena can hear you or if you can hear her." She stopped and frowned. "Actually, it's good you can hear her, because no one else can, not even Tikid. This is not the time to dissect the why of it, all right?" Meeryle pointed an accusatory finger at Leena. "I know you, Leena. You'll sit here, talking for candlemarks, asking question after question if I let you."

Leena was very thankful for the fur covering her body and the fact that cats couldn't blush. She had been about to do exactly what Meeryle was warning her not to do. She was a Healer, wasn't she? Healers needed to understand the whys of things in order to fix whatever was wrong. She couldn't voice her protest, though. Meeryle wouldn't hear it.

However, Leena had an unexpected ally. "*Well, I'd like to know how come she can! It's wrong; only my Mage should be able to hear me.*" Suqi sounded insulted by the very idea that Leena could be privy to her words.

Leena found the attitude insulting herself. "*And just what makes me below the honor of hearing you? Not that you have anything interesting to say, no! You have Healing powers, but you refuse to discuss them with me. You're better than everyone around you, is that is?*"

The goupil hissed. "*The relationship between a Mage and her goupil is private. Little Healers don't belong there, especially little Healers who think they can do everything on their own without proper preparation.*"

"Enough!" Meeryle was livid. "I can't believe I'm hearing this. Suqi, Leena is my best friend and she needs help. You can hear her, so you'll help."

"*But…*"

"But nothing! You've been hinting at the fact that we should be seeing to my training on our own, but now I think you're just jealous."

"*Jealousy has nothing to do with it.*"

"Oh, yes it does. So far, Leena's been more help to me in developing my powers than you ever have, and that rankles, doesn't it?" Suqi's silence spoke volumes. "You told me you had a special technique. Well, I'm not stupid, all right? When I really needed help in the forest, you just made me run around in circles."

"*It was to help you hear earth!*"

"You didn't help at all, I figured it out on my own, thanks to Leena's advice! So from now on, I want you to quit acting like you're the source of all knowledge, admit that Leena is worth something, and help her. Otherwise, I'm going to find myself another goupil."

Leena looked at Tikid, wondering if the dragon was as surprised by this outburst as she was. The red eyes were so wide-opened in surprise that Leena feared they would dry in place. Apparently, Meeryle had been having extensive conversations with her familiar over the past few months. Why had she never told her about them? Probably because Suqi had made her swear to secrecy. Apparently, Suqi was ambitious. From what Leena understood, Mages sought goupils to make them their familiars. Yet it had been the other way around; Suqi had approached Meeryle, called by her power. Now Leena wondered if the little creature hadn't done it in order to have this Mage before any other goupil could. If that wasn't ambition, Leena didn't know what it was. Now where a fox-like creature could go with ambition remained a mystery.

"*Meeryle, I am surprised, and I think so is Leena,*" said Tikid. Her voice sounded frightened. "*There are very strong feelings, and I do not like them. Your colors are flaring in a strange way.*"

The young Mage's eyes had indeed taken a red shade that Leena didn't like. Meeryle seemed oblivious to it. "I'm sorry, I'm losing my temper. But I get the impression that I'm getting used, and I don't like it." She stared pointedly at the goupil, who was sitting on her haunches, staring at the ground. "No matter. We'll go over this later, in detail. I think it's time I trusted my friends more than a *fox*."

Suqi looked up at the emphasis that Meeryle had put on the word 'fox'. "*I am NOT a fox.*" Leena winced at the loudness in her head. The goupil was furious.

"Well, you sure act like one." The red in Meeryle's eyes intensified, and this time, the fire in the alcove popped loudly.

Leena decided to put an end to the fight before Meeryle's temper set fire to everything around them. "*Stop acting like children, the both of you. Meeryle, your eyes are red. Suqi, please relay my words before she burns this cave down on us.*"

"*I would control it!*"

"*Like you controlled the fire in the barn?*"

The goupil stared at her. She sniffed loudly and relayed the warning. Meeryle immediately looked around, panicked. Tikid quickly calmed her. "*Your color is now fine, Meeryle.*"

The young woman crumpled to the ground. "You're right, Leena, you're right. I saw everything red again. I was so mad, I was going to burn everything down, starting with Suqi." She then burst into tears.

The goupil was frozen in place, eyes wide open. "*You... you wouldn't...*"

"*Meeryle is very tired, Suqi,*" cut in Leena. "*She was very sick and hasn't fully recovered yet. Fatigue will make people do and say things they really didn't mean. You should also know that Meeryle has quite a temper and works very hard at keeping it in control. She's a very easy-going person, but I have to say that you're pushing her to her limit.*"

The goupil looked at Meeryle, who was sobbing, rolled up on the ground. "*I will go now.*" Without another word, she left, tail and ears down.

Tikid sighed. "*I think we need to rest. This was very strange, Leena.*"

She agreed, but she couldn't answer. At this point, it didn't really matter what form she wore; Leena was exhausted and her best friend was in even worse shape. She gently bumped her head against Meeryle's shaking shoulder. "Mreow?" She put in as much love and caring in that sound.

Meeryle looked up and smiled. "Yes? You need a hug, big cat?" She sat up and wiped her eyes. "Actually, I do too."

Leena nodded and wished she could smile too. She put her head on Meeryle's left shoulder and her paw on her right shoulder. The chubby Mage hugged her tightly around her fluffy neck and cried some more. Tikid joined them as best as she could in the confined space by encircling them with her tail.

They stayed entwined until Meeryle ran out of tears. At that point, the young Mage's eyes were closing on their own. She probably would've gone to sleep fully dressed if Leena hadn't tugged at her friend's tunic with her teeth. The taste of the fabric left her mouth dry, but she didn't care.

Meeryle curled on her mattress under the covers, against Tikid, while Leena snuggled against both friends. The dragon dimmed the shining light by touching it, and soon, Leena fell asleep.

***

A gasp woke her up. Leena refused to open her eyes, wanting to remain in the warm comfort of sleep.

"Leena, is that you?"

At the sound of Kilaron's voice, Leena's eyes snapped open.

Tikid yawned. "*Good morning, Kilaron. Yes, this is Leena; however, we cannot hear her inner voice*."

Under Kilaron's disbelieving stare, Leena got up and stretched slowly, waking Meeryle.

The chubby young woman rubbed her eyes and yawned. "Good morning, Kilaron." She looked around. "It is morning, right? We can never tell in here."

"Yes, it's morning. What happened to Leena?"

"She changed into cat form."

The elf gave her an aggravated look and sighed. "I can see that. But why?"

"Because she could."

Leena sat and listened. She couldn't participate, as Suqi hadn't returned. Besides, she doubted the goupil would want to cooperate.

"Why didn't you wait for me?" Kilaron stared at Leena, truly upset.

Before Leena could growl, Meeryle stepped forth. "Wait for you? You left her alone after a bunch of bullies threatened her! Why should she wait for you for anything?"

Kilaron stared at Meeryle, as if truly seeing her. "I had gone to think. Saylun and his friends needed to be dealt with as soon as possible."

"*I am not surprised Leena is still deciding if you are worthy, Kilaron. You do not treat her as a person, but as an afterthought. I would not like it,*" said Tikid.

The young man stared open-mouthed at the dragon. His gaze shifted to Leena. "Is this true? You want nothing to do with me?"

Leena didn't nod; all in all, it wasn't true. But until Kilaron made up his mind, she wanted to be as far away from him as possible. She pushed the thought as hard as she could, in the same way she had with Suqi. It didn't hurt, and Kilaron just might hear her.

Kilaron jerked. He stared intently at Leena, who simply repeated the thoughts over and over.

"I… You're trying to speak with me."

She nodded.

"Only Suqi can hear her. Is that something you can do? Speak in other people's mind like Suqi and Tikid?"

"Ah... yes, of course. It's something we learn as soon as we change. Why can't Leena do it?"

Meeryle made a face at him. "For a Healer, you don't know much, do you?"

"What is that supposed to mean?"

"Don't get all huffy on me. You keep asking me why Leena can't do something. You're the Healer, you should know."

Leena shook her head in discouragement. These two would probably throttle each other before they managed to accomplish anything positive. She didn't know if Meeryle was jealous, which was highly improbable, but she acted like Kilaron wasn't up to her standards for Leena. Kilaron, on the other side, had been so influenced by his mother that he didn't know how to react to a human.

Leena sighed. This was taking too long; she was hungry and she wanted to get back into human form. While her friend and her soulmate stared daggers at each other, Leena looked at Tikid and nodded. The dragon understood; she got up and moved forward, forcing the staring match to an end. Leena preceded the lot, glad to be moving.

"What are you doing, dragon?"

"*My name is Tikid and I am leaving. I need to get out and fly.*"

"Wait! You can't leave!"

That stopped them. "*What do you mean, I cannot leave?*" She gave him the full brunt of her red stare and moved close enough to touch the elf with her snout.

Kilaron blanched. Tikid hadn't reached her adult size yet, but she was still very big. "Ah... I meant that Leena can't leave."

And why not? thought Leena as hard as she could, which Meeryle unknowingly echoed out loud.

"Well… what will everyone say?"

"Oh, for love of life, Kilaron, who cares! This is what Tikid meant, by the way. You're not worried about your soulmate, you're worried about your image. Now, if you don't mind, Tikid needs to stretch and Leena needs to find her mother."

"Why?"

Meeryle exchanged a look with Leena. "Why what?"

"Why seek your mother when I'm here?"

Before Meeryle could start another yelling match, Leena put her paw on her friend's hand, hoping she would stay quiet. While she wasn't exactly sure, she had a feeling that Kilaron would do anything before seeking his own mother. The relationship between Kilaron and Safyn was very complex and not healthy at all. However, she was in no position to explain any of this to Meeryle or to question Kilaron about it.

As Tikid was shuffling on the spot, Leena moved things along by jumping ahead and running into the main cavern. She didn't have far to run, but she still found the speed exhilarating.

Herded by Tikid, Meeryle and Kilaron had no choice but to follow, cutting short any argument.

When Leena burst into the cavern, breakfast was still served, though from the small numbers present, she guessed it was coming to an end. She spotted Lyandrin, but before she could make her way to her mother, gasps stopped her.

"Who's golden?"

"Why be a cat here?"

"Especially at breakfast, you know, with no meat served."

Her presence started a rather unusual murmur among the elves present.

Meeryle and Kilaron came out of the tunnel unnoticed. Tikid turned a few heads as she made her way to the entrance, but the golden cat was apparently much more interesting. Once the dragon had taken flight, Meeryle made her way to the food table, also unnoticed. Kilaron hovered on the side, hesitant to join the small crowd. Leena suddenly wanted him to stand by her side. All these green eyes, questioning, wondering who would be strange enough to come to breakfast in cat form… though with Meeryle present and Tikid having passed all of them, no doubt they knew it was the halfbreed.

Leena had assumed that, since elves changed, it shouldn't come as a surprise to see a cat. However, now that she thought about it, aside from Jatoron, she hadn't seen any elves in cat form.

What had she been thinking in coming out here? She should have stayed in Tikid's alcove and waited for her mother. These people saw her as an abomination in human form; what about a golden cat? Apparently, cats were supposed to be white.

When she spotted Ulina, Leena's heart sank. She frantically looked for Saylun, but the beautiful elven girl seemed to be on her own. Ulina made her way towards Leena, a nasty smile deforming her face. Leena sat on her haunches, bracing herself for the impact of the girl's mockery. But Ulina wasn't looking at her; the elf's eyes were targeting something over her. Leena didn't want to turn, as she wanted to seem sure of herself. If she could do so with whiskers was another matter entirely.

She almost jumped when a hand gently landed on her head and the bond between her and her soulmate became suddenly open. The immediate sense of completeness warmed Leena; Kilaron had silently come up behind her and they now presented a united couple.

The bond between was much stronger than Leena had previously experienced. She tried to mute it down, but she couldn't. The fear, outrage and pride that came from Kilaron were overwhelming. Since she couldn't muffle any of these emotions, she sent some of her own. Gratefulness for his presence and pride that he wasn't letting prejudice guide him were the first feelings Leena pushed through. Kilaron was surprised at first, then happy, to the point where he dampened his emotions.

Why wouldn't her mental barrier work? Because he was touching her? Or was the cat form to be blamed?

"So, not only do you have a halfbreed as a soulmate, but also a yellow cat! Did you not tell her when it was proper to change? Or did she want to show how ugly she is?"

The barb didn't sting as intended; Leena was very comfortable with her appearance – usually. She hadn't yet decided if she liked her cat form or not. Until that moment, it hadn't even occurred to her that she should maybe try to see herself in her present shape.

Kilaron, however, was much more affected by the comment. He was sensitive to shots against his soulmate's looks. "Leena is far from ugly, Ulina. I find her quite exceptional. The golden fur she displays, is, I believe, something you've been trying to achieve, is it not?"

How and why would anyone want to change their fur color? Leena really needed to get information about the necessity of shifting shapes.

The comment infuriated Ulina. Teeth clenched, she moved forward, but thankfully Lyandrin intercepted her. "Enough. Ulina, you've made it quite clear that you wanted Kilaron, if not as a soulmate, as least as a permanent mate. Such arrangements are void as soon as the soulmate is found."

"I know!" yelled Ulina.

"Then, child, accept it," cut in Caliana. "You make yourself a nuisance by acting the way you do."

"But he denied me before *that* came," she replied, pointing at Leena.

"That will be enough!" Kilaron's yell quieted the room. "You are speaking about my soulmate. Never, ever, have I ever heard such comments made about someone's soulmate."

"Ah, the remote Healer isn't as withdrawn from his emotions as we were led to believe," said Caliana. "However, I agree. Ulina, jealousy doesn't become you. You should seek your own soulmate rather than attack Kilaron's. Make no mistake, your actions with Saylun haven't gone unnoticed. Threatening a guest, halfbreed or not, is unacceptable."

Ulina's face blanched. She turned and almost ran out of the cavern. Leena expected someone to go after her, but everyone simply stood, some eating, but all looking at Caliana.

The old woman addressed Leena in a gentle tone. "You really have shaken this enclave, child. First as Lyandrin's daughter, then as a Healer, and as Kilaron's soulmate. You might also be the only halfbreed alive, Leena. Lyandrin didn't know it, but here, any such child would have been put to death."

"But why?" Meeryle's question resonated in the silent cavern. "Why would you kill a baby?"

"This is not the time for answering this question, Mage. But you are very much entitled to an answer," said Risalon. The old man had made his way to Leena and her friend. "I have arranged for our Mages to help you purify water, and now I see that we need to cover the mechanics of shifting. It will also be a good time to explain why Lyandrin erred in having Leena." He put his hand up, preventing Meeryle from making any comments or asking any further questions. "You are amongst elves, Meeryle. You will follow our ways. The discussion about halfbreeds is not a public one." He turned to Leena. "I am sorry you weren't able to prove yourself as a Healer, Leena. That Kilaron's soulmate is also a Healer is nothing short of a miracle. You also make a striking cat, young lady, though such show of beauty is usually reserved to travels outside our mountain. But no matter. Please, get some food and follow Lyandrin and myself. I pledge that you will no longer hear any demeaning word about your origins, neither you, nor your human friend. We are at odds with our human neighbors, but it does not mean that we must be at odds with all humans."

He looked around, making eye contact with each person, ensuring they would carry his words to all elves from the enclave. Some met his gaze squarely, but others tried to evade it. Leena tried to identify those, thinking they may not be as friendly if she ever met them on their own, but she didn't recognize any of them.

"Come, Leena," whispered Kilaron.

Meeryle had filled a plate for the three of them and followed Lyandrin, trying very hard not to drop anything. Leena looked around her once more, meeting curious and sometimes mocking gazes. The sheer nonsense of the situation threatened to make her giggle. Here she was, with her mother, a soulmate, in cat form, surrounded by people who despised her for what she was.

As she walked out of the cavern and into yet another tunnel, Leena suddenly missed the silly and everyday problems of the village.

Chapter 10

A few candlemarks later, after a lengthy conversation with Risalon and Lyandrin, Leena forced herself to concentrate on the Tassym's words, the elven Mage who would be teaching Meeryle. The young woman would probably miss half of it and need Leena's help later on. She was hoping that the lesson in Magery would allow her to forget everything Risalon had said. If his information was right, Leena might truly be the only halfbreed alive.

"So." The elven Mage paused and blinked. "Elves do not have them, but I know for a fact that humans do use familiars. Where is yours?"

Right on cue, Suqi came trotting in. Her ears were a bit more perked up than the night before, but the goupil didn't seem as full of herself as usual. Meeryle gave Suqi a questioning look.

"*I will listen.*" Leena wasn't sure what she truly meant, but Meeryle seemed happy with the statement.

The elven Mage looked at his student and her familiar for a long moment. Leena wondered if he had heard the comment. He simply nodded and continued with the lesson. "So." Tassym paused again. "It is my understanding that goupils can store energy for the Mage to use."

Meeryle shrugged. "Then you know more than me. So far, the only thing my familiar has done for me was Heal me."

Tassym frowned. "Is that a normal function of the familiar?"

Leena's ears straightened. Finally, she might get some answers. The goupil had managed to evade her at every turn, but now, if Meeryle was to train, Suqi would have to give out the information.

"I don't know," answered Meeryle. "Suqi?"

The goupil's ears drooped. "*Yes.*"

"Yes," repeated Meeryle. "Just this once, I'd like you to speak to everyone. I don't want to have to repeat everything you say. Leena had to do it with Tikid, and believe me, it was very frustrating."

Suqi's ears drooped even more. "*Yes, I remember. You couldn't hear the dragon and you couldn't hear me.*" Meeryle had to almost die before her power stopped shielding her, preventing her from communicating with the dragon and the goupil. "*All goupils can Heal; we can use the energy stored. In your case, you hadn't given me any, so I had to use my own reserves.*"

"So." Yet another pause, which seemed a rather peculiar part of the elf's speech. "A Mage needs to give his or her familiar energy. This energy can be used by both, depending on the circumstances. Now, the first thing we need to do is to transfer some of that energy." Tassym waited expectantly. Meeryle looked to Leena, begging for help.

"*Suqi, can you tell her how to do it?*"

The goupil stared at the ground. "*No. I just know how to receive it.*"

Leena sighed; it came out as a snort through her cat nose. "*The first thing we need to do, then, is to help me communicate with everyone.*" It would also allow her to discuss Risalon's words with Lyandrin.

"So. You're right, Leena," said Tassym once Suqi had relayed her words. "That you cannot shift back is understandable given your age; we normally shift very young. Your body is probably telling you it needs to recover first. I think you'll be able to change back once you've fully accepted who you are." Leena wanted to cut in and ask details, but Tassym couldn't hear her. Before she could ask Suqi to relay her words, the Mage had continued. "The mind speech, though, is simply a matter of concentration. You can hear the goupil and the dragon, right?" Leena nodded, but didn't point out she shouldn't be hearing Suqi. "So. And the goupil can hear you?" Another nod. "So. I think it is only a matter of setting your mind the right way. Your soulmate should be a big help." The last was said with a very neutral tone. Tassym was not impressed by the enclave's Healer, then.

"Of course, I will help." Kilaron knelt in front of Leena and put his hand on her head. "Touch is always better when first learning the mind speech. Usually, since we learn it as small children, touching our parents helps more than words." Kilaron's touch opened the bond between them; he was filled with positive emotions, making Leena feel complete. "I'm not good with mind speech in elven form, Leena, none of us really are. Something about the different brain shapes. But I should be able to hear you, even if I can't speak into your mind."

"So. Kilaron is right. I would also suggest getting rid of any doubt." Tassym gave Leena a knowing look. Was she that obvious?

Refusing to let the man know he had stung her, Leena sighed and allowed all her muscles to relax. She looked into Kilaron's eyes and wished she could smile. It was stupid, in a way, to feel so good simply by looking into someone's eyes.

Kilaron burst out laughing. "I think so, too."

"*You heard that*?" Leena wasn't sure if she should be glad or embarrassed.

"Yes, I did."

"*Oh. Well. Good, then.*" She was babbling, and probably getting nice and red underneath the golden fur. "*Let's get on with this, then. Meeryle, can you hear me?*"

The chubby young woman grinned. "Yes, and I heard the rest too."

"*Oh, hush.*"

"Like I'm ever going to forget this."

"*Meeryle, I'm wondering how sharp my claws are.*"

The young Mage laughed. "It's good to hear you. You don't need your claws to slice open my throat, your tone will do for sure."

Leena sniffed loudly, and the scent of food, sweat and whatever was used to clean clothes overwhelmed her sensitive nose, sending her in a sneezing fit. Kilaron was trying so hard not to laugh, he was shaking. "*Oh, don't you start, Kilaron. I could try out my claws on you too.*"

"So. You can now communicate." Tassym's blank face betrayed his own resistance to laughter. "I believe you will find it easier with time. At first, you might need to concentrate and recall the state of well-being you felt with your soulmate, then mind speech will become automatic. So. I understand you had a suggestion for Meeryle and her familiar?"

The Mage's dry tone calmed everyone down.

"*Right. Meeryle, you've transferred energy to me, so you know how. I just don't know if Suqi can deal with it.*"

"*Of course I can! Any type of energy is fine. Earth, air, water or fire, just go ahead.*" The goupil was insulted.

Leena rolled her eyes. "*All I'm saying was that Meeryle gave me power to Heal; I don't know if you need it in a more... neutral way.*"

Meeryle threw her hands up. "Just stop it, both of you. Let's try this. But wait. Why do I need to transfer power to you? I mean, all I need to do is just to draw power from the elements around me, no?"

"What if you need to light a fire under water?"

Tassym was serious, but Meeryle laughed. "Why would I want to do that?"

"I just gave you an extreme example. Never turn down the opportunity to gather power. Elves cannot transfer power to goupils, as we have an animal form and we can store our energy in our inner cat, but humans have no choice."

"You are worse than Tikid. None of this makes any sense!"

"*It does, Meeryle. Remember what Tikid said about humans not being part of this world*?" Something was nagging at Leena. "*Tassym, are humans the only ones who don't have an animal form?*"

"I'm afraid so. Elves, melusins, feufollets and sirènes all have an animal form. Dragons are different, as they are more the world than part of it."

"What? Leena!"

Leena ignored her friend. "*Is that maybe why humans can't drink water*?"

The Mage shrugged. "Maybe. I will confess this is a very interesting question, one just as interesting as to why elven Healers are so rare, but this is not the time to discuss it."

So many questions! Leena's mind was bursting with them. Meeryle cut them short. "All right, let's try this, then. Suqi, I was touching Leena when I did this. So do I touch you?"

Kilaron was listening with rapt attention. Maybe he had never seen a Mage work before. Leena blocked them out. She was sure Meeryle and Suqi could pull it off.

Instead, she recalled Tassym's and Risalon's words and analyzed their meaning. Dragons were the world and humans were not part of it. Elves were, though. Is that why elves hated halfbreeds so much? They had a logical explanation for it, but Leena had proven it wrong just by having a soulmate. What Risalon had said about fragmented souls the previous day and in detail earlier was at the base of everything: elves dedicated their lives to make their souls whole. Of course, Lyandrin had explained that depending on the individual, the quest was more or less taken to heart. Some elves never found their soulmates and were fine, whereas others made it an obsession, and turned bitter.

Kilaron's mother was one such; she thought she had found her soulmate. In truth, she had fallen deeply in love. Kilaron was born, and, a few months later, his father found his soulmate in another enclave. Safyn never recovered from it, even once Candron found her. The damage was done. The fact that children born of unsoulmated couples were extremely rare didn't help. Only once his Healer gift appeared did she acknowledge Kilaron and thrive.

Leena didn't agree with the thriving part; Safyn was bitter and the only thing that thrived was an unhealthy ambition seasoned with pride and condescension. Safyn and her son were above everyone else. From what Leena could tell, the woman was so intent about what others thought of her, she had managed to make Kilaron second guess himself ever since the Healer gift made itself known; so, for over ten years. It was a long time of bad habits from which to recover.

It didn't matter; Kilaron was a Healer, his mother was celebrated for it. Children of unsoulmated couples were usually deemed precious because it seemed most of them became Healers. It wasn't a proven thing, and according to Lyandrin, the research in that direction often led to heated debates amongst elves. One thing was sure, for elves to procreate outside the soulmating, deep love was necessary. Leena wondered if the soulmating really meant finding "your one true love", as Navee had put it. The girl had been the village's biggest gossip and romantic. Up until now, Leena had dismissed it as silly, but suddenly, the words had taken on meaning.

Risalon had gone on, explaining that elves found their soulmates and only then had children. A child like Kilaron was born maybe once in each generation. However, when it came to children issued of human and elf couples, things were different. Human women didn't need the extreme feeling of love to procreate, and apparently, Risalon had heard reports of numerous such offspring. Every time, the elven father would tell the woman the child could not be allowed to live; of course, every time, the human woman would respond by casting the father away in horror. The child would come into the world without any problems, but invariably die a few weeks later. Any requests for help from the elven father would be met with refusal.

In the extremely rare event that an elven woman would find herself with child from a human man, she would seek the Healer, who would put a stop to the pregnancy. That part was never shared with the human father; usually, the woman felt ashamed of having almost brought a halfbreed into the world.

The last baffled Leena; all the women she had ever seen were happy to be with child. Corvin had warned her that in bigger villages and cities, some children were not welcome, but she had never seen it. Risalon had explained that no elven woman would want to give birth to a child who could never be whole.

Yet Leena was whole, wasn't she?

All of Risalon's explanations left a sour taste in Leena's mouth. Everything else he added, about why the children died, were details that drowned the basis of the hatred for halfbreeds. A belief. Elves believed that a half-elf, half-human couldn't be complete. Was that a reason to end life before it even began? Yet that belief was truth to them. Kilaron himself had never had to end an unborn baby's life, but he admitted he would have done it if asked.

Only Lyandrin's presence had kept Leena from leaving in disgust. Lyandrin, who had fallen so deeply in love with Parin she had been able to have a child. Lyandrin, who was so happy to be able to love again after the loss of her soulmate, was beside herself with joy to have a little one. She knew men from her enclave had had children with human women and that the babies had all died, but she hoped her child would survive. She was ready to take the risk. She never shared her doubts with Parin. Whether he knew about the risk or not, he never questioned Lyandrin. He was happy to become a father.

Leena survived. Just after the birth, Lyandrin remembered the warning against fragmented souls and the impossibility of the child to ever become whole. But the baby was healthy and beautiful. It seemed impossible for the little girl to grow into the despised halfbreed she's heard about all her life. She couldn't possibly kill her baby or deprive Parin of his daughter.

"Why did Leena survive when no other baby did?" Meeryle had asked.

"The touch. Elven babies need to be touched by other elves in order to live and grow," had answered Kilaron. "Through the touch, elves share sickness, but also life."

"So all the elven men had to do was to invite the human women and the babies to live among elves for a while?"

"Yes. But none of the humans know this, and I think it doesn't occur to elves in general. The touch is so common, so natural for us, we don't give it a second thought," Risalon had explained.

When the elder was finished, all Meeryle could do was shake her head. "Disgusting. You are all disgusting!"

Only the arrival of Tassym and Ordyna, the two elven Mages, prevented her from leaving the room. Leena herself had wanted to go to the warm pool and dive in it to clean away the disgust she felt. In fact, she had been ready to do just that and leave Meeryle to her lesson, when Kilaron had put a gentle hand on her head.

"Leena, please. I can see that you think like Meeryle in this matter. Believe me, now that you are here, I will never, ever end an unborn halfbreed's life. You're the proof that we have been wrong and I will try to change this." Kilaron's eyes had been filled with such intensity, Leena had to believe him.

So she had stayed. Risalon hadn't commented on Kilaron's words; he had simply introduced the Mages and left.

The sour taste wasn't gone. How many children had died needlessly? How many still did? Elves had many enclaves on the mountains across the world, apparently. Could she stay among such people? Could Lyandrin, now that everyone looked at her with disgust?

Luckily, at that point in the conversion, Tassym had broken the uneasy silence and started the lesson without preamble. With Risalon gone, the awkwardness quickly disappeared. Lyandrin had excused herself and left; she was neither a Mage nor a Healer, so she felt she had little to contribute.

Suqi let out a bark and swished her tail, bringing Leena back to the present. Meeryle had successfully given her power.

"So. Now you need to do the opposite."

Meeryle gave her friend a desperate look. "*Hey, don't look at me. I don't have any ideas about this. You gave me power and I used it, not the other way around. You have to figure this out with Suqi,*" said Leena.

The chubby woman sighed. "All right, Suqi. Let's do this." Meeryle sat and closed her eyes. Leena wished she could smile. No matter how hard she tried to fight it, Meeryle was a great Mage. Every time she touched the power of one of the elements, her life song flared and became louder.

Out of curiosity, Leena listened to Ordyna's life song. The elven woman hadn't said anything yet; she had simply listened to everything with a scary intensity. Nothing in her song seemed out of the ordinary, and the same for Tassym.

Leena mulled on his words some more, deliberately pushing aside what Risalon had said. Tassym had mentioned other types of people aside from humans and elves, and those didn't leave Leena feeling dirty.

Sirènes, feufollets and melusins, he had said. What were those?

"So. We are now ready to start." Tassym's statement made Leena jump. She checked Meeryle and Suqi, and both had what Leena called "enhanced life songs", meaning the song was rendered both stronger and louder by the use of power. She put aside the strange names for the moment, concentrating on what the Mage was saying.

"So. How do human Mages work with their power?"

"Um… I don't know about other Mages, but I listen to the elements first." Tassym nodded an encouragement. "Then… I push the power where I need it to go."

"You will have to be a lot more precise than that, girl," said Ordyna. Her voice was cold and hard, like a whip. Leena's heart sank; Meeryle didn't respond well to such teachers.

Meeryle surprised her, though. The young woman had gained assurance with her gift. "Well, then, you'll have to ask precise questions. I haven't really trained my gift; I just went with Leena's instructions and she found them in books. Our library is rather small, so we made do." Her tone was neither rude nor unpleasant. She was merely stating a fact. Leena feared Ordyna might bristle, but apparently, Meeryle's easy-goingness agreed with the elven Mage.

"Girl, you have a lot of work ahead of you. No matter. Which element do you know best?"

Meeryle hesitated and glanced Leena's way. The golden cat rolled her eyes. "*Come on, Meeryle.*"

Ordyna raised an eyebrow. "Is there a problem?"

"No, no. It's just… Fire. Fire is the element I know the best," stammered Meeryle.

"Ah, good. Fire is the best element to purify things."

"If you don't mind, I'd rather use another element."

"Whatever for, girl?" asked the Mage, eyes wide in surprise.

"I…" Tears were forming in Meeryle's eyes.

Leena couldn't stand it. She went to her friend's side and addressed both Mages. "*Meeryle almost killed herself when she lost control of her gift with fire. I've been taking care of heating water on our way here. Please, she needs time.*"

"That is the most ridiculous thing I've ever heard! The fact that you lost control means you need to work with that particular element as soon as possible in order to avoid another accident. Come now…"

"Ordyna, as Healer, I disagree," cut in Kilaron. His tone was cool, professional and a touch haughty. "Force her to do this before she is ready and you will damage her soul." A mind wound, Corvin would have said. Elves used different words, but they described the same thing. Kilaron was right. As soon as anyone mentioned using fire in front of Meeryle, her song shifted and became discordant.

"*I concur,*" she said.

"Oh, you concur, do you?" Ordyna didn't seem to like halfbreeds, especially halfbreeds who contradicted her.

"*Yes, I do. Her life song is off, which means her spirit is not ready to face this yet. If you insist, you will make her sick. I am a Healer, Ordyna, and I know what I'm talking about.*"

The Mage gave Leena a strange look. She didn't care; as long as she didn't push Meeryle the wrong way, Ordyna could give her all the looks she wanted. She turned to Kilaron to confirm her approval, only to find he was staring at her.

"*What?*"

"You just mentioned the life song."

"*Well, yes. I do check my friends regularly, you know. Don't you?*"

"And you just checked now."

"*Of course.*" She listened to his song. "*You're fine, though something is making your heart beat a bit too fast.*" The cat form and its acute hearing allowed her to hear more than usual. Since he wasn't touching her, their bond was muted, but she could feel surprise and pleasure from her soulmate.

"Leena… I can't do this in cat form. I am only a Healer in elven form." This time, he truly sounded amazed and he broke into a grin. "My soulmate… the halfbreed who can do anything!" He hugged her tight.

"So. I find this very interesting. Mages are like Kilaron in this matter; we do not retain our powers as cats."

"*But you can store energy in your cat… whatever it is?*" asked Suqi. "*It doesn't make sense.*"

"It does, little goupil," answered Ordyna. "The cat essence, as we call it, can retain and store a lot of power. We can harness it as cats, then use it as elves. Some Mages need to store while in elven form, which doesn't allow them to store as much power, but it can be done." Her tone said clearly that she wasn't impressed by any Mage who couldn't harness power as a cat. "How it works for Healers is another story, and I am certainly not in a position to explain any of it."

"It doesn't matter," said Meeryle. "Teach me how to use another element. When I'm ready, I'll use fire, but not now, please."

"So. I think we can work around this. Each species has an affinity with an element in particular, I am just not sure which one humans prefer."

"*Tassym, from what I've read, human Mages need to master all elements. Fire usually manifests itself first, that's all,*" cut in Leena.

"Ah. So. Another difference with humans."

"Tassym, I believe you will be able to handle this on your own. I am needed to refresh the lighting systems." Ordyna didn't wait for a reply; she simply left without another word.

"Wow, she doesn't like me, does she?" asked Meeryle.

Kilaron smiled. "In all the commotion about Leena, I had forgotten that humans can be just as unwanted."

"You know, life was much simpler at the village," said Meeryle with a sigh.

"So. Don't worry about her. Risalon insisted she come even though I assured him I could do this on my own."

"*What about the other Mages who cornered Meeryle the night we arrived?*"

"Ordyna is joining them. They need to renew the spell on all the lighting diamonds. We use fire to light them, and fire is not our best element, so we need a few Mages for the spell."

"See, I don't get it. What is a spell?" whined Meeryle.

Leena wanted to slap her. "*Whenever you use an element to do something, that's called a spell.*"

"So when I checked the meat, that's a spell?"

"*No, silly. When you make the fire burn harder or lower, that's a spell.*"

"Oh."

Kilaron stared at the two friends. "You are just… strange."

"Don't you have any friends with whom you can laugh, or have fun, or insult?" asked Meeryle. "I mean, that's what friends do. We help each other and we make fun of each other. Except that Leena's better at it than I am."

The elven Healer gave her a penetrating look, as if trying to tell if Meeryle was serious. "No, I can't say I do this with anyone. I'm not sure I would like it if anyone did this to me."

"Well, you better get used to it with Leena."

"*That's it, you're asking for it!*" And Leena tackled her friend, who fell on her behind, laughing.

"Children, children," said Tassym with a smile. "You are very unruly. I like it. But still, Meeryle, you need to learn control."

He was interrupted by a boy, who came running into the room. Leena examined him, as he was the first elven child she had seen. Thin and pale with messy shoulder-length hair, he was just like any other child she had known. He had a serious look, which told her he probably wouldn't be pulling any pranks.

"Kilaron, you are needed. Childia fell and broke her arm."

The Healer rolled his eyes and shook his head. "Go tell her parents I will be there shortly. Leena, Meeryle, I will leave you with Tassym while I fix this child yet again." He left running. Leena wanted to smile. Her soulmate was a Healer before anything else and that pleased her.

Tassym was shaking his head. "I believe this is the third time the child has broken something. Though she is not much of a child anymore; she will soon be a woman. However, that habit of hers to climb isn't exactly something she can turn into an occupation. So. Let us get back to business, shall we?" He had Meeryle and Leena's full attention. "Elves wield air. Since it exists everywhere, it is readily available, and very malleable."

Tassym proceeded in showing how to use air to create a flexible wall, like the one Jatoron had used to trap the snow and make a shelter. He explained how such walls were made to be flexible in order to allow for emergencies.

"*Such as sheltering a dragon.*"

"Exactly," he answered with a smile. "These spells are keyed to all elves, so any elf can use it and shape the shelter to their liking." Leena blinked; it explained why the wall had moved when she had pushed it. The spell recognized her as an elf.

"But how does that help me in purifying water?" Meeryle was losing interest; her shoulders had slumped and she was playing with her growing hair.

"So. Here is some water. You need to find what makes it poisonous to you, then take it out with air."

"Ah."

Leena agreed. This was not going to be easy.

Chapter 11

It took most of the day, but in the end, Meeryle managed to push out the things poisoning the water.

She dropped on her bedroll, exhausted, but smiling. "There, now I can make sure my water's fine. Even if they forget to boil it, I'll be fine."

Leena couldn't smile, but she moved her tail in what she hoped looked like a happy flick. "*It was very well done, Meeryle. What I'm curious about is those things. What are they?*"

"Leena, drop it, will you? Tassym doesn't know, even if you asked him, oh, a million times?"

Leena only answered with a cat snort. Meeryle was right; however, she was still allowed to be curious, wasn't she?

"Hey, why don't you ask Kilaron? Maybe he'll know."

"*I doubt it. Most of the elves here didn't even know pure water was poisonous to humans. I think you're the first human he's seen up close; how would he know about water?*"

Meeryle shrugged. "Just an idea. How about some food? That Mage thing is hard work, you know. And hard work makes me hungry."

"*Meeryle, anything makes you hungry. Though you're right. Come on. Let's go and get stared at.*"

The last comment was bitter, more than she had expected. The elves' attitude towards her and Meeryle hurt her more than she wanted to admit. She needed to change back into human-elf shape.

She tried, but still couldn't find that purring feeling. Maybe she was going about it the wrong way.

"Leena, come on!" yelled Meeryle, breaking her concentration.

Leena rolled her eyes and followed her friend. She might be more successful with a full stomach.

Much to her delight, Kilaron joined them. He ate slowly, explaining how he had Healed part of that girl's arm. It had however been difficult, as part of the bone was shattered.

"I will have to perform another Healing tomorrow; I no longer have any strength left for today. I need food and rest."

His eyes were indeed sunken and his pale face had grayish tones. Leena's heart sank; if he didn't rest, he would fall sick. She wasn't sure if any amounts of touching would help.

"I'd like to help. All I've done all day was watch Meeryle purify water. It was interesting, but certainly not taxing."

"Healing powers don't work when we're in cat form, Leena," answered Kilaron. Even his voice was tired.

"I can hear the life song, so maybe I can Heal. I mean, it's not like I have anything to lose, right?"

"What if you fail?" he whispered. The doubt, the fear of disapproving looks spiked through the bond. How could he live like this?

Meeryle cut in, mouth full. "If you only try stuff when you're sure you'll succeed, how do you learn?"

He was too tired to get angry, but his eyes lit with a spark, nonetheless. "Oh, and what would you know about success and failure?"

The chubby young woman swallowed and put her fists on her hips. "First of all, I'm a cook. I have to try new things and sometimes, they don't turn out. Second,

I'm a Mage. I didn't get any training, but I still tried my best to help my friends when they needed it, even if I wasn't sure it was going to work."

Kilaron was too weary to argue; he shook his head, though Leena couldn't tell if it was because the human girl bothered him, or to relent. She decided not to ask and simply act as if he had agreed.

"*Come, then. Show me to Childia's alcove.*"

Kilaron sighed. "All right. But I warn you, Childia's parents are amongst the ones who aren't thrilled about you. They are also Sayleen's parents."

Leena's head dropped. Would this ever end? "*Is their daughter still in pain?*"

"Yes. I put her to sleep, but she was still whimpering when I left." He frowned. "They weren't happy when I told them I had to come back tomorrow. But I just couldn't anymore. Was I wrong?" The last words were filled with anguish. Leena knew how difficult it could be for a Healer when nothing else could be done. Others would insist, sometimes even insult the Healer, but something, either the patient was too far gone, or the Healer had nothing else to give.

When she looked into Kilaron's haunted eyes, Leena truly fell in love. Even if he let at times others dictate his actions, her soulmate was a good person, a true Healer, just like her.

At that moment, Leena also realized that no matter how much she pined for the Mage gift, she was a Healer and nothing else. She had watched Meeryle work with air all day, yet what fascinated her was not how the minuscule, almost invisible dark particles flew out of the water, but what they were and why they hurt humans so. This was the thinking of a Healer, not a Mage's.

With that revelation, something clicked within Leena. The life song of everyone in the cavern was suddenly amplified. She knew how tired Kilaron truly was – how close to the edge he had pushed himself. Healers could only use so much power; otherwise, they put their lives in danger.

Kilaron was very close to it.

She also knew that Meeryle really did need the food; working her Mage skills had taken a toll on her body and it needed the fuel. She found out that many elves present had troubled stomachs and that some lacked sleep. Although Tikid was in her alcove, her life song resonated faintly into Leena's ears.

All this flooded her cat senses and she had to blink a few times to take it all in. What did it mean?

"Leena? What is it?" asked Meeryle.

Leena shook her head. "*I was just thinking, that's all.*" She wasn't ready to share her experience yet; she needed to analyze it first. Kilaron felt curious, but too tired to insist. "*So, are we going to Childia? Even if her parents don't like me, I think they will let me help if it means that their daughter will be better.*" As far as she knew, no parents liked to see their children suffer.

"This way," said Kilaron with a sigh. The food had helped, but his life song was still off. Leena pushed his hand with her head, making him smile.

Meeryle followed, mouth full once again.

"Meeryle, perhaps it would be best if you stayed. If they don't like halfbreeds, Childia's parents abhor humans."

The young Mage's eyes filled with red fury, but only for an instant. In fact, it had been so quick, Leena would have thought she had imagined it if she hadn't heard the flare in Meeryle's life song.

"Fine. Anyway, I'm still hungry." She turned back to the food table without another glance.

Kilaron watched her go with a frown. "I'm tired, so I fear I might have imagined it, but…"

"*No, you didn't. Meeryle has quite the temper, but she manages to keep it under control. The last time she lost it, she burned everything down. But the fact that we were able to see the red in her eyes and hear the song flare means that she is very angry. She's also tired from using her gift, so mixing the two is probably not a good thing.*"

"And it doesn't bother you that she might just burn you down?"

"*Meeryle would never do such a thing!*" Leena glared at him. "*She's my friend; I trust her with my life.*" His blank look shocked her. "*Do you mean to say you don't trust anyone that way?*"

"I… No, not really."

Leena wanted to cry. "*Well, now you have me. You might want to make me throttle you, but I would never actually do it. And you know that if anything were to happen to you, I can take care of it.*"

He gave her a weak smile and motioned her to follow. "I am too tired to really think about this. Come on, let's take care of that poor girl."

Leena let it go for the moment, but she wasn't going to forget. Even Teerane, the village bully, had friends. Kilaron didn't seem to trust anyone; that could lead to a very lonely life.

Her thoughts were interrupted when they arrived at Childia's alcove. The curtain was open, as someone had just left and the parents had led them out. The woman's eyes lit when she saw Kilaron.

"Already? You can Heal her fully now?"

The man was more suspicious. "You had said you needed until morning. And what is *she* doing here?"

"I *am here to help*," answered Leena before Kilaron could say anything. "*I know you don't like me, but I can help your daughter.*"

"No, she won't! She'll just kill her!"

Leena's heart sank. Sayleen was the one who had yelled those hateful words. She hadn't seen him in the cavern, but he was still here.

His father became a surprising ally. "You say that because that's what she threatened you with when you scared her. I may not like halfbreeds, but I certainly do not approve of bullying. You had a choice to stay confined to the alcove or leave the enclave. You chose, so you live with it, but you know you no longer have a voice here until she leaves." That was news to Leena.

She wished he had opted to travel to another enclave.

"*I can't kill someone by just looking at them, Sayleen. I lied because you were about to throw me off the side of the mountain.*"

The elf stared at her, mouth gaping.

"Serves you right," said his father, closing the subject. "Now, what is it you think you can do for Childia, halfbreed?"

Leena ground her teeth. The word was spat out as an insult and she was getting sick of it. However, she wasn't here to convince this man that his beliefs were wrong, but to Heal his daughter.

Kilaron didn't see it that way. "Have a care, Daron. She is my soulmate."

"Not that you had a choice, now did you, Healer?"

"Neither did you. Treat her with respect or she will not Heal Childia, and neither will I."

Leena would've gasped, except that cats couldn't, so she hissed. Never would she refuse to Heal someone because they weren't respectful. She was so furious, she couldn't project her thoughts, so she bumped Kilaron on the leg. She hissed once again, because in that touch, she felt the lie. Her soulmate was lying about a Healer's willingness to do his or her duty! When Kilaron put his hand on her head, he pushed *something* in her mind, a shushing feeling. He was right; these people needed the threat, real or not, in order to let her see to their daughter. The concept of Healers needing to threaten in order do their work was so strange that Leena could only shake her head.

It did have the desired effect: Childia's mother simply glared at her soulmate and ushered both Healers in the alcove.

Leena looked around, amazed by what she saw. What had become Tikid's alcove was only a tunnel used for storage, unadorned. The alcove given to Kilaron and her was also empty, just waiting for the occupant's touch, and Kilaron's alcove had been rather bare, filled only with healing supplies. This one was lived in, decorated and very welcoming, which, given the reaction of the owners, was ironic.

This alcove was meant for a family, so it was large and had separate rooms for the different family members. Childia's room was to the right; it reminded Leena of her own room back at the village. Neat, yet filled with things that interested the occupant. In this case, it was rocks.

Apparently, the girl liked to climb for more than just the thrill.

Childia was on her bed, sleeping fitfully. Her life song was a shrill screech that hurt Leena's senses. If Kilaron had already repaired some of the damage, how bad had it been?

She didn't want to waste any time thinking about it. The girl needed help now; to dwell on the reasons for her state were impeding Leena. Kilaron had already assessed the patient, so she could just go ahead to do what was necessary. She trusted his judgment implicitly.

How did she go about Healing in cat form, though? Since as a human, she let her hands touch or hover over the area, she figured doing the same with paws should work.

She needed to hover over the arm, as she didn't dare to touch it. Childia's sleep was induced, but added pain could take her out of it. Leena was sure that touching the arm would hurt too much and make the girl react. However, she wasn't sure how her balance would hold up: standing on two legs was fine, but standing on rear paws was something else entirely.

Leena solved the problem by jumping onto the bed and squeezing herself behind Childia. The girl was on the edge of the bed, so Leena had some space. Her back rubbed on the rock ceiling of the bed, but she had enough room to move.

Sitting on her haunches, left front leg bent so she could stoop, Leena extended her right paw and let it stand over the injured arm. She winced at the screech in the girl's life song. She had heard it as soon as she had seen Childia, but now, up close, it was worse, worse even than

Tikid's wing when it had been torn by an arrow. She had been able to Heal that with Meeryle's help.

She couldn't do this alone. She needed help; Tikid couldn't come, as the tunnels were too narrow for her, but Meeryle could. Yet she didn't want Childia's parents to hear her doubt.

"*Please, we need to concentrate. Could you leave us?*" Leena made her words as firm as she could, while remaining gentle. For a moment, she thought they would refuse, but when Kilaron nodded, they left, closing the curtain behind them. Leena sniffed loudly, insulted that Kilaron's nod held more power than her words. No matter how often she told herself that these people didn't trust her, she still found it hard to accept.

Leena shook the thoughts away. "*I can't do this on my own, Kilaron. I need Meeryle. She can give me power.*"

Kilaron shook his head. "No, you don't. If I was able to get this far on my own, so can you," he whispered.

"*But…*"

"But nothing! I can feel your potential now that we're soulmated. You don't need Tikid or Meeryle anymore. In fact, I'm not even sure you ever did."

"*Some things, like Healing burns to the entire body, are beyond any Healer and you know it,*" she answered, trying to keep her mind voice quiet. How did someone whisper with his or her mind?

"Maybe," he relented. "But in this case, I know for sure you do not need any help, not even from me."

The last comment pricked her pride. Why should she need help from him? He couldn't even hear the life song when he was in cat shape. She was determined to show him she was good, even better than him. It was just a matter of how much better she was.

Leena snorted; if Lyandrin and Jetyaa could hear her thoughts, they would be shaking their heads right now. Pride! How it made people do stupid things. But it also pushed people to better themselves.

Feelings cooled down, Leena concentrated on the thing inside of her that allowed her to Heal. Kilaron was right: it was full of life, more so than before. Now that she had fully accepted herself as a Healer and had soulmated, she was for the first time in her life truly complete. The task no longer seemed as daunting.

Closing Kilaron out, she focused on the arm, moving her paw up and down to find the specific place where the bone needed mending. Leena could hear where her soulmate had repaired the damage. He had fused the bone where all the breaks had been clean, even the smaller ones. However, in two areas, the bone was crushed. What had this girl done to hurt herself so? The most frequent breaks Leena had seen were from falling off roofs or trees. How high were the cliffs that Childia explored?

Leena shook her head. How was she supposed to repair crushed bone? Just like I repaired Tikid's wing, she told herself. But she had used the earth power Meeryle had channeled into her to force the wing to grow. In the case of crushed bone, all the parts were still there, no growing was needed.

Her cat ears were better than her human ones; she could hear subtle differences she normally couldn't – unless it was due to the fact she had accepted herself as a Healer. It didn't matter; she now knew exactly where all the bone parts were. All she needed to do was to bring them back together and fuse them.

Leena took in a deep breath and pushed out her power into the arm. She always felt like that power was an extension of her hands, so she sent out tendrils to scoop the bone parts together.

It wasn't easy, for both Healer and patient. Childia whimpered and her body trembled. Leena knew that if she'd been in human form, she would have been sweating. As a cat, she was panting.

Once all the pieces were gathered, she arranged them in their proper place. She moved them around until the screeching had abated, telling her each part was in the right spot. She then pushed power in, heating the bone parts until they were stuck together.

It wasn't enough. Some of the parts just wouldn't meld with the rest.

A soothing feeling filled her; she looked to the side into Kilaron's green eyes. He pushed some of his power into her and she focused once more on those tricky places.

More, I need more, she thought. She pulled power from every part of herself and from Kilaron. She suddenly remembered he already had given everything he could that day, so she drew only power from herself. His presence was soothing and gave her confidence.

At last, she had enough energy to fuse the remaining bone shards. She blasted it in the arm, willing every part to stay together. The song sent a high pitched note, telling her the body was now whole.

Childia opened her eyes and screamed.

Her parents rushed in and stopped at the sight of their daughter moving her arm without any discomfort.

"I'm fine," she said with a weary smile.

Oh good, thought Leena.

She sighed and closed her eyes, grateful for the break, and almost fell asleep. Childia's movement when she left her bed jerked Leena awake.

Kilaron chuckled. "Come, Leena, let's go to our alcove. You can rest properly there."

Had she slept? She was too tired to tell.

Childia was with her parents, talking in the usual elven low tones. They stopped and looked at her as soon as she stepped out of the girl's room.

"Thank you," said the mother with a smile. "You will always be welcome in this alcove, no matter what."

Daron simply nodded, but Sayleen glared at her. Thankfully, he didn't say anything. Leena was too weary to argue; she just wanted to make sure Childia was fine, then sleep for the next few candlemarks… or days.

"I checked Childia and the bone is fully mended," said Kilaron. "All she needs is time for the surrounding flesh to heal on its own." He frowned sternly at the girl. "This means no climbing."

"Yes, Kilaron, you already said that," replied Childia with a smile. She might be getting scolded, but she didn't care: her arm was now fine.

Leena wished she could smile. "*I'm glad I was able to fix that arm of yours.*"

"Thank you." The girl dropped to her knees and embraced Leena, who wanted to burst into tears. This was the first Healing she performed on someone who didn't know her. Tikid and Meeryle were friends; they trusted her. To Childia and her parents, she was a stranger, yet they managed to overcome their dislike and trusted her.

She was now a Healer both in name and in truth.

Chapter 12

Two days later, Tikid announced that she was ready to leave. "*The snow has finally stopped and you are rested, Leena. Meeryle has been practicing purifying water, so it will be safe for her to drink any water she finds.*"

Leena winced at Meeryle's squeal of delight. High pitched sounds were very hard on her cat ears.

"I can't wait, I can't wait! What are the Whites like, Tikid?"

"*I do not really know, I have never met one before.*"

"Doesn't matter. We need to get our bags ready. Leena, I suppose you'll use the excuse of having paws instead of hands to have me pack your bag, huh?"

Leena sighed. "*Meeryle, it's no longer funny.*" Her latest attempt at shifting back had been unsuccessful yet again this morning. The previous day, Lyandrin had changed into cat form, then back into elven form so Leena to listen to her life song as she did it, but it hadn't helped.

"Oh, sorry. Seriously, though, do you want to have a bag? I'm sure we could find a way to make it fit on your back."

Meeryle was right. Even as a cat, she's need food – she certainly wasn't going to start hunting for mice – and if she managed to change back to her human form, she'd need clothes.

A quick visit with Lyandrin taught them that elves had packs made especially for that purpose. Elves traveled very often in cat form, but they liked hot meals and shifted back to camp, or in areas where humans and elves cohabited, to use inns. Humans did not know elves could transform into cats, so they always made sure humans never saw them in that shape. Now Leena understood that the only reason Jatoron had shown himself to them during the storm was because of Tikid's presence. Otherwise, he would have shifted back to elven form before meeting with them – if he hadn't decided to leave them out there to die.

After the midday meal, Leena, Meeryle and Tikid once again stood outside the entrance cavern. Leena held her mother in as tight hug as her paws allowed her.

"*Are you sure you don't want to come with us? I've seen how you're being shunned, you know.*"

Lyandrin smiled weakly. "I just spend more time with Mundriana, that's all."

"*Mother?*"

"Don't worry about me. It turns out that giving birth to a halfbreed who can Heal in cat form is not such a bad thing after all. Caliana had always been kind to me and it hasn't changed since you arrived. I think she might even be trying to become a friend. She likes you."

Tikid flew off, veering to the west, where the Whites were last seen. Apparently, the White dragons had never made it known where they lived; they just made contact with the elves who happened to be in the area where the dragons were at the time, doing whatever it was they did. Leena hadn't asked what it was; her heart was too heavy. She was useless at shifting, she was leaving her mother behind, but what rankled most was that she hadn't seen Kilaron ever since she had Healed Childia.

He hadn't seemed hurt by the fact that she had been able to finish what he had started, yet he hadn't come to see if she was fine. Not that Leena had sought him out either; after all, he should be the one to make the first step, since she had done her part.

"Meeryle, Leena, there is a trail over there for you to follow. Leena and Suqi will be fine, but Meeryle needs room to walk."

Tikid gave her scouting report from a distance. During the months on the road, the young dragon's ability to see thing from a human's perspective had improved. Leena hoped it included finding trails for a human Mage to tread. Both Leena and Suqi would be able to adapt to any trail – though Leena had yet to walk out in the snow in cat form – but Meeryle might not find it as easy.

"Come on, Leena, we should get going, otherwise, Tikid will lose us," said Meeryle.

Lyandrin smiled. "Go with your friends. I'll be fine, Leena."

No one else had come to see them off. Compared to the welcome they had received, it hurt to see that no one wished her well simply because she was a halfbreed.

No one, not even Kilaron.

***

The way down the mountain wasn't as difficult as the way up. Leena figured it had to do with being on four legs rather than two.

Suqi was trotting ahead, ears up, happy to leave the confines of the mountain. She had confided in Leena – much to the young woman's surprise – that she missed the forest and running. The goupil welcomed the trip with open paws.

Leena looked where she put her own paws; she wasn't sure yet if she liked the snow. Her pads had never been used outside before, so the cold seemed to seep through them. Only where the hair came out between them was immune to that sensation, though she wasn't sure how long it would last.

She had had a few days to get used to moving around in her present shape and she was just beginning to appreciate the possibilities. If the scents and sounds inside the mountain had been louder, outside, they were intoxicating. The small breeze brought smells she couldn't identify. Maybe if she had been back home, where she knew the plants, the trees and the animals, she would be able to tell what she was smelling. Here, all she could do was take it all in. Suqi's scent was amplified by the snow wetting her fur; Meeryle's woolen clothes were still dry, but the bottom of her skirt was getting that wet smell; the food in both packs sent tantalizing tendrils, making her full stomach nevertheless grumble.

A new smell, mixed with food, hit her nose. She wriggled her whiskers – something she had found amazing, as people do not have them – and peered ahead, wanting to see the source of the smell. Even with her keen cat eyes, she couldn't make anything out other than the white snow.

Suqi barked happily, but Leena couldn't tell why and of course, the goupil didn't say anything.

Before she or Meeryle could ask, part of the snow moved and became a cat.

"*Can I join you?*"

Meeryle stopped behind Leena. "Who is that?"

"*This is the first time I am not recognized.*" The wry tone – and the fact that it was male – betrayed him.

"Kilaron!" Meeryle stared. "Wow, you're white. Completely white. Is it just me, or you're shining?"

The white coat was gleaming. Leena sat, surprised that her hair protected her from the snow, and purred. The sound surprised her and she let out a yelping growl.

Tikid prevented anyone from laughing at her. "*Why are you not moving? I cannot land where you are.*"

"*Well, then let's move on until Tikid can land.*" Leena looked into her soulmate's deep green eyes. "*It's good to have you here, Kilaron.*" She hoped he had felt through the bond the emotions that came with her words; she wanted to know why hadn't spoken with her and why he had decided to drop his duties to come with them. However, she wasn't about to have this discussion publicly. Maybe Kilaron could send his thoughts only to her, but she had yet to manage it herself.

For now, she was just going to enjoy his presence.

The dragon was able to land further down the trail in a flurry of snow. She welcomed Kilaron, but didn't seem too surprised by his decision. Tikid was much more focused on finding Whites; since Kilaron was "right" for Leena, she found it normal that he should come.

Leena had yet to get completely used to the dragon's alien thinking. Dragons either didn't have the same types of relationships as people, or Tikid was an exception.

The young Green flew off, guiding her friends ahead on a more or less visible trail. Meeryle was having a hard time; the trail was there, but few animals had used it since the end of the snowstorm. Kilaron took point and cleared the way for her, making easier for the chubby woman. At one point, Leena traded places with him to give her soulmate a break.

Pushing the snow with her chest wasn't all that hard, as the stuff was light and fluffy, but it took its toll on the young Healer. She still wasn't completely used to walking on all fours and unused muscles were complaining. She didn't say anything, wanting to pull her share.

"Um, Leena? Why are you going so slow? Are you all right?" asked Meeryle, concern creeping in her voice.

Leena stopped and looked back, surprised. "*I'm sorry, I didn't realize I had slowed down.*"

Meeryle frowned. "Why did you?"

Leena twisted her nose, wondering if she should admit that her muscles were trembling in fatigue.

"*I think she just needs a break,*" said Kilaron.

"Oh. Then why didn't you just say it, silly? I always said it when I had to stop." Meeryle then proceeded to take out a blanket and sat on it. "Anybody want something to eat?" she asked, while rummaging through her pack.

Leena gave Kilaron a grateful look and slumped down in the snow. They had been going for barely two candlemarks, and she was already exhausted. She wished she could be more like Meeryle and simply state that she was having a hard time, but her pride kept on wondering if Kilaron would think less of her if she did so.

"Leena, really, you should lie on a blanket, not right in the snow."

"*I'm fine, Meeryle. My fur's keeping me warm.*"

Meeryle laughed. "You know how weird that sounds, right? Your fur's keeping you warm…"

Leena shook her head and chuckled. "*It's not the only weird thing, trust me. Honestly, right now, my legs just aren't up to the task. They feel like jelly!*"

The Mage stared at her friend. "Did I hear you right? Your legs are tired?"

Leena nodded with a snort.

Meeryle just blinked for a few moments. "Well. I think we have to note this down somewhere as today being a very important day. Leena got tired before I did!" She burst out laughing.

Leena's mouth dropped open as Meeryle's laughter doubled and she rolled into the snow. "*Did I ever laugh at you?*"

The chubby woman hiccupped and wiped her eyes. "No, but you should see your face. Even as a cat, you looked outraged. You're just too easy to tease, Leena."

As an answer, Leena flicked her paw and sent a flurry of snow into her friend's face.

"Phaw! Hah! My revenge will be swift!" she cried, gathering as much snow as she could, throwing it all in Leena's direction. Leena responded in like, and soon, both friends were covered in snow.

"*May I join you?*" asked Tikid as she landed. The wind created by her wings covered everyone in snow, including the watching bystanders, Kilaron and Suqi.

"Stop! Tikid, I can't see anything," giggled Meeryle.

"*Why have you all stopped without telling me?*" The dragon sounded offended.

"*Because it was time for a snow fight, apparently,*" cut in Kilaron.

"*Oh, hush. I was tired, Tikid.*"

"*How come? You were never tired on our way here. Are you ill?*"

Leena was touched by the concern in the dragon's voice. "*It's just that I'm not used to walking on all fours, that's all. We'll need to stop often.*"

"*I will walk with you, then, otherwise I will find I need to wait for you.*"

Meeryle frowned. "You might not have the space, Tikid. That trail can be narrow at times."

"*We need to continue in that direction,*" she replied, pointing with a claw. "*I do not think you will find any trails, but the way is open.*"

Kilaron stepped up. "*If I may suggest... why don't you open the way, Tikid, and we will follow.*"

Leena wondered why he hadn't said anything before. Seeing her and Meeryle tease each other must have been strange to him, yet he had simply sat there, watching silently. He hadn't said anything about her weakness, either. She hated it, in a way, as she imagined he was judging her and found her wanting. It was silly, really, because he had said she was worthy.

Once they set off, Leena maneuvered for her and Kilaron to be side by side, at the rear of the line. With the dragon clearing the way, they no longer had to walk in a single file and that suited Leena. She wanted to talk privately with Kilaron and since she didn't know how to limit her mindspeech to one person, the only way she could think to keep a conversation private was with distance.

Soon, she was walking beside Kilaron, sneezing away the snow Tikid and Meeryle were sending up. Suqi's small size didn't allow her to tread in the dragon's trail: the snow was too high for the goupil. Meeryle had therefore plopped her familiar on Tikid's back and the fox-like creature was working very hard not to lose her balance.

"*Kilaron.*" Leena sent the thought as quietly as she could – or so she hoped. How did one whisper with one's mind?

"*Yes?*"

The young man looked at her squarely in the eyes, making Leena hesitate. What if he resented her questions?

Her pride soon shook the hesitation off; she had to know why he was acting so remote.

"*Why hadn't you told me you were coming? And for that matter, how come you just disappeared after I Healed Childia?*" The last came out outraged and it surprised Leena. She hadn't been aware of the resentment she bore her soulmate on that matter.

"*I... Leena, you arrival changed a lot of things in the enclave, myself included. I don't dare to discuss anything with anyone. What would they say, as my mother told me over and over. Her attitude showed me I was better off alone. So I don't consult anyone, not even in Healing matters. You're the first one I've trusted enough for it, and the results were...*"

"*Good? Better than you expected?*"

"*Astounding, Leena! No one had ever heard of a Healer doing what you did, let alone in cat form. You saw how far I got with Childia, and I know I'm one of the best.*"

Leena was surprised by the emotions that accompanied the last statement. It was as if he knew he was good, but that he still had to convince himself. While she had had – and still did – doubts about her gift, she never recalled feeling the particular hesitation Kilaron was projecting through the bond.

Kilaron interpreted her silence as doubt. "*I am, you know. I don't know about human Healers, but amongst elves, I'm the best there ever was. I've proved it over and over, but with Childia, you showed that I was wrong.*"

"*And that hurts.*" She made it a statement.

"*Yes. Dealing with the fact that I have a halfbreed soulmate was hard. You don't know of all the comments that were made; and my mother...*" he said, shaking his head. "*But finding out she can do what I cannot was even worse.*"

Leena wanted to cry. He hated her, he resented her very existence.

Her pride tromped over that thought and reminded her that her skill was, according to this proud man, astounding. So she was good after all, halfbreed or not!

Her confidence now regained, Leena continued mercilessly. "*So you just left me on my own, feeling unwanted? What a great way to start a relationship.*"

The sarcasm surprised Kilaron. He gave Leena a startled look. "*It was not my intent! I had to find myself before I could be with you.*"

"*Ah.*" It was all she could say, as his comment puzzled her. While he seemed just too self-centered to even think of others around him, Leena knew some of the turmoil he went through and that he thought himself unfit for company. Looking into his anguished eyes, Leena guessed that Kilaron, spoiled since his gift manifested, suffocated by his mother's constant worry about appearance, had locked himself up in cocoon and was now realizing his personality left something to be desired. Leena wasn't sure if she should be proud or ashamed for that. What right did she have to hurt someone that way? He was hurt, though he didn't say it.

Part of her was happy; it was wrong for someone – especially a Healer – to live as he had. But Kilaron was her soulmate and it was wrong to hurt someone like that, wasn't it?

It wasn't in Leena's nature to be petty, so guilt took over. "*Kilaron, I wouldn't have been able to do that Healing without your help. You gave me strength, something that I suspect wouldn't have been possible if we weren't soulmates.*"

He nodded slowly. "*One can realize one's potential with one's soulmate.*"

"*You just didn't think I would realize mine,*" Leena said, her eyes wide open in surprise. She remembered thinking about it, but she had put it out of her mind. Other things were taking precedence – like being a cat.

"*No, I hadn't. I only thought of my potential, how I would finally truly be the greatest Healer. And now...*"

"*Now you're not.*"

He nodded. "*That hurts too. What I'm not sure hurts the most is whether finding I'm not the greatest or finding out I'm too selfish to think of my soulmate's own potential.*" He snorted. "*I found out I was as bad as my mother, Leena. I'm not who I thought I was, and I think that's what hurts the most. I'm not sure I like the person I am.*"

"*Now I understand what you meant about finding yourself.*"

"*Yes. I don't want to find someone so hateful. I want to be someone worth...*" He faltered, but Leena didn't understand why.

"*Worth what?*"

"*Worth loving.*" With those words, Kilaron moved forward, leaving Leena on her own.

She couldn't be angry with him; she finally understood the reason for his isolation. Leena wasn't sure what to do; she hadn't really ever dealt with such an identity crisis before. Corvin, the Healer to whom she had been apprenticed, hadn't covered that type of ailment, as they very rarely came up in such a small village.

She decided to leave him be, at least for the moment. She would watch him and approach him if she deemed this soul-searching consumed him too deeply. Leena guessed that in the meantime, seeing how he was treading, he might be fine on his own. She wasn't even sure she could help him, really. She should focus on herself, as she had some self-examination of her own to do.

Questions battered her mind. Kilaron mentioned love. She had fallen in love, hadn't she? Did she truly love him? That she didn't know was an honest answer. The fact that she was close to him made her feel elated and, more important, complete. Leena recognized that this didn't constitute love. Over the brief time she had known him, Kilaron had shown himself to be distant, sometimes arrogant, yet very unsure of himself and vulnerable. She recalled his mother's soulmate and his tired appearance. Did he love his soulmate? Safyn was a trial for anyone. As a Healer, Leena felt connected to Kilaron and she had glimpsed a part of him she suspected very few other people had ever seen. He was a good person, she was sure of that. Whether or not she would come to love him remained to be seen.

Leena realized that she did want to spend time with him. His attitude notwithstanding, Kilaron filled a gap she hadn't known she had. Maybe she did already love him. But enough to handfast him? Only time would tell.

Chapter 13

They stopped as soon as the sun fell behind the mountains. Lyandrin's enclave was in the first of a long range, and the lowest. Peak after peak spread out as far as Leena could see. Most were white and some even lost in clouds.

Kilaron activated one of the stones supplied by the Mages to create a snow hut with a touch of his paw. He refused to change back into elven form for Leena's sake. The young woman was touched, and though it made no sense, it lessened her embarrassment at her inability to change back.

Soon, they were all huddling in the hut around the small fire in its center. It had taken a while for the dragon to light it, but she finally managed. Big claws made it very hard to handle the fire-starting tools; yet Tikid had been adamant in her wish to contribute to the camp.

Leena was happy to see that Meeryle was not avoiding the fire altogether. She didn't light it – though she had helped Tikid as much as the dragon had allowed her – nor did she sit very close to it, but she was no longer cowering from it. The short lessons with the elven Mages hadn't cured Meeryle from her fear of fire, but they had given her more confidence. Learning to master air had somehow helped her see that although fire was a fierce element, it wasn't something to avoid. Leena was sure that the only reason they didn't get a warm meal was due to Tikid's dislike of cooking food, otherwise, Meeryle would have treated them to one of her delicious meals. Instead, they ate bread and some sort of dried fruits.

Meeryle purified water under everyone's watchful eye, particularly Tikid's. The dragon had not yet had the chance to see her friend's progress, so the chubby woman showed off her new skill with pleasure.

"*What else can you do with air, Meeryle?*" asked Tikid.

"Well, I didn't have time to learn much, but since I can take out the things that poison water…"

"*For humans only,*" cut in Suqi.

Meeryle gave her a nasty look, and pointedly ignored her. The Mage was still angry with her familiar, then. "It means I can move anything I want with air, including you, if I had the power."

"*I do not need your help to move,*" said Tikid, puzzled.

Meeryle laughed. "You silly thing. Let's say you were caught underneath a bunch of rocks."

"*How could I ever find myself in such a situation?*"

Leena chuckled. The dragon still had a hard time understanding hypothetical situations. She exchanged a glance with her soulmate, who chuckled too.

"*Let me give you another example,*" he said. "*We're in the mountains, with a lot of snow. Sometimes, all that snow will detach itself from the top and fall down the slopes, burying everything.*"

Leena was horrified. She looked at Meeryle, who was just as struck as her. "For real?"

Kilaron was surprised and felt a bit annoyed at the interruption. "*You've never heard of avalanches?*"

"Listen, until we came here, we had never seen this much snow. So no, we didn't know about… whatever you called them."

"*How strange.*"

Leena cut in before Meeryle could get worked up. Leena herself was a bit hurt by Kilaron's reaction to their ignorance. "*It doesn't matter. He's just using an example to explain what you can do, Meeryle. Remember?*" She wanted to ask how likely avalanches were and if they posed a danger. Mostly, she wanted to ask what he would do if he were caught in a mudslide during the winter rains they had back at the village. He probably wouldn't know – if he had even heard of them.

Somewhat mollified, Meeryle sniffed loudly. "Sorry."

"*Please, Kilaron, continue. I want to understand.*"

Tikid's eagerness smoothed the ruffled feathers and the young man continued. "*If you were caught under all that snow, then Meeryle could move it off you so you could get out. Same thing with rocks.*"

"*But could you move me?*" insisted the dragon.

"*She could,*" answered Suqi, giving Meeryle a look. "*You have enough power for that. You just don't want to see it.*"

"Oh, hush. Right now, the only thing I need to move is my bedroll. Good night, everyone."

Thus ending any attempt at conversation, Meeryle made a show of preparing for sleep. Her own stomach full, Leena didn't mind it. She was physically exhausted and was predicting sore muscles the next day. Her mind was too busy to allow sleep, though. As the others followed Meeryle's example, Leena simply rolled herself up in a ball and let her thoughts run.

The question of love had been nagging at her all day. Who decided on the identity of soulmates, anyway? Both people were half of a whole… yet some wholes weren't good ones, were they? Love wasn't necessarily part of it. However, elves could have children with someone other than their soulmate, provided they were in love. Could soulmated couples who didn't love each other have little ones? She would have to ask Kilaron.

He was the result of an act of love, and an exceptional Healer. He could only be a good person, no? Were they truly good for one another? He was so infuriating at times, she could just throttle him. He was so proud, but so vulnerable! Yet wasn't she just as bad when it came to pride? Maybe they were a perfect match after all!

The thought made her smile and allowed her to surrender to much needed sleep.

***

Leena woke basking in warmth and well-being. She didn't move, fearful of losing that comfort. Instead, she concentrated on listening to everything around her. Tikid's heavy breathing filled the snow hut with a regular crashing wind-like sound. She had to concentrate in order to hear Meeryle's soft sighs through the dragon's loud breathing, and gave up trying to find Suqi's.

When she sought Kilaron's breath, Leena wasn't sure at first where he was. A move triggered by a dream soon told her that he was behind her.

Having found everyone, Leena concentrated on her own body. She hadn't felt this good in a long, long time. She wanted to savor each moment and remember it. Having four paws and a lithe body helped a great deal in making one comfortable. As a human, the ground would have been too hard, yet as a cat, she was just fine. The only thing to which she wasn't quite used yet was her tail. She had to really concentrate to feel it, let alone move it.

Since she was relaxed, she explored the feeling. The thing was there, part of her, yet so strange. People really weren't supposed to have tails, she thought. Leena concentrated, willing it to move. Nothing happened. At this point, she was puzzled. She had moved it before, flicked it, though more or less by accident. Why didn't it move anymore? Was she too human? Did this mean that as soon as she got up, she might no longer be able to walk?

Leena shook her head, frustrated with herself. She opened her eyes and looked around. Soon, the reason for her inability became clear. Kilaron had huddled himself against her back, entwining their tails together. He encircled her, paws and tail mixed with her own. Only the head wasn't touching her. She couldn't turn her own head that far, but she surmised that it was right behind hers.

Another dream – or the same – shook Kilaron once again and woke him up with a start. Whereas a human would have yelled, the cat simply snorted. Meeryle, Tikid and Suqi slept on, undisturbed.

"*Bad dream?*" Once again, Leena tried to whisper her thoughts. It seemed to work, as the others didn't wake.

"*Yes. No. I'm not sure. How stupid is that?*"

"*It's not stupid, it just means you're troubled. Now, if you wouldn't mind, I'd like to get up.*"

"*Oh.*"

Leena wasn't sure, but he seemed embarrassed. "*It was nice to be warm with you.*" Her cheeks reddened under fur, she was sure of it. Yet it was true; she was sorry to get up, in a way. Given Kilaron's state of mind the previous day, she needed to share this with him, to let him know he was welcome.

"*Thanks. I hadn't planned to invade your space this way, but this is how we sleep when in cat form.*"

"*It felt right.*"

He watched her silently. "*It did, didn't it?*"

Leena simply nodded and got out of the hut. The sun was still low on the horizon, but the sky was clear. Soon, the sunlight would reflect once again on the bright snow. The previous day, she had had too much on her mind to really notice, but this morning, the light was bothering her.

Her movement and Kilaron's had awakened the others, and soon, the hut was dispelled, breakfast eaten and direction set.

This time, Tikid led them in the direction of a small valley, without going down into it. They simply skirted it, and at midday, she guided the group up the next mountain. By nightfall, they were well on their way to the top. Already, the trees were sparse.

When they stopped for a break at Meeryle's request – for which Leena was thankful – Tikid flew away to scout and to allow Meeryle to prepare a hot meal. The day was very cold and as the clouds rolled in, it became humid, which made the cold seep through to the bones, fur or not. Leena wanted hot food and Meeryle would never cook anything in the dragon's presence. Tikid also needed to stretch her wings, so the arrangement suited everyone.

Leena's muscles had been screaming at first, but as they warmed up, she was able to move without too much discomfort. Now that she had stopped and sat down, the relief was surprisingly intense. It could only mean that she was pushing herself too much. If she continued like that, she might injure herself.

She needed a longer break and it rankled. "*Listen, I think I need to stop. Why don't you all go ahead and I'll catch up?*"

Meeryle stopped stirring the soup in the pot and stared. "Leena, this has got to be the stupidest thing you've ever said."

"*She's right. We're not in a rush, we can take out time and wait until your muscles are better,*" added Kilaron, genuine concern seeping through their bond.

"*You... How can you know that?*" Leena was astounded. She hadn't mentioned to anyone how she was feeling.

"*I've been listening to your life song. At first, it was impossible, but now I can hear it if I really concentrate and if I'm close to you. So far, it only seems to work for you. I tried with Meeryle and nothing happened.*"

Leena was glad and surprised. He could only do this because he was soulmated to her.

"*So I'm no longer as special, am I?*" she teased.

"*Leena, I would never…*"

She laughed, but it came out as a grunt. "*I'm not serious. Truly, Kilaron, have you never been teased before?*"

"*Ah... No, not really.*"

"Well, get used to it. Leena and I always do it," cut in Meeryle.

"*Yes, I saw that. I honestly didn't know what to make of it. You looked like you were having fun.*"

"Wow, you know what you need?"

He hesitated. "*No, what?*"

"This!" yelled Meeryle as she threw a snowball at him. It hit him square on the nose.

Stunned, Kilaron stared at Meeryle. He was obviously at a total loss. Leena's heart squeezed; did he not know how to laugh? Before she could say anything, Kilaron shook himself, jumped over the fire and pounced on Meeryle, who fell in the snow with a shriek. They rolled in a blur of snow. Leena watched them while she sat up in front of the fire, stirring the soup as best as she could with her paws.

When Tikid landed back, Kilaron and Meeryle were sitting on the ground, still both covered in snow, and slurping happily on the soup. Leena had already licked her bowl clean, as had Suqi.

The dragon was distracted: she didn't comment on her snow-covered friends' appearance and she didn't wrinkle her nose as the remnant tantalizing smells of the soup wafted away.

"*I think a storm is coming.*" Tikid was looking at the sky, frowning.

"Another one? How many has it been since we got here?" whined Meeryle.

Kilaron chuckled. "*This is normal, you know. It is winter. We always get a lot of snow during the first two months.*"

Meeryle's shoulders slumped. "So we have to travel during storms?"

"*Well, you won't have a choice. Didn't you consult with the weather watchers before you left?*"

"*No! No, we didn't because, in case you hadn't noticed, we weren't exactly welcome,*" answered Leena with heat.

"*You do not need to get angry, Leena,*" cut in Tikid gently. "*I was the one eager to leave. The enclave's caves were too enclosing for me. I had to leave. I am sorry you came and have to go through this.*"

"Oh, Tikid, don't be silly," said Meeryle. She wiped off as much snow as she could and hugged the dragon's drooping neck. "Don't pretend the snow and the cold don't bother you, because I know they do. You can't travel on your own, you need our help."

"*No one is going or staying on their own.*" Kilaron was glaring at them all. "*The only elves who travel alone are trained scouts like Jatoron, and during the snows, they travel in small groups if they can. When you met with Jatoron, he had been caught unaware, otherwise, he would have been with at least one other. You are all clueless about the dangers of the mountain, so you need to stick together. Leena, you're exhausted and you need the rest, a storm is coming, so we'll stay here and wait it out.*"

His tone brooked no argument. Leena wanted to bristle at this tone, but she knew he was right, and while he had managed in great part to shield his emotions, she had time to feel his concern. "*All right, then, let's set up the snow hut again.*"

It didn't take them long to prepare the hut and get comfortable. They had time to gather wood for the fire, though Kilaron had to go a bit out of his way. Leena felt useless; she didn't have the strength to help gather the wood and she couldn't lay out the bedrolls or prepare the food. She simply sat with Tikid and Suqi, and watched Meeryle bustle about.

She soon got bored; Leena liked to do things, not watch them happen. She took advantage of Kilaron's absence to question Tikid on her views on the elven Healer.

The dragon was slow to answer, but she gave Leena her honest opinion. "*Now that you have been soulmated, your colors are different, brighter. I had not seen Kilaron before, so I cannot say for him, but he is good for you,*

Leena." She sniffed loudly. "*And he does not look disproportionate like Rokin.*"

Meeryle burst out laughing. "I remember that! You don't like muscles on men, do you, Tikid?"

"*I just think it seems wrong. You see, Kilaron doesn't look like he will topple over. He is long, like you, Leena, except for the curves. That has to do with females, does it not?*"

Both girls were laughing so hard, Meeryle was crying and Leena got the hiccups. Before either of them could answer the dragon, Kilaron came back, mouth full of small branches.

"*There, that's the last of it. To find more, I'd have to go too far,*" he said as he dropped the bundle. He looked up at the still giggling girls. "*What's so funny?*"

"*As a Healer, you will appreciate Tikid's view on physical appearances, I'm sure.*"

Leaving out the part about his being right for her, Leena recounted the dragon's description of people. The storm hit in the late afternoon and found them all cozy around the fire, trading impressions on each other. They compared the paragons of beauty for each race – it turned out Suqi's white-tipped tail was an oddity which in turn made her astonishingly beautiful and downright ugly – sipping hot water perfumed with an herb that didn't bother Tikid's sensitive nose, while the dragon infused herself with the energy found in the ground. She glowed with a diffuse emerald light, making odd shadows on the sides of the hut.

A few candlemarks later, the storm was at its fiercest. The wind howled, and though it couldn't penetrate through the spell, Leena still shivered. She concentrated on the fire, willing it to warm her, while Kilaron was snoring softly. It turned out Leena wasn't the only one needing to recover from unaccustomed exercise; her soulmate had been too long without rigorous physical activity. Meeryle was propped up against Tikid, eyes closed, listening to the elements. The elven Mages had encouraged her to continue what Leena had suggested, as knowing one's environment was crucial for Mages.

Leena slowly got up and lay down beside her friend. "*I want to hear too.*"

Meeryle nodded and put her hand on Leena's back. "This is air." Through the wind, a strange rasp and groan reached Leena's ears. "This is fire." This time, a beat, almost like a heart's, thudded through Leena's senses. "I know that snow is made out of water, but it's hard for me to hear it, so let's skip that one. This is earth." Leena didn't have it in her to chastise her friend for choosing the easy way. She simply shrugged and listened to earth's murmur.

It became louder, almost a rumble. She frowned. "*Meeryle, is earth always this loud?*"

Suqi barked loudly. "*This is not earth!*"

Meeryle sat up abruptly. "I know it's not. What is it?"

The goupil's bark had awakened Kilaron, whose eyes widened in fear when he heard the rumble. "*Avalanche!*" he yelled. "*Quick, we have to run and get away before the snow covers us. Meeryle, put your coat on.*"

"But… What about our packs?" asked an astounded Meeryle.

"*There's no time! Go!*" The panic in Kilaron's voice soon became contagious and everyone scrambled to grab their things as best as they could. Within seconds, Kilaron had canceled the spell and they were whipped by snowy gusts of wind. Leena lost sight of everyone, except for Tikid, who was still glowing faintly.

"*This way!*"

Leena was thankful for mindspeech; no matter how loud the wind, words spoken directly in one's mind could be heard. Once again, Meeryle grabbed Tikid's tail while holding Suqi. Leena was close behind her. The only difference with the last time they had been caught in a snowstorm was that she wasn't as cold. The fur was very efficient and since Kilaron had them running, Leena was getting warm.

"*Hurry!*"

Kilaron's words moved them all. They ran, blinded by the snow, the rumble of the approaching avalanche deafening them. We'll never make it, thought Leena. She couldn't see the coming masses of snow, but she had gleaned a picture of it from her soulmate's mind. How could they possibly outrun such a thing? How far up was it?

Tikid was now lighting the way like a bright emerald torch. She was completely infused with the essence of the Greens, fighting the cold as best she could. The dragon had folded her wings, but the wind still managed to catch into them, slowing her down.

Meeryle fell, hurling Suqi in the air. The rumbling grew even louder. Leena stopped by her friend, calling Tikid and Kilaron with her mind. But she knew it was too late; the avalanche would soon swallow them up. Now that she had seen it in Kilaron's mind, she knew it to be even bigger than a mudslide.

"Suqi! Leena, I can't hear her anymore," yelled Meeryle. Leena could barely make her out.

The ground trembled. Leena huddled against Meeryle, wishing she could find a solution. Tikid was still a brilliant green light; if anything, she had been getting brighter, to the point where Leena could hear her life song through the rumble.

The wind suddenly changed, blowing in a much more organized way. The swirls of snow had disappeared; the snow was blown in straight lines, so hard that the rumble hesitated. The air changed again, and this time, Leena was sure of it, the rumble of the avalanche diminished, until she could no longer hear it.

A few minutes later, the group was sitting in a mound of snow, with small flakes falling slowly around them. The wind had fallen, the storm had abated, and the avalanche had stopped.

"*Impossible*," said Kilaron. A huge wall of snow hovered over them. "*It's as if the avalanche got frozen in place*."

"Suqi! Suqi, where are you?" Meeryle was in tears. The black fur of the goupil was nowhere to be seen.

Leena concentrated, listening for Suqi's life song. Soon, a sound unlike one she had ever heard whispered in her ears. She was sure it wasn't Tikid's, yet it had almost the same feel, though a much different sound. She looked around, peering through the snow and moved forward, away from the avalanche wall. She stopped when two red spots appeared.

Leena frowned. What were these red things doing in the snow? Then the red spots blinked, and a head manifested. A white dragon head, with red eyes, just like Tikid's, followed by a pair, then another, until Leena was looking at a lot of creatures.

The White dragons had found them.

Chapter 14

Leena stared at the gathered Whites; they were hard to count, but about a dozen dragons faced them. They didn't exactly shine, but in the fading light of the early evening, they stood out, even against the snow. The stark contrast between their scales and their eyes made these dragons seem very strange. Maybe it was simply because she was too used to the shades of green on Tikid's body.

Yet the red eyes gleamed with an eerie light, making everyone uncomfortable. Leena could feel Kilaron's unease through their bond. Leena vaguely recalled the elves mentioning something about the fierceness of the White dragons.

Tikid seemed shy and Meeryle's face was covered with freezing tears.

"*We have pushed the storm away and stopped the avalanche as soon as we felt your essence, Green. Who are you, and why do you come here with a human?*"

The voice held a harshness Leena hadn't heard in any of the Green dragons, not even in Rutad, Tikid's sarcastic sire.

It didn't deter Tikid at all. "*I am here to meet with your Great One. The human is my friend and her name is Meeryle. She is a Mage and she cannot find her familiar, Suqi. Can you help us find her?*"

A muffled bark sounded somewhere ahead of them.

"Suqi! Suqi, we heard you! Where are you?" yelled Meeryle.

A rumbling laugh answered her. "*You little one is here, human.*" The voice in Leena's mind was younger than the first White dragon's. She peered, trying to find which one had spoken. A smaller dragon – though he seemed bigger than Tikid – was moving the snow around, sending a flurry of the cold stuff all over everyone.

"*Yalad, stop!*" roared the dragon who had first spoken.

Yalad stopped, abashed. "*But I found it.*" He held a twisting Suqi in his paws.

Meeryle ran to him with a sob. "She's alive, she's fine, right?"

"*Do not worry, little human.*" He cocked his head. "*You are little. I thought humans were much bigger than this.*"

The young woman burst out laughing. "You're just like Tikid, you know that? You don't have any clue about humans, do you?" She took Suqi into her arms.

"*No, he does not and for good reason,*" cut in the older dragon. "*Humans are not welcome here. I am surprised to see one in company of elves.*"

"*Well, one of them is only half-elf and she's freezing. Thank you for stopping the avalanche, but could we continue this discussion elsewhere, where it's warmer?*" Leena glared as much as she could, though she wasn't sure if it had the same effect in her cat shape.

The dragon laughed. "*I had forgotten how direct humans could be.*"

"You mean you've seen them before?" asked Meeryle.

"*Yes, a very long time ago and it was not a good encounter. Enough of this. We will take you to our caves.*"

"*Wait, please,*" said Kilaron. "*Before we go, we need our things. Leena and I can't change back if we don't have any clothes.*"

"*I will help,*" offered Yalad.

While Kilaron guided the young dragon – Leena was sure Yalad was Tikid's age – she eyed the big White dragon. He was massive, so she guessed he was old, probably older than Tikid's sire. He had had contact with humans, but he didn't like them. Well, maybe it had been a bad experience, but it didn't mean he had to be rude.

"*I think that while we wait, we can start with introductions. My name is Leena. I'm a Healer. My friend is Meeryle, she's the Mage. Her familiar, I'm sure you've heard, is called Suqi. Kilaron is my soulmate.*"

This time, the dragon burst out laughing, the rumbling of the laughter shaking the very mountain. Leena almost feared another avalanche. "*Ha, for a human to have manners! I cannot remember the last time I heard something as funny.*"

Leena was fuming. A low growl tickled her throat and for a second, she wanted to dig her claws into the big white neck. The desire was so intense, Leena was shocked. What was the matter with her? First, she'd cut Kilaron's cheek, and now, she wanted to tear the dragon apart.

The realization doused her anger and she simply stared at the huge creature in front of her.

"*My name is Qilad. The others will introduce themselves if they wish. Now get ready, we will fly you to our caves.*"

Fly! Before Leena could say anything, Qilad grabbed her with his powerful paws. He reared on his hind legs and started pumping his wings. Leena looked around, to find all her friends were being carried the same way, except for Tikid. A nameless dragon stood by her, probably speaking to her. Leena hoped that the dragon could help her friend with the cold. Tikid suddenly flared with an emerald light, while the White dragon turned a bright silver. Leena gasped. "*What's going on?*"

"*The Green suffers from the cold. Mirid is simply imbuing herself and sharing some of the essence with the young one. No one here can carry her the same way as you.*" Qilad turned to the others. "*Are we ready? Let us go!*"

In a flurry of snow, they all took off. Leena closed her eyes, then she remembered that Meeryle had mentioned wanting to fly. She checked on her friend and sure enough, Meeryle was in the grip of another unnamed dragon, holding on to Suqi, her face split in two by a huge grin. She was truly enjoying this and Leena could do no less. The young Healer therefore resolutely kept her eyes open.

At first, she concentrated on the others. Kilaron's eyes were closed and Leena found Yalad holding on to their packs. Tikid was still an emerald beacon, matched with a silver one, so Leena could only assume that the Green dragon was fine.

Then she looked down. Her stomach lurched and she closed her eyes immediately. Through the gushing air and the flapping of all the wings, Leena still heard Meeryle's squeal of delight. If her friend had said anything, the words were lost in the wind, but the tone was clear: Meeryle was enjoying herself. Leena forced herself to open her eyes; she had to see what made her friend so happy.

The ground was still as far down, but they had moved away from the storm, so in the dying daylight, she could make out what it was they were passing at an astonishing speed. Trees, white slopes and even some sort of animal passed below her. She didn't want to think about the height, but the thoughts still sneaked in and she wondered if the snow could cushion her fall. From this distance, it looked so thick and soft. The past few days had cleared out any questions she might have about snow, though. Now she knew how deadly the stuff could be, and she knew the snow was probably not thick enough to break a fall.

The dragons veered to the left and flew into the setting sun. Leena was blinded by the orange light for a few moments, but soon, she made out the ragged slopes, orange where the sun reflected on the snow and black where the rocks were too rugged for the snow to settle.

Amid the desolation of rock and snow, a dark opening came into view. Soon, Leena made out the entrance of a huge cavern, not unlike the one at the elf enclave where they had spent the last few days.

As they neared the mountainside, the dragons slowed their flight somewhat and prepared to land. The size of the platform in front of that dark gap of a cavern made Leena gulp. It was much too small for so many creatures this size. When Qilad shifted his position to prepare to land, Leena once again closed her eyes. She didn't want to see the mountain from that angle, at that speed. What if the platform broke under all that weight? What if its small size meant the bigger dragons – including Qilad – missed their landing and fell down the sheer slope?

After a few strong flaps and some jostling, Leena was lowered to the ground. She was surprised when her paws touched the ground and she realized how cold she was when Qilad let go of her. The places where his paws had been touching her were very warm and the wind soon chilled her. When she looked at her fur, the parts that hadn't been protected by the dragon were filled with ice.

"We need to get warm quickly, Qilad. I don't know how you stand it, but we're frozen."

"I know, little cat, I know. The Green is in bad shape. Greens are not meant for such cold; only the Purples can stand it." His tone was no longer abrasive; in fact, he sounded worried.

Before Leena could even say a word, they were all rushed into the cavern. The wind was cut off right away, but the cold still lingered. Meeryle's teeth were shattering and Suqi didn't look to be in better shape. Leena herself was cold, but she didn't seem to feel it as badly as her friend.

"The fur helps a lot," said Kilaron very quietly in her mind. The elf was filled with a sense of awe that puzzled Leena.

"What is it? You've been weird ever since the dragons found us."

He shook his head. *"You don't have a clue, do you? I think I may be the first elf ever to set foot into a dragon's lair."*

"Well, we did set out to meet with them, no?"

"Yes, but from what I know, the dragons come to us; they don't bring anyone to their homes, let alone a human. We're all very lucky, Leena."

Leena didn't feel lucky, she felt cold and tired. *"Look, let's get warm, then we can talk about this."*

"Does nothing impress you?" asked Kilaron, a growl in his throat. *"Is there nothing you respect?"*

"I respect people when they earned it. Right now, these dragons haven't done anything in that regard, and honestly, neither have you. Now, can we get warmed up?"

Kilaron sighed. "*I shouldn't get angry with you for being different. It's just... I get frustrated to see you just blunder on without being careful.*"

Leena didn't know what to say. In a way, he was right. She had been harsh to the White dragons, but they had been rude. Maybe she shouldn't let her pride guide her all the time; there was nothing wrong with asking for someone's opinion, especially someone who knew the creatures they were facing better than her.

"*Tikid said that dragons don't kill.*" It was a weak argument, but Leena held on to it.

"*I don't know about Green dragons, but the Whites can be...*"

He was cut off by Qilad. "*Come, all of you, into the inner cavern.*"

Leena and Kilaron exchanged a look and they followed the big dragon into a large tunnel, which turned sharply to the right. It led into a second cavern, this one much darker. Of the White dragons that had flown them in, only Qilad and Yalad went with them into the cavern. Leena barely had time to wonder why when a flurry of small dragons swarmed them.

"*Oh, look, people!*"

"*And big cats! Can I play with them?*"

"*What is wrong with you? Your color is strange.*"

"*You are a strange elf. Why is your hair all frizzy?*"

Leena shook her head while Meeryle smiled at the onslaught of questions and Tikid laughed quietly. "*Just like the little ones in the mounds. But why so many?*"

Qilad gave her a penetrating look. "*How many fledglings do you have at any given time?*"

Tikid hesitated, her head suddenly nodding. "*Around twelve, very rarely more. I count at least thirty here.*"

The big dragon nodded. "*It would seem more White dragons are needed than Greens.*"

"Why is that?" asked Meeryle.

"*What is it you know about dragons, little human?*"

"Whatever Tikid told us."

Which tends to be confusing, Leena wanted to add. Since she didn't want to hurt the young dragon's feelings, she stayed quiet. The Green dragon was no longer a shiny emerald; she was back to her normal color, but it seemed off for some reason. The lack of light didn't help, of course. Leena had the impression that the green was slowly leaching off Tikid's scales. The dragon also seemed to be trying to stay awake, but the fledglings had all gathered around her, asking question after question, keeping her from falling asleep.

Oblivious to how Tikid was feeling, Qilad went on. "*And you, elf, what do you know of dragons?*" he asked Kilaron.

"*I...*"

"*Look,*" cut in Leena, "*I hate to interrupt you, but I don't think Tikid's feeling too great. Is there a place here with earth so she can replenish herself?*"

Qilad lowered his head and blew into Leena's face. The cavern became quiet, as all the fledglings grew still and their voices stopped.

"*I may not know much about dragons,*" *Leena said firmly,* "*but I know you just insulted me. Fine, but I'm a Healer first. I care very much about my friends, even if you don't. So, will you show us to some earth, or will you just stare me down?*"

The dragon blinked a few times in surprise. "*You know this is an insult, but you don't know why, I gather.*"

"*No, and right now, honestly, I don't care.*"

He was quiet for a moment, as if debating whether he should be angry with her, or simply amused. "*Yalad will show you to a cave with live earth. It is very dark, though. We do not need light as you do.*"

"*I have something for that in my pack. Let me change to elven form and I'll light the way,*" cut in Kilaron. He had been very quiet, letting Leena speak her mind, but she felt through their bond – though he was shielding his thoughts tightly – that he wasn't comfortable with her forwardness.

The dragon didn't ask why only Kilaron would be changing. Maybe he hadn't heard, but Leena doubted much got by the formidable creature.

Yalad gestured for Kilaron to join him in another cave.

"*Come with me, Leena. You should try to change back too. It isn't good to remain a cat for too long.*"

More than anything, Leena wanted to turn back into herself. Her muscles were sore, her senses overfilled with smells and sounds, and her head about to burst from the effort of speaking mind to mind. She was worried about Tikid and she was tired. The flight had taken a harder toll on her than she cared to admit out loud. She needed the rest and it just seemed like she couldn't get it in cat form. It was too new, too different.

Yet every attempt had met with failure. Why should it be any different now? If anything, it would be even harder to change back in her current state. She had to try, though. If she didn't, she was afraid she could be stuck in this form for the rest of her life.

The new cave was just as dark as the fledgling cave, if not darker. Leena was grateful for the sharpness of her cat's eyes, otherwise, she might have either tripped a few time or simply bumped into the rock walls.

Yalad deposited their packs on the ground. "*As soon as you have light, we will go to the earth cave for the Green.*"

As soon as he had left, Kilaron sat by Leena. "*You really need to change, Leena. Something in our bond feels wrong because of it.*"

"*No, what you feel is the fact that I'm exhausted.*"

Kilaron hesitated. "*Maybe. Whatever it is, I think it can be fixed by changing. Have you seen someone else do it?*"

"*Yes, my mother, but it didn't help. Her life song changed a bit, but I couldn't really get anything out of it.*"

The white cat sniffed loudly. "*You're the first half-breed, Leena. We don't know anything about what's right and what's wrong with you, but I do know that changing back and forth to cat form is something innate. You can't just be able to do it one day and not the next. You were able to change once, so you can do it again.*"

Leena bit back a scathing retort. He was right; yelling at him and telling him he was saying nothing she didn't already know wouldn't help. "*So, what do you propose we do?*"

"*Lie down. I will lie against your back so you can touch me while I change. Between that and our bond, it might help you.*"

Leena complied and lay on her side. Being off her feet was such a relief, she wished she could cry. She was even more tired than she had previously thought. Resting her chin on the ground, she closed her eyes, savoring the rest. She almost fell asleep, but Kilaron jerked her awake when he touched her back. He encircled her, tucking his front paws under her chin, almost choking her in the process.

"*Are you ready? I will go as slowly as I can.*"

Didn't he realize he hurt her? And he didn't even apologize! However, before she could say anything, Kilaron had started his transformation. Leena quickly concentrated on his life song. It was the same as usual, except for a faint burr. The sound didn't seem wrong, though. It grew louder and became that same purr she had heard within herself. Instinctively, she sought it once again, but it still wasn't there.

Kilaron must have felt it through the bond; he remained at that level, sending encouragements through the bond. Neither of them spoke; Leena wasn't even sure if they could have. She simply let herself go through the link that soulmated her to Kilaron and listened closely to the purr. Somehow, it resonated back to her and came to life in her body.

Leena let the purring sound match Kilaron's. As soon as his became louder, so did hers. All the time, she listened closely to his life song. It flared suddenly, almost blinding the part of her that enabled her to Heal. She instinctively followed suit, as she recognized the sound from her mother's own transformation.

All her senses sang as each part of her body returned to its original form. Her arms and legs lengthened, her spine shifted and her shoulders broadened. None of it was painful; quite the opposite. For the first time in days, Leena felt right.

Both life songs quieted. Leena took in a deep breath, smiling at the fact that the sound she made wasn't as loud anymore. She opened her eyes and briefly regretted her cat-sight, as the cavern was pitch dark to her human-elf eyes. The simple pleasure of smiling quickly dispelled the regret. She was herself again.

Fingers brushed her shoulder and arm lightly, making her shiver and reminding her how cold the cave truly was.

"I can warm you if you like," whispered Kilaron in her ear. His lips brushed her ear and slowly ran down her throat. This time, the shiver had nothing to do with the cold.

Leena sat up. "Tikid needs our help." She tried to keep her voice from faltering. For a brief moment, she had wanted to surrender to that second shiver, even if she wasn't sure about her feelings for her soulmate. She made a face, disgusted with herself for allowing desire to overcome her.

Groping her way on all fours, Leena found the packs. She quickly found hers and proceeded to put her clothes on. Blushing furiously at both the lingering effect of desire and the fact that she was naked, Leena hoped that Kilaron was just as blind as she was for the moment.

From the way the elf shuffled around, she guessed he was at the same level as she was. "Here, there's your pack."

"Thanks," he replied, a smile in his voice. "Can I light a candle now, or do you want to wait until you're dressed?"

He was making fun of her! Leena took in two deep breaths before she dared say anything. "Where I come from, being soulmated means nothing, Kilaron. People tend to love each other, or at least, respect each other before they even think about getting close. You seem to treat it very lightly; I don't."

Kilaron didn't say anything and closed the bond tightly. He fumbled in his pack until he found the lighting device. The scraping sound was soon followed by a bright flame as Kilaron lit the small portable candle. The small flame was blinding after all that darkness. Leena blinked a few times and her eyes accustomed themselves quickly.

The first thing she saw was her soulmate's angry face. His teeth were clenched, his eyes filled with fury. For the first time, Leena wondered if her words might not have been too hasty.

Kilaron put the candle on the ground and grabbed his pack. He was still naked, so Leena got the full brunt of his backside. She blushed, searching for words.

Just before he left the cave, he turned and gave her a venom-filled look. "I knew my first impression had been right: you're a cold-hearted bitch."

He left her on her own, with the fluttering light, wondering if maybe he wasn't right.

Chapter 15

Light in hand, fully dressed, Leena followed Yalad, with Tikid, Suqi and Meeryle in tow. The chubby Mage was still giggling with happiness at seeing her friend back into her normal shape. Leena winced at the memory of Meeryle's hug; that young woman was much stronger than she appeared.

Tikid hadn't said anything – which confirmed that fact that the dragon was not feeling well at all – and if Suqi had said anything, Leena hadn't heard it. She didn't know where Kilaron had gone. The others hadn't noticed he wasn't with them and she wasn't about to bring up the reason for his absence. She also refused to dwell on it for the time being; she needed to take a hard look at herself, but right now, Tikid's wellbeing was more important.

Yalad led them deep inside the mountain. The White dragons had that in common with elves: they liked to burrow. Leena hadn't minded the elven caves, but the dragons liked darkness. She wasn't sure if only Whites had this predilection; apparently, Greens didn't. Poor Tikid was squinting in the dim light provided by the candle.

Finally, the young White dragon gestured to halt. "*This is a very warm cave, rich with soil. You should be fine here, Green. You should all be fine here. Stay as long as you want. If you need anything, you can call for me.*"

"How?" asked Meeryle.

Yalad was puzzled. "*I can hear a call from anywhere in the mountain. Just call.*"

"I think he means with mindspeech, Meeryle," cut in Leena.

"*How else?*"

Leena smiled. "Didn't you notice we're speaking out loud, with our throat and mouth, not with our minds?"

"*But you do both at the same time, do you not?*"

"In a way. Don't worry about it. I can call with mindspeech."

Yalad gave her a skeptical look, but left them to rest.

Tikid flopped on the ground. Meeryle sat beside her and hugged her friend gently. "Is the earth good enough here?"

"*Yes. I can imbue myself in it. I think I might sleep too.*"

The dragon was as good as her word. As she fell asleep, her scales started to glow a muted emerald. It was the first time Leena ever saw her friend do this.

"Does she always glow like that?" she whispered.

Meeryle shrugged. "Every time she's been imbuing, as she says, I think that yes, she does glow, but you really have to look for it. I think she's just really, really tired. Do you know how much energy she used to keep from freezing? I think she needs a sweater or something."

"Maybe you can ask your mother to knit one."

Both young women laughed as quietly as they could, but the dragon was oblivious to anything around her. They talked quietly about the flight here and what they thought about the White dragons so far. Leena's stomach interrupted them and Meeryle took out some crushed bread from her pack.

"Here. It's not much, but it should be enough for now." She shook her head. "We won't be able to stay here very long; they certainly won't offer us anything to eat. They seem worse than the Greens."

"It's the eyes, I think. They just look wrong on them!"

At that moment, the candle sputtered and died, leaving the girls in complete darkness.

Meeryle yipped and Leena swore. "Kilaron's got the fire starter."

"And why isn't he here?"

Leena shook her head and remembered that her friend couldn't see her. Tikid's muted glow only allowed her to find the dragon; it didn't give off enough light to see anything else.

"I'll explain later. Now, let me call Yalad and see if he can convince Kilaron to come here to light this thing."

"Um… Leena?"

"Yes?"

"I can light it."

Leena stared in the direction of her friend's voice. Did she hear her right? Meeryle was volunteering to light a candle with her gift? Even since the chubby young woman had lost control of her gift, Meeryle had avoided anything that had to do with fire, including cooking. And now, she was going to use that part of her gift.

"Are you sure? I mean, no need to rush," she said gently.

"I'm sure. I have to try at one point. I'd rather it be with something this small, with basically nothing around that can burn."

Leena automatically listened to Meeryle's life song. It was the only thing she could do, really. Her gift and Meeryle's were too different.

Meeryle's body was still, her life song normal. Her heartbeat increased, until it was so strong, Leena thought something was wrong. The beat then became different and Leena knew she was hearing fire. A few moments later, the candle came to life and showed a shaking Meeryle.

"I did it, Leena, I did it. I can light a candle without burning it down."

Leena hugged her and smiled. "Let's eat."

They shared the crumbling bread and joined Tikid and Suqi – the goupil was curled against the dragon, sleeping deeply. Leena had to shift around a few times before she was comfortable enough.

That was one aspect of being a cat she missed: all surfaces made a fine bed. Her human body didn't agree. Nonetheless, the day's happenings caught up with her and she surrendered to exhaustion. She barely had time to remember Kilaron before sleep took over.

***

Leena woke to the sound of excited voices. At first, none of the words made sense, but as her mind wakened from the slumber, she realized Tikid and Yalad were discussing the differences in their environment.

"*... in the winters?*"

"*They are not as cold as here. I do not think I spotted any wintering trees here. If you do not have trees, then the Greens do not come.*"

"*What about the warmth? We cannot stand it.*"

As the conversation went on, Leena gathered that Whites and Greens did not meet very often. This was as exciting for them as it was for both Leena and Meeryle.

As much as she wanted to take part in the conversation, she needed a few moments to stretch; her body was stiff – she just wasn't sure if it was due to the lack of bed or the hardship of changing forms.

"I trust you are rested? You slept much longer than the Mage, we were worried you were not well," said Yalad.

For the first time, Leena noticed that both Meeryle and Suqi were gone.

"I told him you were fine, Leena. Your colors were right; I think you were just tired."

"I was, Tikid. This changing into a cat thing is hard on the body. I still need a minute here, so why don't you continue? You were talking about the difference in temperature?"

The White dragon snorted. *"I never really understood why the Greens stayed so far from our mountains. Until today, it had not occurred to me that if we abhor heat, others may fear the cold."*

"You'd never see a Green before?"

"No, I am too young. Others of the Color sometimes go down the mountains during the winter's peak and meet with Greens, but one needs to be schooled for such voyages. I want to be one of them and go not only into Green territory, but also by the Purple's oceans."

Either Yalad was older than Tikid or he was simply better at expressing himself, but Leena's mind suddenly connected all the pieces of the young dragon's words over the last months. "You say Green territory, so you mean the forest, right?" The White dragon nodded. "Tikid's mentioned other Colors before, but I never was able to question her into detail about that."

At the young Healer's reproachful looks, the Green dragon tilted her head in puzzlement. *"But I answer whenever you ask a question, Leena. It is only that your questions never seem to end."*

Yalad's roar of laughter shook the cavern's ground. "*You do not learn quickly, my Green friend. Humans are very curious and always wish to know everything in order to change it to their whim.*"

He was definitely, if not older, at least more experienced. His judgment on humans rankled, but before she could say anything, Tikid hissed in defense. "*How can you know this? Until today, you had never seen a human before. Are these your ideas, or Qilad's?*"

"*I am sorry. You are probably right,*" said the dragon, abashed. "*But every time we ask Qilad about humans, he tells us how they don't belong here.*"

Leena blinked in surprise. People did have a tendency to simply settle where they wished, rather than doing so where they should. In the deep forest, it wasn't so; villages only thrived if they were built where both crops could grow and game could be hunted. Cities were another matter; Parin, Leena's father, had always explained how cities were damaging to the surroundings, how the crops had to be sown further from the buildings every few years, how the game became scarcer if it wasn't managed properly. Yes, humans could be destructive, but to say they didn't belong into the world was… troubling. Tassim had alluded to this, and now, the notion was echoed by a dragon. "I was talking to one of the elves about the humans' lack of animal form and that it might be linked to why humans have to purify their water."

Tikid tilted her head the other way. "*But I do not understand. They are here, are they not? Just like the animals, the plants, the elves, the melusins, the sirènes, the feu-follets. So how could they not be part of the world?*"

"*What you said reflects Qilad's words, Leena. All the sentient beings in this world have two shapes except for the humans. We dragons are the world, yet we are not made to provide water for humans, therefore humans shouldn't be here at all.*"

Leena's mind was in turmoil. It all made some sort of sense, yet it didn't explain why humans were so different. Could anyone know? "Let's think this through."

"*What does that mean?*" asked Yalad.

"*It means she will put everything she knows into words and come up with an answer,*" explained Tikid. The hint of pride in her words was amusing. The more Leena heard, the more it became apparent that the Green dragon was indeed much younger than White Yalad, and just like any youngster, she was proud to show she knew more about something than someone older than her. That she would explain reasoning the way she did seemed strange, but Leena had to put that aside for the moment.

"Well put, Tikid. Now, let me summarize what I know. Dragons are the world, and that means each kind…"

"*Color,*" corrected Yalad.

"Sorry, each Color has a specific task. Greens look after the forests, right?"

"*Yes, without us, the forests would die. Our presence is beneficial to all plants, but we are the trees in truth.*"

"Now, Tikid, you mentioned that the Reds lived in the fire, yes?"

The Green dragon nodded. "*There's fire everywhere, really, but mostly in the center of the soil.*"

"And probably in the volcano lava. Yalad, from what you just said, the Purples are the… ocean?"

"They are. Without them, fish, coral, algae, nothing would live in the sea. The Browns are the earth, the soil, the Coppers are the hard material found in the soil. These mountains are rather bare, so Browns and Coppers are not really needed here."

"What about the Whites?"

Yalad blinked and stared at Leena. "*What do you mean?*"

"What are you?"

"*The air.*"

Of course! Something needed to see to breathing proper air. Did the Whites create air, or did they simply purify it? According to Tikid, Green presence meant healthier trees, it didn't mean no trees at all. The trees around the village were fine, were they not? Yet if the Greens were completely destroyed, would any tree grow? Just how far did their influence stretch, anyway?

"Is this why you like the cold?"

"*Yes. In the cold, we can have pure, clean air that our wind can carry far and wide. All living things need air. I think the Whites hold the greatest number of individuals in all of the Medley.*"

Meaning that without White dragons, nothing could survive. It also explained the numerous fledglings they had encountered when they arrived. Air for an entire world required quite the workforce.

"Let me sum all of this up; some dragons make the air, others the soil. I think the material the Coppers create might be metal, in some form or other. The Reds… they what, heat the world?"

Tikid flapped a wing. "*They just... are.*"

Leena rolled her eyes. "Never mind. So the Purples are water, then, are they not?"

"*Yes*," said Yalad. He gave her a look. "*Are you finished thinking?*"

She smiled. "Well, you could say that. If Purples are the water, how come humans can't drink it?"

The White dragon chuckled. "*You cannot drink water from the ocean, no one can. You drink water from the lakes and the river.*"

Since Leena had never seen the ocean, how could she have known its water wasn't potable? "You shouldn't laugh at someone for not knowing something, Yalad," she gently scolded. "But now I have another question: who makes the drinkable water, then?"

"*Oh, I never thought of that*," said Tikid.

"*Rivers and lakes start at a spring, and there are many in the mountains. Maybe as we purify the air, we purify the springs too, but I am not sure. It is a very interesting question, Leena. I like this thinking thing you do.*"

Leena smiled. "Why, thank you, Yalad."

"*We can ask the Great White One, Leena.*"

Tikid's words got Yalad's attention. "*Do you think the Great One will come here? I have never seen her.*"

"*I met with the Great Green One and he told me to come here. Then I do not know if I am to seek the other Great Ones.*"

"Don't worry about it for now, Tikid. First, make sure you're completely recovered. Then we'll see about arranging a meeting with the Great One, as you say."

The Green dragon stretched, taking the time to unfurl each wing to its fullest and declared herself fit.

"*But what about you, Leena? You slept, but you have not eaten. You should seek Meeryle. I am sure she found some food.*"

Yalad looked embarrassed. "*We are not used to visitors, so we do not keep any edibles here. I think the fledglings found mushrooms.*"

The Healer's stomach chose that moment to make the loudest noise. Yes, she was quite hungry.

"Can you take me to Meeryle?"

"*Of course.*" Yalad was quiet for a moment. "*She is with the other elf. Come, I'll show you the way.*"

Leena's heart sank as she followed the dragons. If only for a few candlemarks, she had been able to forget about her soulmate. However, she had to face him at one point; she couldn't just hope he would go away, now, could she?

Squaring her shoulders, Leena took in a deep breath and firmly told herself that everything would be all right.

Chapter 16

A delicious waft of cooking mushrooms made Leena's stomach growl once more.

Yalad grunted in surprise. "*What is this?*"

"That is Meeryle's doing. You give her something edible and she'll transform it into something delicious."

"*She makes many things just so I can smell them,*" added Tikid.

"*But you do not eat them?*"

"*Not unless you like dead live things.*"

Yalad grunted once more, but whether it was in agreement or not, Leena couldn't tell.

In order to accommodate their guests, the dragons had somehow put luminescent things throughout the cave in which Meeryle had set up her makeshift kitchen. Leena didn't get a chance to get a good look at them because as soon as she saw her friend, Meeryle thrust a tin cup full of food in her hands.

"Here, you must be starving."

"Yes, I am."

Both friends sat by the small fire on which Meeryle had placed a flat rock. The fire was too small to give off enough heat, yet the mushrooms were sizzling. Should she question Meeryle about this? While it was a good thing for her friend to experiment anew with fire, close scrutiny might discourage her to continue, which would be a shame. Did the lighting of that candle really cure her of all her fears in that regard?

"Kilaron told me."

"What?" The statement took Leena off guard.

"He told me that… well, that you're not getting along."

Leena blinked and realized that her soulmate wasn't in the cave. Was she so afraid of what he represented that she could so easily erase him from her conscious thoughts? The White dragon had said that Meeryle was with the other elf, yet the enticement of the food, the strange lights and her friend's experimentation with fire had conveniently allowed her to forget about Kilaron. Leena was angry with herself. How often had she criticized others about denial? Meeryle had been her chief victim over the past months! And now, she was just as guilty. For the first time, she understood why people would change the subject when they were uncomfortable addressing something that troubled them. It wasn't cowardice, as she had surmised, but a sort of protection, a way to deal with a jumble of feelings.

"Leena?"

"Sorry, Meeryle. It's... difficult."

The young Mage smiled. "Really, I couldn't tell."

Leena blinked in surprise; never before had she heard sarcasm from her friend. She was usually the one with acerbic comments. "Serves me right!"

"I never thought I'd be able to return the favor, Leena. You helped me with my gift – against my will, I might add – and now, I can help you with your mate!" She giggled. "I have to say, saying 'your mate' is funny. You, with a mate! Rokin will not be happy."

"Oh, hush. Healing sometimes takes a different turn. I healed you in that sense; it hurt, but it was necessary."

Meeryle nodded gravely. "I'm just realizing it now, but ever since I've started to consciously use my gift, I've been feeling right about myself, like this who I really am. I'm not completely there yet, but give me time."

"Are you saying I should do the same?"

"Oh, Leena, you know these things so much better than I do! But you should have seen him. He's hurting so much."

"What?" Why did it surprise her that he should be hurt by her rejection? She knew just how poor his confidence in himself could be; if only she had checked the feelings that came through the bond! But she had unconsciously blocked him off, and had done so very tightly. Now that she realized it, she let the wall down a notch – the emotions were unmistakable. But his comment, his reaction, was infuriating, no matter how much she tried to be rational. It felt safe to tell herself he was at fault, not her.

But try as she might, Leena couldn't just dismiss that little annoying voice in the back of her mind. He was a Healer, one who cared deeply for the well-being of others, but most of all, his remoteness and the near arrogance which hid his lack of confidence notwithstanding, he was a good person – a person with whom she was more than probably in love.

"Why don't you like him? Aside from the obvious, of course," said Meeryle with a loud sniff.

Leena burst out laughing. "What, you're not head over heels for him?"

Her friend arched an eyebrow. "Don't change the subject."

"*I am not sure what you are discussing*," interrupted Yalad. "*Is there something wrong with the other elf?*"

"*He is Leena's soulmate*," answered Tikid.

"*What is the problem, then? Elves are happy when they find their soulmate*."

"It's not so simple, Yalad. I'm not a pure elf, so I'm not a good soulmate."

Both dragons and Meeryle gasped, then all spoke at once.

"Don't be an idiot."

"*You are a soulmate or you are not; you can't be good or bad.*"

"*But Kilaron is good for you; your power glow is better since you know him.*"

Leena reeled under the mental voices of the dragons, and Meeryle's shock touched her. "Stop, all of you. Tikid, thanks for letting me know. You're confirming what I have felt." Never before had she felt so confident about her gift. "Yalad, it's a bit complicated to explain."

"*Please do.*"

The request took her aback. The things that were bothering her were very personal. While she liked the White dragon, she didn't know him enough to confide in him.

"*You have much to learn about humans. Relationships are a complex thing,*" explained Tikid. "*Come, I will tell you what I know while Leena eats her meal. I am not comfortable with the smell any longer.*" Yalad followed the Green dragon out of the cave, leaving the girls alone.

"Well, I guess Tikid's learned a thing or two from us. I know for a fact that once she likes the smell of something I cooked, she never gets sick of it." Meeryle made a face. "I can't decide if I'm proud of her for her diplomacy, or horrified that she lied."

"Our little dragon, all grown up. Let's shed a tear."

The chubby woman laughed. "You're horrible."

"Sorry, but it just feels good to laugh. She's right, though, I needed the space, so to speak. I like Yalad…"

"But he's not a friend yet."

Leena sighed. "I'm having a hard enough time telling this to my best friend."

"So, what is the problem?" asked Meeryle quietly. "He asked me what he could do in order to warm your heart. Aside from the fact that it sounds terribly romantic, it also sounds sad and very much like you."

"What?"

"Oh, come now, Leena. Rokin was all over you and you never batted an eye." Meeryle forestalled Leena from making a nasty comment with a hand gesture. "And don't mention me, this is about you. Why were you never so much into him? You always said he wasn't right for you, but how did you know?"

"It was… a feeling."

"That's it?"

"Well…"

"Well what?" Meeryle glared at her, fists on her hips. "Out with it!"

"I… we… we tried once."

The young Mage's eyes were so wide with surprise, Leena was afraid they'd pop out of her head. "But you never said anything! Neither did he!"

"That would be because it just didn't work out." A fiasco, more like it. How could she tell Meeryle?

"He always courted you, though. Tried to, anyway."

"Yes, I think he was hoping I'd give him another chance."

Meeryle sighed. "Leena, I'm not a Healer and I'm not experienced, but I do know that getting intimate takes some work. What went so wrong that you weren't even willing to try again?"

"He… I had to…"

Meeryle's eyes went wide with shock. "He tried to force you?"

"No, nothing like that! Otherwise, I certainly wouldn't have been nice to him. And he would have had a terrible time trying it again," she said wryly. "I just couldn't surrender, let him… do anything."

Her friend's face crunched in concentration. "I'm sorry, I want to help you, but I don't know what to say. I just can't really understand."

"I can," said a deep voice.

"Kilaron. You heard?" asked Meeryle.

"Yes."

"Oh," said Leena.

"You could have told me, you know. Though it's obvious once one gets to know you."

The elf's restrained tone set Leena on edge. "Told you what, exactly?"

"That you can't bear to lose control."

Leena stared at her soulmate. The blank look on his face disappeared under her gaze and was replaced by a longing so deep, Leena could feel it through the bond she thought she was blocking.

He was right, of course. She had to control everything in her life, and if she couldn't, she concentrated on the small things she could manage effectively, always giving her the impression that whatever was happening was her decision. When she had allowed Rokin to touch her, he has awoken intense feelings that she couldn't control. How could she let go? That day, she had learned that, should she be willing, she could probably pleasure a partner; however, she just couldn't allow him to do the same to her.

"Leena, you have a knot inside you. Now that we're soulmated, I can feel it. Something inside you is wound up tight. You won't let it unwind, so you can't accept physical intimacy, but more importantly, it means you may not be able to achieve your potential as a Healer."

"That's all this is about, isn't it," hissed Leena.

"Leena, don't get mad," said Meeryle. "He's trying to help." She had forgotten her friend was there. The words – and her presence – calmed her down. She was right, of course. Kilaron's face was filled with concern; his frown told her he was listening to her life song. If she dared open herself to the bond, she would know for sure – but she wasn't quite ready for that.

"Sometimes, Healing means you have to surrender to the power, to the song, in order to achieve your goal," he explained. "You have to be at ease with yourself, know yourself, in order to do that." He smiled. "It includes sex, you know."

The kindness in his voice brought tears to her eyes. Kilaron reached and wiped them gently before they could run down her cheeks. "Tears are part of it too."

He was right; she hated to cry. When she had lost her apprenticeship, when she had learned that she didn't have the Mage gift, when she found out Meeryle had it, she'd fought hard to keep the tears at bay and had resented the ones who finally won their way out.

"Leena?"

"It's all right, Meeryle, she needs time."

"Oh."

Leena's heart clenched at the sadness in her friend's voice. Was she this pitiful? "Stop it, both of you. I'm fine, I just need to figure things out."

"There's nothing to figure out. You're my soulmate, but you just can't accept it."

"So I have to be as open-minded as you?" she asked sweetly.

"By the life song, Leena, you're as stubborn as… as a human!" yelled Kilaron. Leena glared at him, and he left the cavern without saying another word.

Meeryle sighed. "That went well."

"I just can't help it. Every time he says something, it just rubs me the wrong way." Her friend looked at her in silence. "What?"

"Well, he's not the only one to blame here. You're very… forceful at times."

Leena stared at her friend, torn between anger and laughter. Her pride was getting the best of her again. Laughter won. "You're putting it mildly, but you might be onto something."

"Hah! And I'll have you know I told Kilaron the same thing about himself. Go talk to him and really listen, will you? Ever since you joined him, or whatever you call it, you seem, I don't know, better, almost like you're confident."

Leena gave her friend a hug and nodded. She would make things right with Kilaron. Even if it killed her, she wouldn't let her pride get in the way. The illogical thought made her giggle and she left Meeryle by the small fire in search of her soulmate.

***

She found him with an excited Yalad and Tikid.

"*She's coming here!*" said the White dragon, his tail swinging back and forth, the tip hitting Tikid. The Green dragon didn't seem to even notice, as she as just as excited as Yalad.

"Who?"

"*Kiqod!*"

Leena arched a questioning eyebrow to Kilaron, who smiled. "The Great White One has apparently confirmed her arrival."

"Oh, so she'll be here in person, not through another dragon?" Seeing Tikid's sire change personalities as the Great One of the Greens took over his body had been unsettling.

"They can do that?" whispered Kilaron, eyes wide.

"*Yes, but it will not be the case here. The Great One wants to speak to me and see me through her own eyes.*" Tikid's voice was muted with excitement and awe.

Leena smiled. "You came here to meet with her, didn't you?"

"*Yes, but now it seems unreal. Meeting Murod was... and now Kiqod... I have no words.*"

The awe in the young dragon's eyes humbled Leena – she couldn't recall ever feeling anything remotely close to what her friend was displaying. Was it her pride, a lack in her character, or simply because she had yet to meet anyone who could inspire such respect?

"*I cannot believe you will have met two of the Great Ones in person,*" said Yalad, just as awed.

"*If Murod has his way, I shall meet all the Great Ones.*"

"*I do not think any dragon in the Great Medley has ever done so.*"

Both dragons stared at each other, stunned into a frightened silence. Kilaron arched his eyebrows. "Well, just take it one at a time. Murod was kind, was he not?"

"*Yes, yes, he was,*" nodded Tikid.

Leena nodded. "From what I recall, he was very kind to Meeryle and that was within Rutad's body. I don't care what you say, I can't believe one's personality can be completely taken over like this. Some residual personality must remain, and Murod was kind enough even with Rutad's…" Leena hesitated, as she didn't want to insult Tikid's father.

"*His mean side. You can say it, Leena. Now that I know more about humans, I notice more about dragons. Yes, Murod was very kind. But what about Kiqod?*"

Yalad shook his head. "*I have never met her, so I cannot tell you.*"

They all stayed silent for a while, mulling over the meaningfulness of the occasion.

A bark shook them back to the moment. Suqi sat on her haunches, giving the arriving Meeryle something akin to a hopeful look.

"Well, what is she saying?" asked Leena.

The young woman's eyes came unfocused for a few moments. She blinked and stared at the goupil, then at Leena. "She told me Qilad had something to say to me. He just spoke to me in my head about the White Great One. He says that I need to use these skills of mine to prepare an area outside, as the Great One won't fit into the cavern. Is he right, Yalad?"

The White dragon was nonplussed. "*Of course she would not. But why prepare anything?*"

"Because Tikid and Meeryle can't stay out in the cold for very long," explained Kilaron. "Leena and I can shift to cat form, but they can't." An offended bark reminded him that not all furred people were protected against the cold. "And Suqi can only withstand the low temperatures for so long," he quickly added.

"*Oh. I do not think we ever had guests like you. I will find an appropriate place*," said Yalad. The young dragon simply left them without another word, his speed impressing Leena. How did he manage not to hurt his wings? It seemed dragons needed to flare their wings, even a little, when they moved quickly. Did they know the caverns and tunnels that well? Had they adapted to the point where they knew instinctively how much space they had?

"So, what did Qilad want you to do, Meeryle?" asked Kilaron, startling Leena out of her endless string of thoughts. She mentally rolled her eyes; when would she learn to stop asking questions, querying everything? When she died, probably.

The short woman sighed. "I need to create something like the hut in which we hid from the snowstorm."

"Meeryle, that'll be one huge hut. And we don't have the rock with the spell," said Leena, eyes wide.

"Well, if I learned Tassym's lessons correctly, I won't be doing a hut exactly."

"What will you be doing, then?"

***

Leena's question was answered a few candlemarks later, after climbing furlongs inside the mountain. How many tunnels did this mountain have? It seemed so riddled with holes, caverns and passages, it was a wonder it didn't collapse on itself.

The thought brought on a sudden pressure into Leena's lungs. She quickly took in a deep breath, reminding herself that her mind was imagining things. This mountain was solid.

Wasn't it?

Before fear of being crushed truly spread, they reached the top. After the darkness of the tunnels, the daylight was blinding. What time was it? All these candlemarks spent in the darkness of the caves seemed long, but it probably was late morning only. So much had happened in little time…

They were in a large depression near the top of the mountain with a rather flat surface. The sun reflected on the snow, making Leena's eyes water. Tikid had walked up with her, Yalad, Meeryle, Kilaron and Suqi, but apparently, the other White dragons had already made their way to the platform by flight. The sun lit their scales, showing different shades of white, including pearl and some silver. They were magnificent.

All the red eyes were looking at the sky. Leena shaded her eyes with her hands and sought the reason for their concentration. Soon, the clear blue sky wavered and became a huge dragon shape. Leena blinked a few times in disbelief. How could a dragon simply appear?

"*She travels as the wind,*" explained Yalad when questioned.

But before Leena could ask him to elaborate, the Great White One was preparing to land. The dragon didn't flap her wings the way Tikid or any other dragon did, she simply gently tucked them in as she slowly landed on the ground – as if the air was gently depositing her. Was that what Yalad had meant?

The Great One controlled the wind. It made sense, since the Whites were the air. Leena sighed; her questions would probably have to wait. She hoped the Great One would be friendlier than the other White dragons.

Once the big dragon had settled, all the Whites converged towards her, shifting the snow around, making it blur everything.

"*I come to seek the Green,*" said a deep female voice. "*I am Kiqod of the Whites.*"

"*I am Tikid of the Greens,*" answered the young dragon, voice filled with awe. She moved forward toward the Great One, forcing the Whites to part for her. Only then could the young Healer truly appreciate her size. Tikid was young, Yalad a bit older and bigger and Qilad was huge by comparison. Kiqod dwarfed them all. She seemed as tall as the mountains. Leena tried in vain to find a reference point, but none of the buildings in the village matched her height.

Tikid became a bright emerald. The cold was already affecting her.

"*We are very high in the mountain, you need shelter.*" Kiqod's head slowly turned towards Leena, Meeryle and Kilaron. "*Murod said you are a Mage.*"

"Yes, yes I am," replied Meeryle, gulping nervously.

"*Proceed. I can wait.*" The huge dragon slowly looked away, almost as if she were sluggish.

All the red eyes focused on the group of friends, the look carrying curiosity, disdain and impatience. While none spoke, the White dragons let their emotion flow freely. Never before had Leena experienced such an intense wave of mixed emotions. Could all dragons do this?

In order not to get overwhelmed by the onslaught, Leena focused on differentiating the feelings projected by the dragons. They were so numerous! But while she did feel hostile emotions, a concentration of curiosity and eagerness did manage to make its way through, allowing her to relax. So Qilad's way of thinking wasn't unanimous. Or maybe the curiosity was directed at the Great One, not towards them.

Meeryle took in a deep breath. "All right, here I go."

Leena wondered if her friend didn't feel all these emotions, or if she simply decided to ignore them. "So how are you going to do this?"

"I think I need to form a barrier in order to keep the heat trapped in."

Kilaron arched an eyebrow. "From what I know, the snow shelters are made of two barriers of air trapping snow. Are you going to do this here?"

"I'm not sure, actually. As long as it can stay warm enough, we should be all right for a little while. It's just…" Meeryle hesitated, looking overwhelmed.

"What?"

"It's going to be a huge shelter," she said. "Now that I see her, I'm not sure."

By her, she obviously meant Kiqod. Anything Leena had envisioned based on Tikid's shared memory of meeting Murod had been dissolved by the White Great One's presence. What had Meeryle planned before being confronted with reality?

"*Start anyway, Meeryle,*" encouraged Tikid. "*We will help you.*"

The confidence in the Green dragon's voice made Leena smile. Their friend took their potential for granted and had become a source of assurance for both Leena and Meeryle.

The short woman strode to the center of the platform and closed her eyes. While Leena loved to touch her friend when she wielded magic, she didn't want the dragons to think Meeryle needed Leena's support. This time, the only thing she could do was listen to her life song in order to witness her work.

The rasp of air invaded every aspect of Meeryle's life song, yet she didn't sound wrong. Arms extended out, hands wide open, the young Mage closed her eyes and pulled air to her. Leena was both listening to the life song and looking at her friend, and it seemed air was filling her and surrounding her. Slowly, the snow at Meeryle's feet receded, moving out, pushed away by air. Soon, the Mage was standing on bare rock, in the middle of a perfect circle of snow.

The mood within the White dragon mass shifted; disdain and indifference changed to panic, and curiosity to wonder.

All of them had suddenly a comment to make.

"*How can anyone use air like this?*"

"*This is wrong, only Whites should control air thus!*"

"*Do you think she can clear the entire area?*"

"*What! Impossible!*"

"*Never trusted humans…*"

"*Continue!*"

"*More!*"

"*Stop!*"

The onslaughts of words and emotion startled Meeryle. Immediately, her life song returned to normal and the snow stopped moving. She gave Leena a desperate look. How could anyone blame her? Who could concentrate in such conditions?

"*Silence!*"

That single word somehow carried a blast of cold wind, which stung Leena's cheeks and froze her lashes with ambient humidity. Tikid almost immediately emitted a brighter emerald shine to protect herself from the intense moment of cold, while Kilaron shook his head in surprise. After a few blinks to clear the ice crystals from her lashes, Leena surveyed the now very quiet plateau. Meeryle's hair was white with frost and from the slight discordance in her life song, she was shaken.

Who wouldn't be?

"*You will let the Mage work.*" Kiqod's words were now far from languid. Her eyes were lit with anger and small bursts of wind burst out of her, circling and hitting the crowd. All the White dragons were still, taking the hits, some without flinching, others with a blink or two of their red eyes.

For the first time, Leena truly understood the power of the dragons. Tikid was a very gentle being and, for all his acerbic humor, so was her sire, Rutad. They each had their personality, like everyone, but truly, the Green dragons were a quiet, beneficial power – they nourished and offered shelter, just like the forest.

The Whites, on the other hand, were the wind – soft and cooling, but also harsh and destructive. What Leena had thought to be torpor from Kiqod was really her personality at rest. The brief outburst of anger gave way to the coldest moment Leena had ever experienced. During the blizzard when they had almost died, the cold had been insidious and slow. The wind that had just hit them all could have very easily killed them.

That it hadn't was a measure of her restraint, wasn't it? Biting her lip, Leena suddenly wondered if letting the humans know about dragons was such a good idea. While the Green dragons had given humans a cold reception, they had become quite curious and open with their neighbors. She wasn't so sure about the Whites. So far, Yalad had been the only welcoming dragon – though the comments she had just heard had shown he wasn't alone. Could the White dragons who thought like Qilad be trusted? Did all of them have the ability to do what Kiqod had just done?

Leena didn't dare ask any of the questions that suddenly crowded her mind. The giant red eyes were still gazing around, flashing with anger.

"*Continue, Mage. They will all respect your skill*," said the Great One of the Whites, as the swirls of wind slowly disappeared.

Meeryle resumed her stance, and once again, air rasped within her life song. The circle of snow continued to widen, albeit at a much slower pace. The young Mage was probably having a hard time now that she was on the receiving end of resentment from the dragons. But she continued, eyes closed. Leena was proud of her friend.

"Leena," whispered Kilaron, "this is too slow for Tikid." Sure enough, the emerald light of the Green dragon was now muted.

"*I want to help. Tikid told me how she fed you power, Leena. I can do the same to Meeryle, can I not?*" asked Yalad.

The Healer and the Green dragon exchanged a look. "The best way is to see it done, I think," said Leena. "I'm not sure how to explain it properly." She didn't want to say out loud that Tikid's explanations might not be clear enough.

"*If we need to show Yalad, we must do it very soon. I am going to run out of power to share soon*," said Tikid.

Leena rolled her eyes. "You wouldn't happen to have a dragon who needs Healing on hand, now, would you, Yalad?"

She had spoken louder than she intended, and heads turned her way, including Meeryle's. The Mage's face filled with hope, and Leena's heart clenched. Was this exercise beyond her friend's capabilities? The elves had been teaching her, but Meeryle could be so stubborn at times. What if the time with the elven Mages hadn't been enough?

"Show us, Leena, quickly," said Meeryle as she briskly made her way to her friends. "This is more difficult than I expected," she added quietly.

"You can't be serious! Just who are we supposed to Heal, anyway?" Leena couldn't decide between laughter and anger.

"*This one.*" A dragon made her way through the crowd, sheltering a limping fledging with her wing. "*A while ago, Dut wandered into a cave where rocks were loose, and now the front leg is misshapen.*" The White dragon's voice was tinged with sorrow.

"This is your little one?"

"*Yes. Can you Heal it?*" The hope in the dragon's words squeezed Leena's heart. These creatures didn't have Healers; they let nature take its course in case of injury. It still angered Leena and Meeryle both. If they could only trust Healers – human or elf – this young dragon wouldn't have been in pain for too long.

"Of course. Tikid, let's do this before you freeze."

The Green dragon gestured to the fledgling, who limped the rest of the way to Leena under the watchful eye of its dam. Tikid sat beside it and wrapped her tail around Leena, who had knelt in the snow.

"*It doesn't look as injured as Meeryle had.*"

"No, so this shouldn't take long. Meeryle, put your hand on my shoulder. Yalad, do the same with Tikid. As soon as we're done, you'll know what to do," said Leena with as much authority as she could. She didn't want anyone to see how close tears were, how much Tikid's simple words affected her.

The fledgling was indeed in much better shape than Meeryle had been after they'd found her in the debris of the burned barn. Only the shrieking discordance of her life song had enabled Leena to know her friend was still alive; as soon as Tikid had extinguished the flames with Green power, she had known her exact location in the rubble. The dragon had then been able to remove debris and at first, Leena hadn't been able to believe that the shape in front of her was her friend.

But the blackened figure with legs bent the wrong way had indeed been Meeryle. As she put her friend to sleep, Leena had wept freely, knowing that such Healing was beyond her and beyond Corvin, the village's Healer.

Tikid had refused the prognosis and insisted she give Leena her power to help Heal their friend. When Meeryle had fed Leena earth power to Heal Tikid's shredded wing, Leena had experienced something wondrous, something she had dreamed about for many nights, something that had finally allowed her to believe in Healing, in her own power.

But being suffused with Green power had been even more wonderful. The thing that allowed her to Heal, to knit bones, restore shredded skin, kill deadly fever, that which enabled her Healing power had become so rich, so intense, she had almost wanted to get lost in it. The power being fed to her was almost inexhaustible, as it came from the trees and the plants, not solely from Tikid, so Leena had been able to mend the broken leg and the burned skin all at once, without needing a break, without having to let the patient suffer while she recuperated until her power was replenished. Healing Meeryle had been a truly wonderful thing.

This time, when Tikid's power filled her, Leena wasn't surprised to see everything with a green tinge. What did amaze her was how each dragon gave off an aura. She remembered seeing a bit of it around the villagers when they helped clearing the ruins of the barn, but at the time, she hadn't paid attention. Now, it was clear that this aura reflected the power beheld by each living being. Did she dare look at Kiqod? Would she be blinded?

"*Go, Leena. I am feeling the cold.*"

Tikid's words helped the Healer to focus on the moment. She sought the little dragon's injury and pushed the power into its body, showing it how to fix the crooked bones. The break had mended in the wrong position. How long had this youngling been like this? It would take weeks, if not months for something like this to heal on its own.

Pushing away the anger, Leena focused the power on detaching the fused bone and mending it straight. Where the elven child's had been crushed, this one was neatly severed and simply stuck the wrong way. Normally, such an injury would be remedied by breaking the bone again, then Healing it. But with the green power, Leena was able to disassemble the bone and reassemble it all at once. The fledgling only hiccupped once and its life song was once again harmonious.

"*Now you know*," said Tikid.

Yalad nodded. He was still touching Tikid, who was no longer infused with green power, so Leena didn't see the power aura around him. Rather, he became a silver beacon, filled with the rasp of air. His life song, like Tikid's, was extremely vibrant, almost overwhelmingly so.

Suddenly, under her hand, Meeryle's life song resonated the same way as Yalad's. The Mage once again became filled with air, but this time, she overflowed with it. For a brief instant, Meeryle's eyes flickered with silver and dismay, but only for an instant. Very quickly, the Mage bit her lips in concentration and the entire plateau cleared of snow. The sky suddenly became white and the air warmer.

"Tell me when you're warm enough, Tikid."

Leena's mouth opened in wonder as a whisper of the beat of fire mixed with the rasp of air. Meeryle was using her internal power to heat the very air. No fear, no doubt flickered on her face. The young Healer wanted to whoop with pleasure: her friend had conquered her fear of fire.

"*I am fine now, Meeryle, thank you.*"

"Actually, I'm getting hot with all my clothes," smiled Kilaron.

All at once, Tikid, Yalad, Leena and Meeryle let go of each other and the fledgling, who bounded back to its mother, laughing with pleasure.

"*Look, look! I can run, I can jump!*"

Leena and Meeryle smiled at each other. "I did it, Leena. Just like I did with you, only it was…"

"Intense?"

"Yes, and some!"

Kilaron gaped at them. "Do you both have any idea how much power you just wielded?"

"A lot," answered Leena. She wasn't able to keep the smugness out of her words, but she didn't care. Not only had she been able to Heal a too-old wound, but Meeryle could wield fire without fear or losing control.

"You… This is just…"

"*Amazing*," cut in Qilad. His usually acerbic tone was gone. When Leena looked around, all she could see was intense respect in the red eyes of the White dragons.

Kiqod chuckled, the vibration so strong within Leena's bones that she feared another avalanche. "*Murod was right to send you here. The Healer can wield Green power, the Mage White power. I wonder, can the elf do the same as the humans?*"

The Great White One was back to her languid state, projecting pleasure. Her question was motivated by curiosity, but Kilaron bristled.

"Why would an elf be lesser than a human?"

Qilad chuckled. "*I forgot; your enclave is among the ones who won't touch humans, just like us*."

"I'm half human, half elf," interjected Leena. She didn't want Kilaron's pride to ruin everything. "If I can do it, so can he."

"*It doesn't matter*," said Dut's mother. "*The Healer had shown that dragons do not need to suffer through injury. Had you listened, we would have sought the elves long ago and helped Dut and countless others*." She turned to Kilaron. "*You could have helped it, couldn't you?*"

"Yes, of course, though it wouldn't have been as quick."

"Unless you're fed White power to help Healing," added Leena.

Kilaron frowned at the thought. "From what I understand, the Green dragons are closely linked to the earth. Things that grow need earth, but also water and air, so why not?"

"We could…"

A burst of warm air interrupted Leena. "*Enough, young one, and listen. What Murod did not say to Tikid, but probably thought, was that what you have accomplished with this young Green one proves something that many have been debating over the years: that humans belong in this world and dragons should welcome them.*"

Chapter 17

The ensuing uproar caused by Kiqod's statement still rang in Leena's ears as she made her way back into the dark tunnels. The rocks muted and absorbed all sounds, but the dragons' roar somehow continued to ring, hiding the noises Tikid, Meeryle and Kilaron made. None of the White dragons had followed them in; in fact, Leena wasn't sure any of them realized they had left – except for the Great White One. Very few things must escape the huge dragon's notice.

The deeper they went into the mountain, the quieter Leena's ears grew, until finally, the aftereffects of the din cleared completely. Never before had she heard such noise.

"That was very scary," said Meeryle in hushed tone.

"Yes, it was," agreed Kilaron. "We are taught how fierce the White dragons are, but I never really knew just how frightening they could be."

"*They are the wind*," added Tikid, as if her statement explained everything. Maybe it did.

"But why do they hate humans so much? We're here, aren't we? Why would they refuse to welcome us, as Kiqod says? I don't understand."

Kilaron chuckled. "Most of the elves in my enclave agree with the dragons, but I think their reasons are much more… material."

"How so?"

"Since you came to be born, some elves do keep company with humans, but in this part of the world, it isn't so. You see, these mountains are very rich with stones, which elven Mages use to trap spells. This is how we light our alcoves, how scouts like Jatoron can carry shelter with them. However, for centuries now, humans have been trying to get these stones. First by trade, then by force. It has been decades since we've been left in peace, but we've learned never to trust human avarice."

Leena exchanged a glance with Meeryle. "But why do they want it? I didn't know that human Mages used stones for spells."

"The Mages didn't show me how to do it," added Meeryle. "And I forgot to ask."

"Oh, they don't need it for Mages. They want it for currency. What we call spell stones, humans call diamonds."

Diamonds! Leena knew what they were, even if she had only seen them drawn in books – no one in the village could afford such a thing. "How many diamonds are we talking about?"

"You've seen how every corridor is lit? These are raw stones, stuck in the mountain. All the Mages do is blow in the spell and let it run throughout the mountain. All the raw stones are close enough to each other, or even connected to each other. We do have a special place where we remove the stone to use them and trade them with other enclaves whose mountains are bare of stones, but mostly, we don't need to touch the rest."

"But… but that's…" stuttered Meeryle.

"Impossible to imagine," finished Leena. Her understanding of such things was limited – she didn't care at all about precious stones or any sort of riches – but even she knew that such a mine was indeed something any human would covet.

Now she was beginning to understand the White dragons' attitude towards humans. They had only seen relentless greed for something they couldn't fathom –

dragons had no material needs. They had witnessed centuries of bloodshed for what? Nothing, at least in their eyes.

"But why not trade for diamonds? If the mountains contain so much of it, can't someone have negotiated something?"

"Other enclaves need them too, for lights, heat, you name it. These stones are a finite resource that needs to be managed; they can't be used for superficial matters. Humans just couldn't understand it, though."

"Doesn't surprise me," muttered Meeryle. Kilaron gave her a sharp look. "Well, it's true. Did anyone ever explain to whoever started all this what the elves did with the diamonds?"

"I would hope so." His condescending tone made Leena cringe, but she let Meeryle continue.

"Hey, how can you know? Maybe the first ones knew but didn't care and then as each generation continued, that little fact got lost. Before you know it, one side says that the other is just too greedy to share, while the others just don't understand why they can't be left alone. Your people don't strike me as very knowledgeable about humans. I mean, no one in the enclave seemed to know about the water."

Kilaron stopped and glared at Meeryle. "Healers don't like to be reminded of their shortcomings, human Mage." His smile took the sting out of his words. "However, you do have a point. I've never been one to really take interest in this, though; the scouts have that responsibility. In fact, this conflict is the reason they exist. I've heard other enclaves don't have the need for scouts."

Leena resumed their descent, wondering what could be done. If these humans and elves could get along, maybe the dragons would respect humans? She knew how to deal with sick and wounded people, with their families, but she had no idea how to make two people sit and talk things out. One could order sick people around, but somehow, she doubted the same could be done with leaders.

"I'm hungry," announced Meeryle. "We all need a real meal and this place is stretching my abilities. Maybe we should go to Sharitown as planned and see how people react to Tikid."

"Then what? Do you think that would help opening a dialogue between humans and elves?"

"Leena, we didn't even know about elves until we got stuck in that storm. I'm saying we should just continue introducing the dragons. Kiqod approves, so does Murod. We can't fix all the problems."

"*Meeryle is right; you heard how the Whites disagreed. Waiting for them might take too much time. I would like to continue. Maybe Yalad will want to come with us.*"

Would having two dragons in the traveling party help or hinder them? What about her soulmate? The tug of their bond was always there, reminding her that she was no longer alone. How far could it stretch? Would he want to come? Would she?

All her questions remained unanswered, as Meeryle, in her typical fashion, made the decision for all of them. "I'm serious about the food; what I have in my packs back in our dark cave is the last of it."

"Well, then, let's at least get back to my enclave. Sharitown isn't very much further, but we'll need good supplies, especially for Tikid, Meeryle and Suqi. Leena and I could shift, but I'd rather we didn't, as we don't want humans to know about this yet."

Leena didn't know which emotion to feel first – resentful since she didn't make the decision and was therefore not controlling the situation, relief that she wouldn't have to change into cat form, or elation that Kilaron was coming.

Something must have shown on her face – or the bond betrayed her – because the elf smiled and winked. "Let's see if Yalad would like to come; it would do my people good to see how the halfbreed and the human befriended a fierce White dragon."

***

"*I am not sure it is right to leave without saying anything to the elders*," said Tikid.

"*They know, I told them*," explained Yalad. "*The discussion is still ongoing; Kiqod has not yet left. I grew tired of it during the night, as did others, especially the ones who think like I do that we should not hide from humans*."

Leena wasn't bothered by leave-taking without proper goodbyes; she was more concerned about the elves. Would they welcome them like the first time, or would they only see the halfbreed? And the Sharitown humans, would they attack on sight?

From the flurry of activity, she seemed to be the only one with doubts. Meeryle was already set to go, Kilaron was fussing with his pack and her own, Suqi was running back and forth, eager to be on her way, while Tikid and Yalad discussed dragon leave-taking etiquette.

Soon enough, they were stepping out of the cavern and onto the platform. The light and the wind were overwhelming, but only for a few moments. Meeryle quickly lifted her arms and surrounded them all with warm air.

"Well, this seemed like a great idea last night, but now, I'm not too sure what to do. I can't fly us out of here, and I'm not sure how long I can maintain this heat bubble." The young Mage didn't seem too worried; she wore the same look she always did when trying to figure out which herb would best serve in a dish.

"*We will help, of course*."

Dragons came out of the cavern, crowding the platform. Leena recognized the one whose fledgling she had Healed, but the others were strangers. Or maybe they had carried them in and she didn't remember them.

"*While others still argue with Kiqod, we would like to meet other humans*," said a big dragon. "*I was always one to question rules, and yearned to see these creatures. Mage, the Great One respects you and now I regret complying for so long*." Given her size, she was probably the oldest of the dragons on the platform. Her red eyes were fixed on Meeryle in such a way that Leena was wondering if the dragon wasn't begging.

Trying not to be alarmed, Leena cleared her voice. "Um, thank you. However, I'm not sure if the elves can accommodate many dragons without prior warning." Let alone the humans, she thought. If anything, Tikid had taught her that dragons didn't realize how fearsome they were. In fact, the young Green dragon had been insulted when youths from Leena's village had been afraid of her. Even if Whites were fiercer than Greens, they couldn't be prepared for humans' reaction.

"*They need not cater to us; we are easy guests*," replied another dragon.

"Oh boy," said Meeryle.

Leena wondered whether she should laugh or panic, and since Kilaron's expression mirrored her feelings, neither of them ventured a word.

"*We should go before I get too cold,*" said Tikid, who was giving off an emerald halo. "*We can sort out all this once we reach the elf enclave.*"

Could any of the dragons even understand what Leena had meant? Her soulmate had alluded to the fact that the elves would be awed because she and Meeryle had befriended White dragons. Would they still be impressed when a dozen adult dragons came to their doorstep?

In the end, laughter overtook Kilaron. "Come on, then. It's true, only the Green will need warmth; the others can find room higher in our mountain."

Suqi barked when Yalad picked her up. Some of the dragons grumbled a laugh at the goupil's words – words that Leena didn't hear. Once again, she was angered by Meeryle's familiar. She could communicate with anyone she wanted; only she usually chose not to do so with Leena. The Healer was quite irked by it. Was she not good enough for the goupil?

General movement prevented her mood from going sour. Brooding over Suqi's attitude was useless; only her pride was hurt, really.

"Suqi had a great idea," announced Meeryle. "All the Whites will feed me power so I can keep us all warm during the entire flight."

"*That will be wonderful! I will not need to infuse myself, then.*" Tikid glowed a bit more brightly with pleasure.

The idea was actually phenomenal. Even in her cat form, Leena had been freezing during the flight here.

Now that she was in human form, she wasn't looking forward to the trip back, but if Meeryle could feed fire into air to maintain the heat bubble, the flight might be enjoyable.

"Are we going to fly directly there?" asked Leena. They had trekked almost two days before the avalanche overtook them and the White dragons rescued them. Could they fly this long while carrying such weight? When they had first flown away, the only thoughts Leena had had were about height and a possible fall. Now that she was rested and warm, her methodical mind was busy analyzing everything she hadn't considered then.

"*No*," answered the big dragon. "*Not with so much weight. We are also not sure how long we can maintain shared power with the Mage. We will therefore stop along the way*."

Her name was Talid and Leena quickly took a liking to the dragon. She reminded her of Jetyaa, her stepmother. Both of them were soon in deep discussion on the particulars of the trip.

Leena was impressed by the attention to detail; the dragons knew exactly how long they could fly and the time needed to recover during breaks. It wasn't a new exercise: injured dragons had to be carried back to the comfort of the caverns to recover. The tricky part was estimating the weight.

"*You are heavier than a fledgling, but lighter than a youngling. It makes guessing our flight time hard, but we will manage*," explained Talid.

Leena had to restrain her curiosity. Since neither Meeryle nor the dragons knew how long she could sustain her heat bubble, questions had to wait.

This time, they didn't need one of the bigger dragons to carry Tikid, which was fortunate, as the one who had wasn't present. "*He follows Qilad*" had been the only answer given. Talid would carry Meeryle, while Kilaron and herself would be in the claws of Lorad and Satid. The argument about who would have the honor of carrying Suqi exasperated Leena; she had to remind herself that Whites never had the occasion of meeting with goupils this high in the mountains. Meeting this creature was quite the event, and they didn't care whether her personality left anything to be desired or not.

Suqi herself cut short the discussion by jumping into Meeryle's arms, explaining to everyone who could hear – but not Leena, of course – that a familiar's place was with her Mage.

"But Suqi, I need my hands to start the bubble. It'll collapse when we take off, I just know it. Once we're in the air, I'll be able to concentrate and reform it."

The Mage argued with her familiar, the discussion bringing Leena onto the edge, but with a few deep breaths, she managed to calm herself enough to gather that Suqi was offering to help control the amount of heat Meeryle would mix to the air. Each dragon gave his or her opinion on the matter – after all, they were the air, so they evidently had to pronounce themselves – thereby lengthening the entire argument.

Meanwhile, Tikid's glow was getting brighter and brighter. The Green dragon was so intent on the discussion, Leena wondered if she even noticed. Since she herself had more than once become so engrossed in what she was doing that she never noticed that she was hungry, she could understand. But how long before the dragon froze?

Kilaron must have thought along the same lines; he gave Leena's arm a small squeeze and said: "We need to end this soon."

The elf rummaged with their packs, emptying one of them.

"Here, Meeryle, put this on your back. Suqi can ride in it, so you won't need to hold her. She can touch you with her nose. Honestly, this is too big for her, so her head will be the only thing that comes out."

The pack itself was tight on Meeryle; it was the type meant for an elf in cat form, but the chubby woman made do. She wriggled into it, declaring it fine even though the straps were clearly cutting into her shoulder. Since Meeryle couldn't put her familiar into the pack, Suqi deigned to let Kilaron pick her up and drop her in, while Leena was holding the pack open.

They had to work fast, as Meeryle had collapsed the heat bubble while she was struggling to put on the pack – thus confirming that the Mage did indeed need to have her hands free. The wind was behaving most peculiarly, blowing one way, then the next, blowing their hair in the way, freezing their hands, making them both miserable and clumsy.

"*Enough!*"

The mental call and the simultaneous roar startled them; luckily, Suqi was already in the pack, so Kilaron didn't drop her.

"*Control yourselves,*" said Talid. "*You are affecting the wind, and hurting our friends.*"

The wind suddenly dropped and the air stilled. Leena was surprised how quiet the plateau had become; she had been so intent on getting Suqi into the pack that she hadn't noticed how loud the wind had whistled.

"*Sorry*," said a young White. "*We got really excited.*"

"Don't worry, we're fine," replied Meeryle with a smile. "Are we ready to go, or do I need to summon another bubble right now?"

At that point, Leena was just as eager as Meeryle to be on the way. The platform was simply too small for her liking, and the mountains loomed the wrong way, in her opinion. The elven enclave was much more welcoming, even if its inhabitants weren't.

All the dragons shuffled around to get into place, making Leena even more nervous about the lack of space. Satid gestured for Leena to join her – the White dragon was thankfully closer to the mountain than the platform edge – and the young Healer briefly shuddered with fear when the huge claws encircled her waist.

"*Do not worry, I will not drop you*," said the dragon in a gentle tone. Leena couldn't bring herself to tell her she had been afraid of the claws themselves. Instinct was not something one could control, and having huge talon-like things grabbing for one's body was just wrong. She simply nodded with a smile.

"*Yalad and I will go first*," announced Tikid.

The Green dragon took flight, the White dragon close behind. At that point, Tikid was a bright emerald beacon, telling Leena that the dragon was very cold. Yalad, himself imbued with his environment, was a beam of silver. He extended a paw, which Tikid grabbed and suddenly, the Green dragon's hue was muted. They both hovered in place, waiting for the rest to join them in the air.

Leena and Kilaron were next with their dragons. They flew close to Tikid, and as soon as they were in place, Meeryle and Suqi joined them in Talid's claws.

The Mage opened her arms, eyes closed, and once again created a bubble encompassing everyone around her.

All the other dragons – Leena counted fourteen – took flight and placed themselves around Tikid, Yalad, Talid, Lorad and Satid, forming a circle.

"*Now*," called Yalad.

All the dragons became silver at once. The claws holding Leena shone, radiating a sensation of cold and heat at the same time. *They are the wind.* Air could be both hot and cold, so it made sense that a White imbued with her environment should emit such a feeling, did it not?

Before she could delve more into the thought, Yalad called for the dragons to link.

Leena had linked with Tikid, but never with a White dragon. While she wasn't linking with them, Talid was touching her, so she was engulfed in silver power.

Whereas the Green power had been almost soothing, the White power had a raw, mighty feel to it. The inside of Leena's body thrummed with both cold and warmth, buffeted by a mix of breeze and blizzard. The sensation was disorienting; she automatically engaged the part of her that enabled her to Heal, but the two powers were not compatible. The jarring between the powers made Leena cringe; gusts of cold seeped into the very center of her being, while air filled every part of her until she felt ready to burst.

Desperate to escape this endless energy before it killed her, Leena sought Kilaron through their bond. It wasn't much, but it was enough to help her overcome the panic. She was still both hot and cold, but her insides no longer felt like they were going to be shredded apart by the wind.

The elf gave her a reassuring smile; in fact, her soulmate seemed exhilarated. For a brief moment, Leena wished she was in cat form in order to be able to speak to him and hear how he would describe his experience. Since the elven Mages were experts at wielding air, did it mean all elves had the same affinity? And since she was part elf herself, why couldn't she connect with White power? Was she too human?

The thought reminded her of Meeryle, but the Mage didn't seem bothered. Her eyes were closed and her face was a frown of concentration, but she was faring much better than Leena. Force of habit made the Healer check Meeryle's life song. It was almost drowned with the rasp of air, mixed with the beat of fire. While the rasp seemed to fluctuate, the beat was stable; Suqi was true to her word and controlled the heat.

Now that she wasn't as overwhelmed by the White power – thinking of other things had helped – Leena noticed that the ambient temperature was quite comfortable. She was still buffeted by wind, both inside and outside, but it was bearable. Checking dragons' life songs threatened to overwhelm her again, so she concentrated on the scenery passing below her.

The day was clear and bright, showing mountains blanketed with snow. How high were they flying? Wasn't air supposed to be sparse at a certain altitude? While she had never seen any such patients in her village, Corvin had mentioned people suffering from height sickness when they went up too quickly in the mountains. They obviously hadn't known about White dragons.

The more time elapsed, the more Leena grew accustomed to the power surrounding her and engulfing her. She found that if she shut off her Healer sense, the experience was very interesting physically. The ambient heat was mixed with a cooling breeze, while sometimes gusts would make her long hair lash at her. Now that she had witnessed how the dragons' emotions could affect the wind, Leena could tell which gusts were due to flapping wings and which came from an overexcited dragon.

Between the scenery, her general observations and the White power filling her, Leena didn't notice how quickly time passed. The dragons made their descent as soon as the sun started to lower in the horizon.

They all landed in a flurry of snow, blinding everyone around. While Meeryle maintained her heat bubble, Kilaron used a spell stone to build a big snow hut. As soon as Tikid entered it, the Mage let go of her weave and collapsed to the ground.

"Meeryle!" yelled Leena as she ran to her side as quickly as she could in the snow.

Kilaron had been closer and was hovering a hand over her friend's head. "She's exhausted, and the goupil isn't in any better shape."

Sure enough, Suqi was unconscious in her bag. It was lucky that Meeryle had fallen on her side and hadn't rolled on her back, otherwise, she would have crushed her familiar. Leena scooped the bag and carried the goupil inside, while Yalad and Kilaron did the same to Meeryle under Tikid's worried and watchful eye.

"*Why did she not tell us she was tired?*"

"Maybe she didn't realize it herself. Or maybe she was too stubborn." Leena covered her friend with a blanket and tucked Suqi underneath, against the Mage. Both their life songs were stable, if a bit weak. The only remedy was rest, so Leena started a fire, while Tikid shuffled around, getting as comfortable as she could.

The White dragons settled outside, making all sorts of noises, from shuffles to grunts, and even a roar. If they spoke to each other, they had shielded her from their words, for which she was both thankful and resentful. It would have been nice to be included, but at the same time, she wasn't sure she wanted to eavesdrop on them.

Tikid had dug herself a hole, and much to Leena's and Kilaron's dismay, what made up the floor of the hut partly ceased to exist as soon as the dragon's claws touched it. However, before either of them could say anything, they realized that only the area directly affected by Tikid's work was deprived of the spell; the dragon had settled herself into the resulting muddy mess, while the rest of the hut remained dry. She fell asleep quickly, tired from the extended flight, glowing a soft emerald.

"I'll have to mention this to the Mages," said Kilaron as he poked around the wall and the ground. "She broke part of the spell as she dug, but as soon as she stopped, it repaired itself. I wonder if that's normal."

"Well, I'm just glad it fixed itself so quickly, otherwise, we'd be soaked with melted snow." As it was, the spell covered the snow on the ground, flattening it.

They prepared a cold meal and sat, talking for a long while. Yalad and Talid checked on them, more out of curiosity for their shelter than out of concern; the White dragons seemed fascinated by the need for heat. During the flight, Kilaron had overheard some of the questions Tikid had been asked, and he related them to Leena with a few sarcastic comments which both annoyed and pleased Leena. They were very similar; she could hear it in his comments – she had made the same remarks about her fellow villagers.

When the time came to sleep, Kilaron opened his blanket invitingly with a small smile. Leena hesitated briefly, but his words about her being unable to lose control came rushing back. She wanted… too many things came to mind. The only thing about which she could be sure was that she wanted to be his soulmate. *One step at a time*, she told herself. He was right; she needed time. But she had to start somewhere, so she cuddled with him beneath the blanket.

***

The next day was the same. Yalad and Tikid took flight first, and the rest followed. Once again, Meeryle created a heat bubble, only this time, Leena and Tikid had made her promise she would take breaks. It meant being frozen for a while, but neither Healer nor Green dragon cared. Seeing Meeryle collapse had affected Tikid deeply, and Leena was worried about her friend. Her eyes still sported purple circles and she wasn't her perky self quite yet.

The White dragons assured them they would hold on to the heat as best they could so their passengers wouldn't freeze too much. So far, they had been true to their word. Leena didn't have a good way to keep track of time, but she estimated that every candlemark, Meeryle released her weave to rest. As soon as the heat bubble disappeared, the ambient temperature dipped, but not drastically.

"*I am concentrating as much power as I can into my paws*," explained Talid. "*In fact, we are discovering that being linked while with are imbued with power allows us to do much more than we thought possible.*"

"What do you mean?" asked Leena as loudly as she could, hoping the dragon could hear her through the whistling wind.

"Remember I told you we were not sure if we would be able to carry you, the elf or the Mage for lengthy periods? We were comparing you to fledglings, but we never imbue ourselves while carrying young ones, so we had never learned that imbuing ourselves would allow for almost limitless strength. Kiqod is right; it is a good thing that you came to meet with us."

Leena observed all the shining dragons without seeking to hear their life song – she had learned her lesson – and while the engulfing power was still a bit disorienting, it wasn't anything as bad as the prior day. None of them displayed any signs of fatigue. Over the months, Leena had been able to observe Tikid and find the telltale signs.

The Green dragon was the only one whose shine fluctuated. The Healer quickly surmised that while Tikid borrowed some power from Yalad when Meeryle collapsed her heat bubble, it wasn't enough to protect her completely. The dragon would slowly increase the amount of Green power to shield herself against the cold, until an emerald shine would bounce off Yalad's silver glow. The Mage must have been watching the same way as Leena, because at that point, Meeryle would create a new heat bubble.

This newfound strength amongst the White dragons allowed for great traveling time. Soon, Leena thought she was able to recognize the mountain on the horizon. Her guess was confirmed when one of the young dragons broke from the formation to fly ahead.

"*He will tell the elves we are coming,*" said Talid. "*Kilaron suggested that such a warning would be welcome.*" Her puzzled tone made Leena giggle. Even with advance announcement, she doubted the elves would be thrilled. One Green dragon had been a happy event, but over a dozen of White dragons? Any community would be appalled, really. Adult dragons were *big*.

Her musings were soon interrupted by the return of their herald. However, as he got nearer, the general atmosphere changed.

"*Something is wrong*," he said with an anguished roar. "*There are many, many people on the mountain. They are running up, some are falling down. And there is a very strange noise, with fire*."

Leena's heart stopped and a dreadful cold filled her. What the White dragon described could only mean one thing.

Kilaron's enclave was under attack.

Chapter 18

The dragons immediately made their descent and landed near a frozen stream. Kilaron bombarded the returning dragon, Nilad, with questions.

"What kind of people did you see? Were they dressed in light-colored clothes? What color was their hair? And the fire you saw, where did it come from?"

The White dragon was taken aback by the onslaught of questions; he blinked and looked to Talid for guidance. The older dragon – and all the other dragons, including Tikid – seemed just as confused; all stayed silent, looking at the elf.

Meeryle was the first to recover. "One thing at a time. Nilad, can you describe the fire?"

"*It was not only one, but many. The fire came with great noise.*" The dragon shuffled on the ground, tail lashing. "*I am sorry, Kilaron. I am not sure how to answer your questions.*"

The elf Healer shook his head. "Don't worry. I forgot that you're not familiar with my world. Meeryle, pray continue. I need to know."

"Tell me, Nilad, did the fire come out of long tubes made out of iron?" asked the young Mage.

"*Yes, it did.*"

"Cannons. They have cannons. I've never seen one, but my brothers talked about them in detail," she stated.

"Why now?" asked Kilaron to no one in particular. "It's been years! Why are they hurting us now?"

"Because they can," answered Leena softly. "Now they have cannons and they want the diamonds."

"*What are cannons?*" asked Yalad.

"A way to throw Mage fire without a Mage. Fire spells are stored in a thick tube of a special metal; then all you have to do is to release the spells one after the other," answered Meeryle.

The dragons looked at each other, crestfallen. "*This is what Qilad meant about humans.*"

"*I do not care what Qilad says. I have learned that humans make good friends,*" said Tikid.

"*But your friends are not... destructive.*"

Leena bit her lip. "We can be. To protect our families, we can do quite a bit, actually."

"This taking what is not theirs is typically human, Leena. My people are getting hurt! Are we going to sit here and waste time explaining it to the dragons, or are we going to do something about it?" Kilaron was pacing within the circle made by the White dragons.

Tikid, Meeryle, Suqi, Leena and her soulmate were in the middle, protected in part from the wind and the cold by the dragons' extended wings. Meeryle was too agitated to create a heat bubble, and soon, the Green dragon had to imbue herself, the emerald light reflected on the white scales of the other dragons.

"*What can we do?*" asked Nilad. "*I have seen these cannons; they are dangerous things.*"

Talid rose on her hind legs and roared. "*We are the air, we are the wind. It is passed time we show our might. Come!*"

It was all the warning Leena had before the White dragon seized her in her paws; the other dragons did the same so quickly that Meeryle barely had time to scoop Suqi in her arms. They took flight in an instant, their wings and Talid's outrage creating strong gusts tossing Leena's hair in her face.

With this flight, Leena realized how leisurely their pace had been, how much of an effort the dragons had made for their gliding to be smooth. This flight was even worse than the first one, and this time, she wasn't covered in warm, protecting fur.

The wings were constantly pumping, gathering more and more speed, to the point where Leena had to close her eyes and hide her face in her arms to protect against the whipping air. She couldn't check on the others, not even Kilaron through their bond; with each wing beat, Talid accumulated more power, until all Leena could see was the silver light the dragon emanated, even with her eyes closed.

Outrage and anger saturated the very air in such a way that it affected Leena. She was surprised at the intensity of it – she hadn't known Kilaron's people meant that much to the White dragons. Leena herself was outraged, but by principle. Waging war for territory was an old story, but it didn't make it right. Now she knew the people who were getting hurt. Would Kalianna be safe, deep in her caves? Would she see her mother again? What about Childia, the girl she had Healed so well? Had it been for naught?

The wind, the cold, the rage and her fear would have enveloped her if not for the White power; its rasp somehow helped keep the cold at bay – though not completely, as her teeth chattered and her fingers felt like icicles. In it also lay hope, though what kind, she wasn't sure. What could they do? Dragons abhorred violence, Kilaron was a Healer, just like her, and while Meeryle had unleashed a destructive fire, it had scared her in such a way that Leena doubted the young Mage would be willing to try it again.

A strange noise broke through the White power, a coughed roar. The dragon's speed suddenly relented and the stinging wind diminished. Leena opened her eyes and gasped.

The mountain was indeed covered with people; the snow was now a brown mess with red highlights. *Blood*, thought Leena. With the dragons so close and imbued with so much power, she didn't dare listen to any life song. Would she be able to hear it from so far above?

From her vantage, Leena could spy the entire battle: humans in dark clothing were running up the mountain, shouting and waving their arms. At that distance, she couldn't see the swords, but the gesture was clear. Others were stationed with the cannons, long, black tubes whose cough echoed every time a fire ball escaped. Wherever it hit, elves would fly with snow and soil. The mountain slope was riddled with brown craters around which bodies were strewn. From their color, their dress was elven.

Somehow, with the havoc wreaked by the cannons, human troops had managed to get behind the elven lines. It seemed as if the elven Mages had blocked the entrance, thereby stopping the humans from moving further, but had done it before all the elven forces had time to retreat.

Leena didn't dare look at Kilaron.

The closer they got, the gorier things became. Soon, Leena could see the swords, see them hack hands, arms, see them run through flesh. The results of the cannons were also much clearer; bodies in pieces, the depth of the hole each fire ball had made.

Tears ran down Leena's cheeks. Wrong, it was so wrong! Every time someone fell, she didn't care if it was an elf or a human – it just hurt. Hurt to see a life extinguished, hurt to think anyone could do this to another person.

"Stop!" she screamed as loud as she could. "Stop, all of you!"

Her words were lost in the din of the battle, in the whistling of the wind. None heard her, none stopped.

"*They will listen, Leena*," said Talid. "*They will listen to the wind and stop this*." She gave some sort of signal that Leena couldn't see or hear and all the dragons landed with a roar. Their passengers were promptly deposited onto the ground – Kilaron was dropped – and left in the muddy snow.

Wings extended, bodies shimmering with a silver light, the dragons advanced on foot. With each step, the wind picked up. A first, it was a small movement of air, barely noticeable – and the fighters were too busy to perceive the change in the air.

However, the ones closest stopped in their tracks at the sight of the dragons. Both elves and humans stood, mouth gaping, swords and daggers still, at the sight of the shinning creatures moving towards them.

As they proceeded, the wind picked up. Soon, it was whipping hair and clothes, stinging everyone's face into paying attention. In a matter of moments, the fighters had all stopped moving and were staring at the shining creatures. The elves knew dragons; their faces, partially hidden by their moving hair, were filled with awe.

The humans, however, were on the verge of panic.

"Leena, they're going to hurt them, I just know it. That's how Tikid got hurt. We have to stop them!" said Meeryle, eyes wide.

She couldn't agree more, but stop whom? The humans or the dragons? Which ones would listen before further blood was shed? The swords weren't much of a threat, but the cannons… Leena shuddered at the thought.

"I don't know what to do, Meeryle," she admitted, fists tight in frustration.

"Meeryle, get their attention," said Kilaron.

"What? How?" Suqi barked and the Mage smiled. "Great idea."

Before Leena could ask about this bright idea, Meeryle moved her arms and a very warm *whoosh* of air exploded in front of the dragons. They blinked and looked at each other, projecting their puzzlement.

Meeryle's hands moved again, and another, yet much larger, heat bubble exploded close to the fighters. The elves smiled at the touch of the warm air, and the humans looked for its source, just as puzzled as the dragons.

Leena took the opportunity to move forward, Kilaron and Meeryle at her side, and in the sternest voice she could muster, she yelled "Enough!"

This time, all heard her. The wind stopped and with it, all the noise. For a moment, an eerie silence set over the mountain slope, as if Leena's simple word was making them all question themselves.

However, groans from the wounded put an end to the calm. The elves moved towards each other – the ones who could get up – while the humans did the same, although at a much slower pace, wary of the dragons.

"They will not hurt you," said Leena. "All they want is for the… this butchery to stop."

One burly human limped his way forward. "What are they, child?"

Leena bristled at the term; she certainly wasn't a child. Even Corvin, the Healer to whom she had been apprenticed, had never called her anything other than by her name. Yet from the harassed look on the man's face, any objection she might have would be lost, so she clamped her teeth and simply answered them.

"They are the White dragons and they strongly disapprove of violence, especially against elves."

The man blinked at her, at the elves, at the dragons. Had he understood her? Leena put aside her anger and checked his life song; it was surprisingly jarring for one such as him. His leg had sustained an injury, but the rest of his body was unhurt. Yet something was making his life song discordant in a vaguely familiar way. After a few moments, she was finally able to identify it: fear, but a fear with a completely different intensity than she had previously heard. If this man was a seasoned warrior, the dragons could not account for it – in fact, he was the only human who had stepped forward, showing a certain bravery. What could frighten him so?

"Until this day, I had thought dragons were only stories. But here they are. Now, what hold do the elves have over them?"

Talid stepped forward. "*No one has any hold over dragons, human.*"

His eyes widened, as did the ones of the other humans nearby. "It… what…"

"They speak. Dragons are people, not animals for anyone to train. White dragons are the wind. Without them, you wouldn't have any air to breathe," said Meeryle. "And this is Tikid, a Green dragon. Greens are the trees, but they don't like the cold very much. Can we agree to stop all this bloodshed and find shelter from the cold?"

Tikid was indeed a bright emerald. Leena guessed that Meeryle hadn't dared create a heat bubble for their friend until she was sure the fighting wouldn't resume.

The man was taken by the Mage's direct words. Anger briefly flashed in his eyes, but eventually, he smiled. "This is a strange day indeed. Creatures out of stories, elves and humans standing together, and children telling me what to do. Had I listened to my son, none of this would have happened. Let's call a truce and find this shelter of yours, girl."

Another man sounded a horn; its signal brought all the humans together, even the ones who had stayed further away – and the ones who had run from the dragons.

An elf cradling his arm made his way towards Leena and her group.

"Jatoron!"

"Well met, Leena. I see you found the dragons."

"Your arm is hurt, let me see."

"A deep cut. Kilaron, please take the stone and raise the shelter. The Green one's light is dimming."

From his tone, Leena guessed the scout was expecting an acerbic comment from the Healer, yet Kilaron complied without a word. He seemed worried, but about what, Leena didn't know.

Soon, a very large snow hut was protecting Tikid, Suqi, Meeryle, Leena, Kilaron, Jatoron and the man from the cold. Talid had joined them, though of course, the cold didn't bother her, and Yalad had managed to squeeze in with them. The young White dragon was so eager to participate, none had been able to refuse him.

"Please," said the man, "can we make this quick? I would rather my son didn't die without me at his side."

Kilaron exchanged a look with Leena; he had heard this man's fear as well. "We are Healers. Let us see to your son."

"And to any who need care," added Leena.

Jatoron gave both soulmates a look. "I will gather the elves who are in dire need of care."

"You can also tell the others to open up the caverns," said Kilaron. "Tell them the dragons are here and that we are all safe."

The scout got up, cradling his arm, and left without another word.

"Can we trust them?" asked the man.

"Can we trust you?" asked Meeryle. "You're the one who attacked, remember?"

"*Do not worry; the wind will not allow any more blood to be shed this day*," announced Talid.

Everyone was silent for a moment. Leena certainly didn't want to feel the cold air again, and from his expression, neither did the man. Should she tell him how Kiqod had frozen everything around them? Or would it only fan the fear?

The man shook his head. "This day gets stranger by the moment. Come, follow me."

They left Tikid in the snow hut, along with Suqi. Meeryle had insisted, as she feared some of the humans might mistake her for a wild animal. Leena was just happy not to have her underfoot. That she could think of the goupil at this moment was a sure indication that the day was indeed strange.

As she followed the limping man in the muddy, blood-brown snow, Leena was in a daze. Surely, these people weren't bleeding. This man wasn't dead, an arrow through his eye. Elves did not have blood red hair.

Yet the smell was very real. Never before had Leena seen so many people hurt at the same time. And worst of all, while she had read about it and Corvin had shared his limited experience with her, it was the first time the young Healer witnessed the results of sword- and arrow-inflicted wounds. For a brief moment, Leena feared she would be sick.

"I can't believe anyone would do this," said Meeryle, tears running down her cheeks.

Kilaron walked beside her and put a hand on her shoulder. "Close your mind to it and move on. Worry only about where you step."

"That's just disgusting."

"Yes. Healing often is."

"You've seen this before," stated Leena.

He nodded. "Once, when rocks came off the mountain-side. The wounds were worse than this."

"But how can it be worse?" asked Meeryle.

"Think," answered Leena. "What do rocks do? They crush."

"Oh."

The man stopped beside two other men kneeling in the dirty snow, tending to a third one. "Here's my son."

He was a few years older than Leena, his round face pale and sweaty, his eyes closed. The hair plastered to his forehead was dark like his father's, minus the gray streaks, and his features were softer, but no one could doubt the young man was indeed the limping man's son. He didn't have the same seasoned warrior look, though. In fact, the young man seemed to fit better in a scholar's hall than on a battlefield. But what did she know about such things? He was hurt, that was all that mattered.

His wound was shocking to Leena: where the left arm should have been, only a red, shredded and shining mess remained. Even with her limited experience, the young Healer knew no arrow or sword had caused this.

"It was the cannons," she stated.

The man nodded. "He had told me we needed more practice with them. I don't know who let the fireball go, but I hope for his sake that he died in the battle."

Since she didn't know what to say, Leena concentrated on the young man. His life song was so faint, she could barely make out the shriek of the wound.

"Move, I'll stop the bleeding," intervened Kilaron.

"You stinking elf, get away from him! You'll just kill him!" yelled one of the warriors tending the man's son.

"Easy, Lago. They're Healers and they will help."

Lago and the other man's eyes opened in astonishment. "Healers? On a battlefield?"

"And this one's an elf. I didn't know elves had Healers," said the other warrior.

"There is much you don't know about elves," said Kilaron. "We'd be delighted to enlighten you, but first, please, let me tend to him. His life song is almost gone."

Lago blinked a few times. "He speaks true, my lord. Only Healers know about the life song."

Leena gritted her teeth. Why must they doubt? And why wouldn't Healers be on a battlefield?

Putting aside her question, she knelt with Kilaron beside the injured man. "You do it and take whatever strength you need from me. I'm just a bit overwhelmed here," she said with a gulp.

Her soulmate nodded. "I remember how I felt after that rock fall. You just need a bit of time."

Leena sincerely hoped he was right. At the moment, she was fighting nausea as best as she could. Why was she feeling this way? She didn't recall feeling sick when she had been faced with Tikid's injured wing. Maybe it had been the lack of light, or because she and Meeryle had been the only one present. Or maybe – and that disgusted Leena, because it was probably the real reason – facing a severe injury on a human felt worse than seeing a shredded dragon wing.

Kilaron invoked his power and put his hands closely above the wound without touching it, pushing the blood together, forcing it to thicken and harden. Since the life song was so weak, it meant the body barely had the energy to heal on its own, let alone participating in a deep Healing. Leena invoked her own power, and putting a hand on his shoulder, guided it to Kilaron. She didn't dare try to participate directly to the Healing; every Healer had a way of doing things, and while some could truly work in tandem, she had yet to do it with the elf.

Kilaron removed his hands and sat on his heels. "There, the blood flow is staunched. You need to clean the wound and bandage it. I can't do anything more until he's recovered more strength."

"Will he live?"

The life song was now a little bit louder, which was a good sign. "If you get him out of the cold, clean him and manage to feed him a little bit," answered Leena. "The body will rebuild the blood he lost. It will take time, but yes, he will live."

"Aye, but my son will never write again," said the man. At the blank looks Leena and Kilaron gave him, he smiled briefly. "He's special in many ways, my son. He uses his left hand to write. His right hand, he reserved for the sword, which he hates."

For a moment, Leena thought he would cry. So had been right; this young man wasn't a warrior at all. Yet from what she could gather, he was responsible for the cannons' presence. Would lacking an arm stop him from ever trying to use another cannon?

"Elf Healers are just like humans ones, aren't they?" he asked after a while.

Kilaron raised an eyebrow. "What do you mean?"

"They can't make limbs grow back, can they?"

"No, I'm afraid not. Though I wish I could."

The elf and the man shared a sad smile.

"But Leena can," said Meeryle.

Chapter 19

All the faces turned towards the forgotten young Mage.

"Be very careful what you say, child," said the man. "I'm not fond of Mages in general, but since they're the ones who got us in this mess, I like them even less."

Meeryle tightened her hands into fists, and for a very brief moment, her eyes flashed orange. Leena almost wished her friend would fry the man with fire.

"That was rude, sir," she said as calmly as she could.

"And this Mage is the reason the dragons didn't unleash a freezing wind on you," added Kilaron.

"All right, all right!" The man threw his hand up and sighed. "Can you regrow his arm?"

Leena bit her lips. "Meeryle and I regrew Tikid's wing."

The man and Lago exchanged a look. "Child, your words show that you're indeed a Healer. You can never get a straight answer out of them! What does that mean, exactly?"

The young Healer blinked a few time in surprise. What was unclear about her words?

Kilaron chuckled. "Tikid is the Green dragon who stayed in the shelter." His smile disappeared when he turned to his soulmate. "You told me about Healing her, but you never said anything about regrowing her wing. We can only repair what's there, we can't create new tissue."

"But you can make it grow, given the right power," explained Meeryle.

"This is… impossible!"

"That's what Corvin had said too."

Leena had to smile at Meeryle's barb; the village Healer had rubbed her the wrong way for too long.

A shadow loomed over them, interrupting further discussion. "*The Mage, the Healer and the Green dragon have shown that many things we thought impossible were in reality unexplored skills. Murod sent them to seek Kiqod, who is more familiar in dealings with other species.*"

The man scratched his head. "Are you Healers too?"

Talid cocked her head. "*Of course not. Why do you ask?*"

Meeryle burst out laughing. "It takes a little while to get used to understanding dragons. And for dragons to understand humans, too. I would love to give your son a new arm, but we shouldn't be doing this out here."

"Agreed," said Kilaron. "We need to move him into the caverns. We also have to see to all the wounded. Then we can see this miracle happen."

Moving the young man proved to be problematic; the transfer to the makeshift stretcher Lago produced brought moans from the unconscious man, which alarmed both Leena and Kilaron, and the ground was too slippery to allow for a smooth walk up to the elven caverns. In the end, Yalad and another dragon each picked up an end of the stretcher and flew the short distance to the entrance of the cavern.

The sight of two White dragons carrying the wounded human into the elven dwelling cave shocked the other humans into cooperating with Jatoron and gathering all the wounded in the caverns. The few who protested were curtly silenced by Lago, who seemed to have a lot of authority.

The entrance had been damaged by the fireballs, but the elven Mages had already cleared the rubble away. Tikid had found her way inside and stood as far away from the entrance and the cold as she could while remaining in full view of the outside, probably on the lookout for her friends. Suqi bounced to Meeryle with a bark as soon as the young Mage had made her way inside.

Kilaron guided the two warriors now carrying the stretcher inside the large cavern where Leena and Meeryle had eaten. This time, it was filled with people, humans on one side and elves on the other, all staring intently at one another. None of them were happy with the situation. Would they all manage to put aside decades of hatred and allow for the Healing of all of them, or would the hostility take over? Leena felt suddenly drained of energy. How could she Heal and make sure someone didn't set off more bloodshed?

Caliana, all the while directing people, came toward Leena with Jatoron at her side. The cave soon filled with the smell of blood and Leena was thankful she wasn't in cat form.

"Ah, Kilaron, Leena. Jatoron tells me you're to be blamed? Thanked? For all of this," said the elven woman as she gestured towards the wounded. Her face was stern, but the sparkle in her green eyes spoke of happy mischief. The older woman was enjoying this, though Leena hoped she was pleased by the forced collaboration and not the attack. Her matter-of-fact attitude might be what was needed to defuse any animosity, at least for the moment. Who knew how long it would last once the warriors were back on their feet.

"Caliana, we want to help everyone."

“The Mage said that this Healer could get my son’s arm to grow back. Find us a place where she can work,” interrupted the limping man.

The elven woman bristled at his tone. “You are not master here, and I am not a servant, so use another tone with me, sir. What is your name?”

He hesitated. “Talin. My son is Elnyon.”

“Well, Talin, know that elves prize courtesy. I am Caliana and I was put in charge of this… effort. I will see to others who came in before you, unless of course the Healers say otherwise.” She nodded to Kilaron, acknowledging his skill.

Then her head whipped back to Talin. “Did you say grow his arm back?”

Her words had been spoken loudly; since elves were quiet by nature and the humans were hushed in the presence of the wounded and so many of their enemies, all heard them and stared.

Tikid moved forward. “*Leena and Meeryle fixed my wing; they will fix his arm*,” said the young dragon.

Human and elves gazed in silence.

“Oh boy,” muttered Meeryle.

The elven Mages abandoned whatever it was they were doing and converged on Meeryle. “You never mentioned this,” said Tassym, a reproachful look on his face.

“Um… well, it never came up, really.”

“And it never came up in my discussions with Kilaron either,” added Leena.

“I don’t care,” interjected Talin. “Just do it, please.” His eyes were begging her.

“What about the others? He’s stable for now, but they need our help.” She pointed at the wounded lying everywhere on the ground. They were all looking at her, at least the ones who could sit up. Among the humans, Leena spotted her mother, whose eyes were filled with curiosity and wonder, rather than with disbelief and – at least from some of the elves – disgust. When she met Kilaron's eyes, they betrayed impatience. Their bond also carried eagerness. Somehow, through it all, the elf had lost his fear, his hesitation and had accepted her and all that she could do.

"Let's do this, Meeryle."

At her command, everyone moved back to give them some space. Leena only allowed Tikid and Suqi to remain close by; the latter because she might be useful, and the former because as the only other patient to have undergone this particular type of Healing, she had a right to be there, if only by default.

As for Kilaron, Leena beckoned for him to sit beside her. "Listen closely," she whispered, not wanting anyone else to know how unsure of herself she was. "I don't think you should touch me, though, since I don't know how all the power would react."

He nodded and smiled. "Ever since you came into this cavern, the impossible is feasible."

The words and the intent warmed her inside. For a brief moment, she heard and smelled everything as distinctly as she had in cat form. She was a Healer with her best friends and her soulmate by her side.

She really could do anything.

Meeryle and Leena both knelt beside Elnyon. Leena placed herself by the left shoulder of her patient, while Meeryle settled beside her and put her left hand on her shoulder.

Only a few months ago, they had done the same for the Green dragon now sitting on her haunches, eagerly awaiting to see her friends work their magic. Leena recalled how scared she had been to hurt the dragon, how much Meeryle's idea of sharing power had shocked her. Her best friend's impulses had served them well, it seemed.

Focusing on the task, eyes closed, Leena placed her hands over the wound without touching it. The life song was a bit stronger, but still far from normal. The wound itself was still screeching, though not as loudly as she had feared. Kilaron had not only stopped the bleeding, he had also started the basic natural healing process.

Where to begin for the unnatural process? Tikid's wing membrane had been shredded and Leena had forced the earth power Meeryle had given her to grow and match the surrounding tissues. This case, however, was much more complex. She needed to grow bone, muscle and skin, not to mention the veins and the nerves. What if she forgot something?

Her eyes opened and panic set in. Meeryle squeezed her shoulder and smiled, unaware of her friend's alarm. Kilaron, thanks to the bond, knew. He simply looked at the young man's right arm and raised his eyebrows. Of course! As long as she had a model, she shouldn't miss anything.

"Just say when, Leena," said Meeryle quietly.

The young Healer nodded. "Give me a few moments. You can hear, right?"

Meeryle nodded. "Just like with Tikid. As long as I touch you, I hear the life song." Kilaron breathed in sharply, but stayed quiet. Another thing that was supposed to be impossible, then.

Once again, Leena closed her eyes and listened to Elnyon's life song. This time, she focused specifically on his right arm, letting her power get an imprint of every part of the arm. As soon as she was absolutely sure she had touched every building cell of the arm, she switched to the left. "Now, Meeryle."

The Mage had been waiting; right away, Leena heard the strange murmur that was earth power. Soon, it was rushing into her body through her shoulder, filling every part of her. It caressed every fiber of her being, thrumming her senses with its murmur. While it didn't have a harsh quality, it was nevertheless unrelenting. Leena was briefly reminded of winter mudslides – nothing stopped earth when it moved.

The Healer waited until she was completely saturated with the power before harnessing it and guiding it out of her into the unconscious man. Once there, she directed it towards the left shoulder, concentrating it all in the same area. Soon, the screeching of the wound changed; it was still discordant, but mixed with the steady murmur of earth.

Slowly, the song of the wound and the earth increased in volume, and as soon as it became loud enough to make her wince, Leena pushed it gradually away from the shoulder. Drawing on the power she had used to examine the right arm in detail, she used the earth power to grow the arm, pushing and twisting it until she was sure it matched the right arm – or the memory that her power, and therefore she, had of it.

Under her hand, the shoulder became a rounded thing, which in turn grew longer. It was working. Slowly, steadily, just like she had done with the dragon's wing, Leena was making Elnyon's arm grow.

However, when she reached the elbow, for some reason, the earth's murmur was growing fainter. Was she running out of strength, or was Meeryle? She didn't dare stop, or even open her eyes, for fear she would lose the pattern of the right arm.

Suddenly, the murmur flared and the power increased. Through it all, Leena heard the Green dragon's distinct life song; Tikid had joined them and was adding the Green power to the Healing. But how long could she last? When she had last given Leena power, Tikid had been in the village, a vast clearing among the trees, on firm ground. How much Green power could these mountains yield?

It wasn't the right time for questions. *Concentrate, Leena*, she thought to herself.

So she continued to draw on the earth power through Meeryle, on the Green power given freely by Tikid through Meeryle.

And the arm grew.

When she reached the wrist, both earth and Green powers diminished, but only for an instant. They were boosted up almost immediately with another power, this one sharp and cold: the White power. Could it be used to Heal? After a while, Leena knew that it wasn't truly the White power. It was Green power, mixed with White. How could that be?

It didn't matter, really. She took advantage of the renewal of power and pushed it into the young man. Cold sweat trickled on her closed eyes; she was suddenly feeling the drain of this Healing. How much longer could she last?

Since she didn't know, she gathered all the power she could. "I need all that you can give me, right now." While she couldn't see them, she knew that all who were linked to her had heard her and were ready. Taking in a deep breath, Leena pushed all the power that came to her into the wrist, telling it to grow into a palm, into fingers. Within a few breaths, the power became so strong, so loud, Leena backed out with a shout and went from her knees to her behind.

Everything was quiet; people were barely breathing.

Kilaron sighed. "You did it, Leena. His left arm is whole."

When she opened her eyes, the first thing she noticed were Tikid and Talid, Green and White leaning against each other. Meeryle was sitting, blinking, face pale, but smiling. "See, look!" Sure enough, Elnyon's arm was there, complete with a pale pink and smooth skin. "Too bad you didn't grow the sleeve back too."

Leena stared at her friend and they both burst out laughing. When she finally found her breath, the young Healer realized that their laughter had been the only noise in the cavern. Sure enough, all eyes were turned towards her, staring with disbelief and awe. Meeryle shrugged in silence, just as unsure as Leena.

The silence was broken by Lago, who had managed to make his way beside them. "My lord, I can't believe I'm seeing this."

Talin simply shook his head, tears running down his cheeks.

"Um, why are you calling him 'lord'?" asked Meeryle.

"Because he is," answered the man, a puzzled look on his face.

Leena looked to Kilaron, who seemed just as mystified.

Finally, Talin cleared his throat. "All the humans here call me lord, except for my son. I'm the duke of Sharitown, answerable only to the king."

***

The following candlemarks were spent Healing elves and humans, none of whom dared protest the situation once their liege's son had been Healed in that spectacular fashion. Kilaron had insisted that Leena rest, for which she was thankful. As soon as she had settled in an out-of-the-way corner of the cavern, an extreme fatigue had set in, reminding her that what she and Meeryle had accomplished was indeed quite the feat. The young Mage had ensconced herself with Tikid and Suqi in the alcove they had used during their original stay among the elves, while Talid had remained by the entrance. The White dragon was rolled like a huge cat, her red eyes following the flurry of activity.

Yalad and Kilaron had paired to Heal anyone who needed it. While the power of air wasn't as effective as that of earth, it was nevertheless enough to give Kilaron an almost endless supply of power, especially given the nature of the injuries.

At first, the Healer had hesitated. Yalad knew how to feed power, whether to a Mage or a Healer didn't really matter to him, but Kilaron had never used energy from a dragon. Talid had pointed out that life needed air, and since elves were particularly well attuned to that element, he should be able to use the power without any problems. Leena surmised that was why Talid had been able to link to Tikid and help give her the power needed to rebuild Elnyon's arm.

So her soulmate's life song was filled with the rasp of air and his eyes glowed with a soft silver light as he and

Yalad moved from one wounded to the next. The White dragon was imbued with the power of air, adding a silver light to the cave.

At one point, the silver light dimmed, and Yalad's life song changed. The dragon was getting tired. Just like Tikid's power had limits, apparently, so did the White's. But air was everywhere, wasn't it? Shouldn't he be able to replenish himself? However, Leena was too tired to ask her questions and before she could even decide whether she should say something at all, another White dragon made its way towards the pair, imbuing itself with power. As soon as it touched Yalad, the White dragon regained his own shine.

Talid's half-closed eyes turned to Leena. "*We can replenish ourselves quickly, but in order to do so, we need to let go of the power.*"

Leena was too far away from Talid to answer her; she would have to speak very loudly and she didn't think the others would be interested in hearing this. She therefore smiled her thanks to the dragon. The White dragon had learned quite a bit in a short time if she could read Leena's face. Maybe she always had questions on her face.

The more time went by, the more dragons joined Yalad. As the last of the wounded was Healed, nine dragons occupied the cavern, much to the dismay of some of the humans.

"Tell me, how did you come to meet with these dragons?" asked the duke as he slowly lowered himself to sit beside Leena.

Eyebrows arched, she stared at his leg. "Why haven't you had Kilaron see to your leg?"

"Ah, he was busy. It's such a novelty to have a Healer on hand, I just couldn't let myself deprive my men of the pleasure. This will be the first time they get such quick care, whereas I always have Healers within reach."

"You see, I don't understand this. Why wouldn't Healers be part of a warrior unit?" Leena had never studied warfare, so she grasped for terms.

"A company, you mean? The Healer's Guild saw to it. At one point, during one war or another, many Healers were forced into serving on the battlefield. The enemy figured that if their opponent couldn't recover quickly, they would be beaten more easily, so the Healers were targeted. None had any combat training, of course, so they were killed. From that day on, the Guild forbade the use of Healers on the battlefield. They would remain at the established camp, and they would go only if they were willing, given specific combat training for defensive purposes and if the fees were doubled. Needless to say, very few lords were willing to spend so much time and money on Healers, so for a while, warriors only got basic care. It was the Healers themselves who insisted the part about the fees be dropped. According to them, it wasn't the warriors' fault if the lords were stingy, yet they were the ones suffering. The Guild lifted the condition concerning the fees, but they still insisted about the Healers remaining at the camp."

Leena was dumbstruck. "But… this goes against being a Healer!"

Talin laughed. "Some agree with you and do come, but after they suffer a few injuries, they tend to change their minds. A battlefield is no fun place to be."

She snorted. "I figured that out for myself."

They sat in silence for a while, watching the dragons make their way out of the cavern now that most were back on their feet. Some, like Elnyon, had suffered greater injuries and needed to rest in order to allow their bodies to recover from the shock of both sustaining an injury and having it Healed.

"So, the dragons?"

"Well, we met Tikid in the forest. She became our friend and eventually, she came to our village, along with some of her kin. The Great One of the Greens sent us here, to meet the White dragons and so here we are."

The duke burst out laughing, startling the resting people. "This has to be the most concise report I've ever heard. You could give a few lessons to some people I know."

"There is a lot more to it, but frankly, right now, I'm a bit tired. Later, I can give you all the details," she offered, hoping she hadn't offended him.

"Rest, child. You deserve it." He looked at her with a strange expression on his face. "Today, thanks to you, I discovered quite a few things."

Before Leena could ask anything, Kilaron came and crouched in front of Talin. "You're the last one. That man of yours told me to Heal you whether you wanted it or not," he said with a smile. "Of course, if you wish to continue limping, I won't force my services on you."

Once again, the cavern echoed with the duke's laughter. "Ah, I wish my Healers had a sense of humor. Go on, man."

Kilaron knelt beside Talin's extended leg and laid both hands on it. While touch wasn't necessary to Heal, when fatigue set in, it helped to ensure that the Healer could hear and feel the wound properly. Leena bit her lip to stop herself from telling the elf he should rest; he knew it, of course. They were all exhausted, even the White dragons, whose scales seemed a bit gray.

"It's a nasty cut through the muscle. How did you come to get it?" asked Kilaron, a puzzled look on his face.

"You're going to laugh: when the fireball hit my son, the aftershock made me trip on my sword."

Leena wasn't sure if Talin was telling the truth, but what did it matter? They all smiled while Kilaron Healed the duke's leg. A sense of humor did a lot to lift the spirits.

Once he was done, Kilaron sat beside Leena and sighed. "I'm tired. But I have to say, having Yalad giving all this power…" He stopped and shook his head. "Incredible."

"Where is Yalad?"

"He went back outside. They all did."

A brief look around confirmed the elf's words. She must have been even more tired than she had thought if she missed noticing nine – no ten, as Talid had left too – dragons leaving the cavern.

"Do you think these dragons of yours would be willing to show my Healers how to do this?" asked the duke.

Leena exchanged a look with Kilaron. "Well, Kiqod did say she thought it was time for humans and dragons to get along, didn't she?"

However, before the duke could ask what she meant, a roar came from the outside. They all got to their feet, Talin testing briefly his leg, and made their way out to find out the reason for the commotion.

The side of the mountain was besieged with people, all human, all clean and free of wounds, all holding weapons. Where did they come from? Reinforcements for the duke?

The roar had come from Talid, who was protecting another dragon with her wings. Leena couldn't tell who it was, but she could see the telltale traces of blood in the white scales: one of the dragons was injured and from the shouts coming from the people, Leena was pretty sure humans were responsible – no elf would injure a dragon.

"No, no! Stop, don't harm them!" she yelled a loudly as she could.

Kilaron and Talin ran forward, echoing her shouts. "They're friends! Stop!"

However, all the humans were also shouting, and no one could make out any words.

Suddenly, Talid was shining with power. Leena was sure the white dragon was about to freeze the lot of them, which would probably kill them. She couldn't let this happen! Making her way to the infuriated dragon, Leena yelled for her to stop.

Somehow, the dragon heard her, even with the noise. The creature turned her head towards her, which guided the oncoming crowd toward Leena. "They're friends, don't hurt them!" Doubtful faces exchanged looks, probably puzzled by the presence of a human girl – Leena knew she looked more human than elf, and that probably saved her. One archer stared at her face; puzzlement, then recognition, though tinged with confusion. Leena could almost hear his question: what is this girl doing here among elves and monsters?

He turned his gaze to her left, where Talin and Kilaron were running, both shouting. The archer's eyes widened in recognition when he saw the duke, and he lowered his bow. However, at that very moment, Talin lost his footing. Kilaron tried to grab him, but his hand could only reach his shoulder and the duke rolled down. In that brief moment, it had seemed as if Kilaron had pushed Talin down the slope.

Before she could even utter a sound, the archer, his face deformed in a rictus of hate, had lifted his bow, pulled the string and loosed the arrow.

Leena screamed at it flew and hit Kilaron's chest.

Chapter 20

Leena wasn't exactly sure how she got back into the cavern; one moment she was witnessing Kilaron being shot, and the next, she was sitting by the prone body of her soulmate. Her mother was holding her hand, saying words that didn't make sense.

All she could hear was the screeching of Kilaron's life song – he wasn't dead, then. The arrow… the arrow was gone! Who had dared remove it? Didn't they know how dangerous it was to remove a projectile from a wound without the assistance of a Healer? He could bleed to death if she wasn't there to staunch it.

"Who did this? Who?" she screamed, startling the people surrounding her. Where did they come from? They hadn't been there a while ago… Had they?

"One of the warriors, Leena. He thought… it was a dreadful mistake," said Lyandrin.

"I meant the arrow. He could die!"

"Easy, child. Lago removed it; he knows what he's doing," answered a man. He looked familiar, but she couldn't place him.

"But… I need to…"

Tears blurred her sight. He was so pale, his song so wrong. Grabbing his hand, she listened for the wound, but something broke her concentration. Cold sweat broke out as pain slowly exploded in her chest, gradually spreading to her arms, her fingers. She was so tired, she had to lie down.

"We need more people touching Leena!" yelled someone with panic in her voice. Immediately, something sparked and she felt better.

"*I want to help and so does Meeryle*," said Tikid.

The pain receded enough for Leena to recognize her friend's voice, but she didn't understand what was happening. When did she get hurt? Someone else was wounded, someone very important to her, but whom?

"Leena, can you hear me?"

She blinked, allowing her tears to fall and her vision to clear. "Mother."

"Yes. Kilaron is wounded, this is why you're not feeling well. Your bond as soulmates lets you feel what he's feeling, though why you're even conscious, I can't even guess."

"I see two possibilities," said another woman – Caliana? "Either her human half is keeping her from oblivion, or they didn't complete the bond."

"How could that be?"

"Did you see them together? They seem friends, but not lovers."

"Enough! I'm here, you know." Something in her mind had cleared, making her behavior during the past candlemark seem remote. She was lying on the ground of the cavern, surrounded by elves, all touching her. Kilaron was on her right, a bit apart, also encircled by a group of elves. In his case, though, it seemed the entire enclave was trying to touch him.

"What happened to me?"

Caliana frowned. "It's more what didn't happen to you. When a person is gravely hurt, his or her soulmate usually collapses and two people need tending. However, you're still conscious, though you were delirious."

"The touch is helping."

"Yes. It's also helping to keep Kilaron somewhat stable, or so the human Lago says."

“He knows what he’s talking about, lady,” said Talin. “He’s the closest thing to an expert on battle wounds that I have – next to an actual Healer, that is.”

Leena closed her eyes. She needed to concentrate, but having so many people touching her and invading her personal space was making it very difficult. However, if they stopped, she would probably become delirious with pain once again.

“What do I need to do?” she asked her mother. She had lost a soulmate, had she not? Yet she was alive, even if she had tried to kill herself.

Lago waved over the elves around Leena. “He needs Healing. The arrow hit too close to the heart for me to be able to do anything else. Even if the bleeding seems to have stopped on the outside, I’m sure it hasn’t on the inside.”

Caliana sighed. “This enclave has not one, but two Healers, and of course, they’re the ones who need Healing. The touch is obviously helping you, Leena, but I doubt you’ll be able to Heal anything.”

“It’s distracting, to say the least,” she admitted. “But if you all stop, I won’t be able to do anything either and he’ll die.” She bit her lips to stop herself from crying.

“*The touch is power, Leena. I can provide it*,” offered Tikid, her head towering over everyone else.

Would it work? “Are you sure, Tikid?” Leena didn’t want to lose whatever coherence she had.

“*Your glow is almost normal when they touch you, yet their power is different than yours. I do not see why mine would not have the effect*.”

Caliana and Lyandrin looked at each other. “What in life is she talking about?”

"*Dragons can see the aura of power every being emits,*" offered Talid. Leena couldn't see the White dragon behind her wall of elves, but she must have come back into the cavern at one point. She just hoped the big dragon hadn't hurt any of the humans.

"Do it, Tikid."

A green scaled tail made its way between two elves. Leena grabbed it, hoping fervently that her friend was right. Soon, her sight became tinged with green. While the elven touch had helped her, it was weak in comparison to the power of the Green dragons. Underlying pain disappeared completely; her lungs seemed suddenly able to fully expand and whatever fatigue had been holding her down was gone.

"I'm fine, you can let me go," she said with a smile and a nod of thanks.

Not trusting herself to stand, Leena hobbled her way to Kilaron's side on all fours while holding the dragon's tail in her hand. The crowd of elves touching Kilaron parted; some had to completely move away to make room for her. Leena was surprised to see Ulina's tear-stricken face. The young woman wasn't looking at her with her usual disdain, but hope. Leena simply smiled and Ulina responded with a hesitant smile of her own.

Safyn was kneeling beside the younger elf, her eyes closed, both hands on her son's forehead. When Leena touched her shoulder, the older woman blinked in confusion.

"You're awake."

"Yes. Now I'll Heal him."

"Oh." Others helped her get up and gently guided her away, and soon, Kilaron was lying by himself, with only Leena at his side. Caliana, Lyandrin, Lago and Talin kept close, but gave Tikid room to approach. Meeryle joined her and grabbed Leena's shoulder.

"What do you need?"

"Well, I'm not sure. Be ready with earth, just in case."

Meeryle nodded and her life song was suddenly filled with the murmur of earth.

Tikid shuffled behind Leena and wrapped her tail around her waist. "*That way, you will have both of your hands for Kilaron.*"

Kilaron, who was right for her. Kilaron, who was lying, pale as snow, his life song so weak, she had to strain to hear it. Kilaron, whom she didn't want to die, because, she realized suddenly, she loved him.

Kilaron, her soulmate.

Leena clenched her teeth; he wouldn't die, because she wouldn't let him. Putting her hands on his chest, she closed her eyes and sought the wound. Deliberately ignoring the screeching sound, she let her power seek the damage done by the arrow. Luckily, it had been a simple cutting arrow, not the barbed kind that could inflict so much harm both coming in and coming out. Lago had indeed known what he was doing – had the arrow been barbed, he wouldn't have been able to remove it.

Muscle and veins were cut, but the heart itself was sound; all she needed to do was seal the neat wounds. Such a procedure was so simple compared to what she had done lately, she almost burst into tears with relief. Instead of having her power examine the wounds, she forced it to seal them, to push the flesh together and bind it close. Meeryle's power wouldn't be needed after all.

A few moments later, Kilaron's life song was back to normal, if somewhat weak. Leena was feeling much better, as if in Healing Kilaron, she had Healed herself. Taking a deep breath, she smiled and took the time to examine him from head to toe. He had managed to pull a muscle in his right leg, nothing that wouldn't heal on its own, and his spine wasn't aligned properly, probably something with which he had been born. However, something in his head wasn't quite right. She had heard the sound before, and thought it was part of his life song, but now that she was imbued with Green power, she could hear everything much more clearly.

The slight discordance was so diffuse, she almost didn't find its source. Since she was too stubborn to admit defeat, she probed until the elusive dissonance became clearer. She still couldn't pinpoint it, but now she could hear it better, it would be easier. Yet it still managed to elude her.

Leena gritted her teeth and out of pure frustration, she challenged it. Come on, show yourself, she thought.

Surprisingly enough, it did. The discordance was suddenly there, not in a particular spot, but in her power, as if it was trying to grab it. While such an occurrence would normally require study and, most of all, caution, Leena didn't wait. This was Kilaron, she need to Heal this, whatever it was.

Once again, she guided her power. This time, instead of mending something, she made it destroy whatever it was that had invaded Kilaron and her.

Her power flared brightly. From the gasps around her, she gathered it wasn't just behind her closed lids, but outside of her. While it wasn't commonplace, it could happen. The Green power must have had something to do with it. Leena tried to tone it down, but her power kept on, burning brighter and brighter.

What was wrong? What was it that Kilaron had that needed so much power to Heal?

Suddenly, she felt the jolt that meant the Healing was complete. Only this time, it was much, much stronger than it had been the first time she had Healed him. Life sang throughout her entire body, filling her with joy.

A hand touched her cheek. "Leena."

She opened her eyes to see Kilaron's face and eyes lit with muted power. Was she glowing the same way?

Kilaron didn't give her time to think of any more questions. He sat up, gathered her in his arms and kissed her. Power once again flared up, but this time, she could feel Kilaron's. Briefly, she wanted to examine this, to ask questions, however her soulmate's passion crawled through the power. For a moment, she resisted. But the feeling was so strong, so warm, so filled with need, Leena pushed her questions aside and surrendered.

From far away, she heard Caliana's voice: "Their bond is now complete."

***

Sitting on the floor, Leena looked at what Kilaron called "their alcove". It was still empty of anything but the basics, except for one of her mother's paintings. Lyandrin had picked a blanket-size abstract of greens, reminding Leena of the forest around the village. It exuded spring and summer warmth, allowing her to forget about the bitter cold outside and the colorless snow.

It still didn't feel like home.

But where was home? At the village, with her father and Corvin? Thinking of the old man who had taught her everything he knew, Leena realized how far she had come since the day she and Meeryle had Healed Tikid. That moment was when she had truly become a Healer. Her thirst for learning would never be quenched in such an isolated place.

Was the elven enclave any better? It was Kilaron's home, but his privileged status as a Healer and his mother's influence had made him someone whom she hadn't liked. While he had changed by his own admission, would the enclave allow him to continue?

What about her status as a halfbreed? Most of the elves had conveniently forgotten she was a Healer and Kilaron's soulmate when they learned of her heritage. People didn't change easily; such an ingrained prejudice couldn't disappear overnight. Life among elves would be extremely difficult.

Leena sighed. She didn't have a home. Could she impose another on Kilaron? The elves had been quite clear on this; the soulmate bond did not allow the couple to be physically apart over great distances for very long. If Leena wanted to travel, it would have to be over short distances and short periods of time.

The thought of traveling filled Leena with a surprising longing. It made sense, did it not? How else could she learn? Things wouldn't come to her, so she had to go to them. Even the dragons, who could cover a lot of ground, didn't like to explore too much. Only a few, like Tikid and Yalad, wanted to venture out of their known element.

Wasn't it the same for people?

"Leena?"

Meeryle's voice, muffled by the curtain that served as a door, was a welcome interruption.

"Come on in."

The Mage stood at the entrance and took in the alcove. "Kind of empty, no?"

"I guess. I'm not sure I want to fill it, though."

"I figured you'd be moping about this. How long have you been sitting here, anyway?"

"Too long. Meeryle, I just don't know what to do! Stay here? Leave?"

"Well, what does Kilaron think?"

Leena snorted. "I haven't asked him."

"Why?" asked Meeryle with a puzzled look on her face. "It's been three days since you've Healed him. I know your mother's been busy acting as a go-between with the elves and the humans, but Kilaron hasn't been involved and neither have you. So what have you both been doing with your time?"

It was a fair question. "Moping."

Meeryle burst out laughing. "You're impossible! Only you could mope at such a time. These people are finally talking to each other, the dragons want to continue to meet with humans and you're just sitting on the floor, wondering if you should stay with Kilaron or not."

Leena blinked a few times. Her friend had hit the mark too closely. "The thing is that I have to stay with him."

"Ah, yes, the bond thing."

"Don't forget the halfbreed thing, too."

"You think too much. You're a Healer, all you need is the sanction of the Guild, right?"

"Right."

"Well, get it, then! Once that's done, figure out where you and Kilaron want to set up your place. From what I've seen with you, Healers have to Heal, otherwise, they go crazy."

Meeryle's words struck a chord. Was it possible that Kilaron had been chafing as a Healer? By their own admission, elves didn't get sick or hurt too often, so a Healer really didn't have a permanent place anywhere. She had never asked what other elven Healers did, but maybe they should be traveling.

"Let's go ask him," she said, getting up with a grimace. She had been sitting for too long.

"Ask who and ask what?" Meeryle confused look made Leena smile.

"Ask Kilaron if he's going crazy."

Now that their bond was complete, Leena knew exactly where her soulmate was, and his general mood, even if she blocked him. At the moment, Kilaron was in the great cavern, and until a few moments ago, he'd been bored. A flare of interest, then complete excitement overwhelmed her briefly. She quickly shielded herself against it and sped up.

Seated around the central table were Risalon, Caliana, Lyandrin, Kilaron, Talin and his son, while Tikid and Talid were sitting on their haunches at each end of the table.

Elnyon was still pale, but his life song was strong.

"Ah, here are our miracle workers," said Talin when he spotted Leena and Meeryle.

Elnyon got up and grabbed Leena's hands. The grip on his left hand was weaker. "You'll need to exercise that hand," she said with a frown.

The young man smiled. "You truly are a Healer. Anyone else would have said hello."

Leena wasn't sure if she should be insulted or amused. The glint in Elnyon's eyes spoke of someone who liked to laugh, so she opted to do the same. "And I bet you're a nightmare patient, what with being here instead of home, resting."

"Guilty! But in all honesty, as soon as I could move I wanted to meet the ones who had given me back my arm. Some Healers from the Guild came with me to make sure I would be fine."

Leena looked briefly around, but the only humans were Talin, Elnyon and Meeryle.

"They're waiting outside," explained Kilaron. "They had… difficulty accepting that an elf could be a Healer." While he didn't voice his outrage, it permeated the bond.

So he had found out how it felt to be doubted. She let her satisfaction fill the bond and he gave her a surprised look. Eyebrows up, Leena smiled. He ruefully returned her smile.

"Aren't they cold?" asked Meeryle.

"They deserve it," said Talin. "I'm the one who sent them out when they insulted Kilaron. Damn Healers, they're almost as bad as Mages."

When he caught Meeryle's and Leena's stare, the man burst out laughing. "Sorry, the comment didn't apply to you. Come, sit and listen to what I have to propose."

Leena sat beside her mother and Kilaron joined them. Lyandrin's face was strangely blank, but before Leena could ask anything, Talin had started to speak.

"You see, the reason why I make such outrageous comments about Healers and Mages is because all the ones I know are old and set in their ways. When I saw what Leena and Meeryle did for my son, I decided I needed new faces in my court. Since I experienced first-hand that an elven Healer is ten times more effective than my supposedly best Healer, I figured it was time the Guild changed."

Leena was stunned. "Are you saying you want to depose the existing Guild?"

"The one in Sharitown, yes. I have the authority. For the rest, it rests with the king."

"We're Healer, not politicians," said Kilaron. "I know nothing of human politics, but I can tell that what you want to do will not go over easily with the Healers." Yet Leena couldn't help but notice that he didn't say he didn't want to do it. "Talin, when you said you wanted Leena and I to come to Sharitown, you didn't mention anything about removing the Healers in place."

The same excitement he had felt earlier was back and hope stirred. Kilaron wanted to leave!

"Caliana and Risalon didn't give me time to explain," answered the duke.

The older elven woman arched an eyebrow. "You would take both our Healers away. That is not acceptable."

"But what if they want to go to Sharitown?" asked Meeryle. "Healers don't have a lot of work here, so wouldn't it make sense for them to go where they're needed?"

"Young lady, you may be a talented Mage, but you do not know what you're saying. An elf belongs with his own kind, not among humans, especially a Healer," explained Risalon in a rather condescending way.

Before Meeryle could express the anger that had changed her life song, Lyandrin spoke. "But he would be with his kind. Leena would be with him, and so would I."

Caliana and Risalon stood to express their dismay, but Lyandrin stopped them with a raised hand. "Where my daughter goes, I go as well. Nothing more is to be said on the subject."

The elves sat down, exchanging looks. "It is not our place to question your decision, Lyandrin. It's just…

surprising, as you hadn't mentioned you wanted to live amongst humans once again." What Caliana didn't say, but was clearly on her mind, was that Lyandrin hadn't been able to stay with humans the first time. Leena took her mother's hand; this time, she would be among her kind: she would have her and Kilaron.

Talin cleared his throat, startling them all. "I owe this woman for the loss of her husband. I offered her a place, and she's accepted. She also agreed to become the elven ambassador to my court."

From Risalon and Caliana's faces, Lyandrin hadn't shared this news. She had also neglected to tell Leena, but since she had been avoiding everyone in order to decide what to do with her life, she couldn't complain.

"*The duke has also offered a similar appointment to the White dragons*," announced Talid. "*While Yalad has volunteered, we are still not sure if he will be the one to fulfill it. Tikid and Meeryle explained how the Greens have dealt with such a situation. We might do as them and appoint different individuals for a set period of time*."

Leena's jaw dropped. "You mean to say that after all this time, dragons are going to walk openly among humans?"

"*It is Kiqod's wish*," stated Talid.

"*And Murod's as well*," added Tikid.

"But I'm not sure you realize how many people live in the city." She turned to Talin. "How will you prevent panic?" The memory of Tikid's shredded wing made her gulp.

"You will all arrive together and be presented at court," explained Elnyon. "We've put a great deal of thought to this."

"So I see," replied Risalon. "I do not appreciate how you're orchestrating all this. While it is good that our relations have resumed, you're imposing too much on us."

"No, he is not," cut in Lyandrin. "The only true change to the enclave will be Kilaron's absence. I had left. Upon my return, I was welcome, but I had become a stranger. Meeryle and Leena are only visitors and so are the dragons. You cannot control everything, Risalon. Things are changing, yes. You have to accept it."

The two elves stared at each other, both seething. "Very well, I accept it, but I do not like it."

Something nagged at Leena. "What about the diamonds?"

All the elves tensed at the reminder. "They are not for sale," said Caliana.

The duke frowned. "I had hoped that some trade…"

"No." Caliana's tone brooked no argument.

Meeryle sighed. "You're going to start fighting again. Talin, the elves use the diamonds for spells. All the light you see here comes from spells imbedded into diamonds. This mountain is one of the main sources of spell stones for all the elves in the world. What could you possibly trade in exchange?"

Talin didn't answer. His son gave him a quick glance. "We need to discuss this with our Mages. This is unexpected."

"Mages!" Talin swore, "All they will do is nag, ask questions, make unending demands…"

"Father, enough," cut in Elnyon. "I will find a Mage who is willing to be open minded."

The duke snorted. "Good luck."

"Maybe I can help," offered Meeryle. "I can introduce you to the elven Mages."

“I would like that very much,” said Elnyon with a wide smile. Both stood and left the cavern.

“Humans!” exclaimed Risalon. “Rude to the very end. They didn’t ask permission to leave or even to seek the Mages.”

Caliana gave him an offended look. “I wasn’t aware anyone needed permission to see the Mages, or anyone else for that matter. Soulmate mine, you need to focus.”

Leena stood. “Look, a lot of things happened here and during the last few days. How about you let in your Healers, Talin? They must be frozen solid by now.”

The duke blinked. “I admit, I completely forgot about them.”

Talid’s chuckle made the table vibrate. “*Dragons are looking after them. Some managed to start a conversation.*”

“There’s hope yet! Come then, let’s work with what we have, shall we?”

***

How the duke managed to make the peace hold, Leena never knew. She didn’t ask either. It was all about politics and she found them frustrating. People always wanted more, and for nothing. Elves and humans weren’t that different. She suddenly understood why Meeryle liked the dragons so much; the huge creatures’ way of thinking was indeed very different and very refreshing compared to that of the humans’ and elves’.

Leena’s mind was still reeling from the few days since the attack on the enclave; the fact that the hostilities had ceased were nothing short of a miracle. People didn’t put aside years of hatred so easily, but she didn’t question the duke. It was too much for a simple Healer like her.

Over the last week, heated words had been exchanged between Risalon and Talin, tempers had been cooled by Caliana and Lyandrin. Leena had also caught glimpses of Elnyon and some of the elven Mages, but she hadn't been invited to join any of the discussions, for which she was thankful.

Her own life had been changed in these few days, and it took up all of her thoughts. The new closeness that she enjoyed with Kilaron could not be denied. He was smiling now, his confidence had soared. Their bond was so much more comfortable that neither one of them felt the need to shield themselves.

That bond still rankled at times – but it was part of accepting that she couldn't control everything, that she could share her own doubts with her soulmate. Kilaron was also learning to ask, discovering that questions led to knowledge, something for which he'd been thirsting for so long without knowing it.

How could she possibly have time to see to the peace between humans and elves? When asked, Lyandrin told her to trust the duke. Leena was uncertain; however, Elnyon's openness and willingness to learn told her that the son just might take after his father.

She would leave all this in the capable hands of the leaders and focus on what Talin had offered her and Kilaron: a Healer's shop in Sharitown.

"What could you possibly have left to pack?"

Leena was jerked out of her thoughts by her soulmate's voice. "Nothing. I was just thinking, that's all." She sighed. "But we will need more things, you know. I guess we'll find everything in town."

Kilaron's excitement filled the bond. "I don't care. For some reason, this place feels stifling now."

"I think it's my fault. These mountains feel… enclosing."

"Come, you need to help your mother pack, I need to reassure mine, then we can be on our way."

"So, will Yalad come with us?" asked Leena. The young White had been adamant about coming.

"Talid will come too."

"Ah," was all she said.

Things would be very interesting in Sharitown.

***

Leena was helping her mother close the last bag when Meeryle burst in, followed by Suqi.

"You won't believe it!"

Mother and daughter smiled at the young Mage's excitement. "All right, I'll ask," said Leena.

"I'm not coming with you to Sharitown!"

Leena was dismayed. "How is that good?"

"I'm going to the capital with Tikid, Suqi and Elnyon."

Lyandrin nodded her understanding. "It's the duke's idea, isn't it?"

"Yes. He gave me a letter to explain to the king who I am and who Tikid is. Then we can show the Mages how to link with dragons."

"That man is very cunning."

"What do you mean, mother?"

"By appointing his son as an envoy to the royal court along with Meeryle and Tikid, he's also making sure his actions against the Sharitown Healer's Guild will be pardoned by the king."

"Isn't it a bit farfetched?"

"Not if you're familiar with politics, which I am. Remember, Danpiron was a diplomat and he always discussed such things with me."

"See, the elves have the best ambassador! Oh, Leena, this is so exciting." Meeryle suddenly stopped and her expression became thoughtful. "You will be going to Sharitown for sure?"

"Yes. We're going. Getting a Healer's shop is a great idea. We're not sure how we'll go about it, but Talin swore he'd help – that is, once he's dealt with the Guild." Leena's eyes filled with sudden tears. She embraced her friend tightly. "Don't do anything stupid, all right?"

"Elnyon will keep me out of trouble," Meeryle said, sniffling.

"I think he fancies you," teased Leena.

"You're being silly. He's the son of the duke and I'm…"

"The best Mage this world has ever seen. Don't forget that."

"Only if you always remember that you're the best Healer there is."

Seeing the confident look in her mother and her best friend's eyes, Leena couldn't possibly doubt herself any longer. She was a halfbreed, probably the only one in the world, who had inherited a wonderful gift from both sides. She had a soulmate – even if he could be infuriating at times. While she had yet to meet with the Healer's Guild – the idea of standing in front of them asking to be received made her very nervous – she was sure the work she could do with the White dragons would help alleviate the inevitable tension the dragons' presence would bring. Along with Kilaron, she could build a life, with her mother at their side, and face whatever the city and its people would throw at them.

The home she had in the village with her father seemed so far away...

It didn't matter where they made their home, really. Caliana had made it clear that their alcove would always be there for them should they wish to visit. Whether in Sharitown or in the enclave, they would have a place to stay, but Leena now knew that having a home wasn't as important as knowing who and what she was.

And she was a Healer.

Acknowledgements

I would like to thank Joelle Duran for having the courage to read the first draft and make her astute comments; Sandra Leigh for helping me making this story even better and my daughter for wanting to read over my shoulder while I was writing…

But most of all, I would like to once again thank Melody Peña for creating her wonderful sculptures. *A Dragon Medley* was directly inspired by her beautiful dragons, who have invaded my home and are constantly staring at me in the hopes that I will tell more of their adventures and ways of life…

www.ingramcontent.com/pod-product-compliance
Lightning Source LLC
La Vergne TN
LVHW030909080826
845145LV00010B/2824

* 9 7 8 1 7 8 6 9 5 4 7 6 3 *